THE STREETS HAVE NO KING

JAQUAVIS COLEMAN

ST. MARTIN'S GRIFFIN

NEW YORK

THE STREETS HAVE NO KING. Copyright © 2017 by JaQuavis Coleman. All rights reserved. Printed in the United States of America. For information, address St. Martin's Press, 175 Fifth Avenue, New York, N.Y. 10010.

www.stmartins.com

Designed by Omar Chapa

The Library of Congress Cataloging-in-Publication Data is available upon request.

ISBN 978-1-250-08127-8 (trade paperback)
ISBN 978-1-4668-9314-6 (e-book)

Our books may be purchased in bulk for promotional, educational, or business use. Please contact your local bookseller or the Macmillan Corporate and Premium Sales Department at 1-800-221-7945, extension 5442, or by e-mail at MacmillanSpecialMarkets@macmillan.com.

First Edition: April 2017

10 9 8 7 6 5 4 3 2 1

This book is dedicated to BMF juice. You taught me so much and I will use those lessons to navigate through this thing called life. Rest in Peace and I will always love you.

Love,

Coleman

PROLOGUE

The stars never shined so bright. Well, that's what it seemed like on that cool summer night. A couple sat on top of the rooftop admiring the beautiful night's sky. They sat on a picnic blanket while bottles of bubbly and fruits accompanied them. The smell of a sour sweetness filled the air as the young lady took another pull of her tightly rolled joint. As the beauty inhaled the smoke, she glanced over at the man, who stared at her with a slight grin.

"Why are you staring?" Moriah asked as the weed smoke filled her lungs. She smiled and blew a smoke stream out of the corner of her mouth. Her full lips made the simple act of blowing smoke seem so seductive, so sexy. Everything about her screamed sensual. She never rushed . . . always smooth. Her cat-like hazel eyes and her neat hair wrap looked natural and pure. The way she let a couple of strands of her neatly twisted dreads hang out of the sides of her wrap got him every time.

Her soft baby hairs, which rested perfectly on the edges of her scarf . . . Basil absolutely loved Moriah. He loved her in the purest form, because he was in love with her spirit. His deep love was reciprocated; she'd fallen in love with his soul as well. See, that's the thing . . . they had a different kind of connection. He was mesmerized by her inner beauty, and her natural outer beauty was only a plus. She had him at hello and vice versa.

"Because I love you . . . I'm staring at you because I love you," Basil said confidently, half smiling as he reached over and swept the dreads from over her left eye. Basil then gently cupped her face and stared into her eyes.

"I love you more," she replied as a huge smile spread across her face, displaying her perfect white teeth. They said nothing, but their eyes told each other that they were looking at the person who completed them. They were soul mates. They burst into laughter when they both made a funny face at the same exact time and Basil leaned in for a deep but tender kiss that ended with a soft peck on the lips. Basil stood up and then walked to the ledge, picking up a bottle of champagne in his hand and popping the cork, causing a small volcano-like eruption as the sound of the popped cork echoed through the air. He held the bottle up and looked back at Moriah, offering some to her.

"Not in the mood to drink tonight," Moriah said smiling.

They were on top of the roof of the Regency projects on the south side of Flint, Michigan. The Regency was in one of the worst parts of the city. However, you couldn't tell them that; not at the moment, anyway. This was their secret place, the place where they had their first date. They were also standing on top of the most lucrative drug operation in the city. While so many bad things were going on underneath them, so many good things were going on, on top of that roof. But today, they were celebrating their two-year anniversary as lovers. As Basil looked out over the skyline, Moriah looked her man over in admiration. His Italian-cut suit and thousand-dollar pair of Prada loafers made her grin. His slightly loosened tie and the way he stood reminded her of her father so much. Basil had the bottle of champagne in one hand and the other hand slyly had slid into his left pocket. She had witnessed his transformation over the last two years. The projects that he was overlooking were his. He ran Regency with an iron fist; the smooth operation didn't run like a typical trap. He ran that motherfucker like a Wall Street stock exchange. However, instead of stocks and bonds, heroin, pills, and crack cocaine were his commodities. His structured way of moving work was comparable to that of a Fortune 500 company. The streets had crowned him king and at that moment, Moriah knew it was true. She stood up, took one last drag of her joint and then tossed it. Walking up behind him, she hugged him from behind, while resting her head on his muscular back. She closed her eyes and inhaled the scent of his cologne. The expensive fabric of his suit felt soft beneath her cheek and she wanted to stay like this forever, but she could tell he was in deep thought.

"I'm tired of sneaking around with you like we are teenagers. I'm tired of hiding," Basil said, referring to their secret relationship. He looked again at the city's skyline and took a sip of his drink, then sat the empty glass on the rooftop's edge. Basil turned around and placed both of his hands on her cheeks. Moriah felt the exact same way, even though she knew that their love was forbidden. Her father was Basil's mentor and business partner. They had crossed that line and were at a point of no return. They were made for each other and so deep in love, so deep that it hurt. However, it hurt so good. Kane had always explained to him that family was off limits in any business relationship. Kane understood how love clouds the brain, which in return could cause a problem in business; especially street business. However, Basil fell victim to his own heart.

"We have to tell him," Moriah said.

"Let's tell him tonight," Basil demanded. "I can't wait any lo—"

Moriah placed her finger on his lip, stopping him from saying another word. "First ... I have to tell you something." She looked deep into Basil's eyes and her own eyes began to water. Basil frowned at the sight.

"I'm pregnant," she whispered as the first tear skipped down her face. "We are having a baby."

"Wh ... what?" Basil asked, his eyes instantly dropping to her belly. He then carefully placed his hand on her midsection.

"I said, we are pregnant," she repeated as she placed her hand on top of his. All of a sudden, Basil smiled and scooped Moriah off of her feet. He spun her around once, causing her to laugh out loud. Basil was smiling from ear to ear, beyond excited. He gently placed her back on the ground then kissed her passionately. Moriah continued to cry as she smiled as well. It was one of the happiest days of her life. She hadn't been sure how Basil would take the news, but by the expression on his face, it was clear she didn't have to worry.

"Oh my God. How?" Basil asked while rubbing her stomach in a circular motion. "Well, I know how but . . . ," he said, at a loss for words. They kissed passionately and Basil hugged her tightly. He was so overcome with joy and warmth; a warmth that he had never experienced before. Something was happening that hadn't happened since he was a little boy. Basil dropped a tear. They cried together while smiling at each other. It was beautiful . . . it was pure.

Basil looked down at his watch and noticed that it was a couple of ticks before 9:00 P.M. They still had time to catch Kane Garrett, Moriah's father. He was being honored at the mayor's ball and Basil wanted to tell him their big secret. It was a perfect time to do it, on the day that he was being honored by the city. Basil was tired of hiding his love affair and was ready to step up to Moriah's father with the news. Basil knew that Kane would disapprove; however, he also knew that Kane would respect him. They had a father-son relationship. The new news would only make that official, so Basil was more confident than ever on this night.

"Come on, let's catch Kane at the ball and tell him the good news," Basil said.

Moriah smiled and nodded her head in agreement. Basil scooped Moriah off of her feet and carried her to the rooftop exit. They smiled and giggled all the way down the stairs as they were on mental highs. Although Basil was known to be calm and collected by everyone else, tonight he was ecstatic. He was ready to get the weight off of his chest of sneaking around with Moriah, and that added to the fact that he would be a father would make this night legendary.

When they reached the outside exit, Basil gently set Moriah's feet on the ground after walking her down eighty flights of steps. He was winded, but didn't care. Moriah chuckled, seeing the small beads of sweat that had formed on his forehead. She took her palm and wiped off his perspiration as she looked into his eyes and grinned in admiration. They hopped in his all-black Range Rover, which was parked in the rear of the building, in the alley. Basil started up the car and looked over at Moriah, who was smiling. But her smile quickly turned upside down and it seemed as if she had seen a ghost.

"What's wrong, Mo?" Basil asked, still grinning. He had never seen Moriah make the face she was making. Her eyes grew big as a man with a ski mask crept up on the driver's side. She let out a bloodcurdling scream and it all happened so fast, Basil had no time to react. Gunshots rang out as the gunman dumped his entire clip into the vehicle. The sound of shattering glass filled the air. Bullets flew into Basil's chest . . . six, to be exact. He still had the awareness to pull off in the car. The tires screeched and his Range Rover scraped the sides of the alley's buildings. He sped off as his truck fishtailed through the project's parking lot. Pains in his chest began to form and he breathed heavily while gripping his chest with his free hand. He sped out of the projects, away from the brutal scene and the pandemonium. He ripped open his shirt, displaying his smoking Teflon vest, and noticed that no bullet had passed through it. He raced around a few blocks, then parked to gather himself. His heart was pumping rapidly but he thanked God that no bullet had penetrated him. *Thank God . . . thank God . . .*, he thought as he realized how close to death he had come. Basil took a deep breath and looked over at Moriah. He saw her leaning against the window as she struggled for air. Blood was oozing from the corner of her mouth and pure terror was written all over her face. He then looked down at the maroon-colored circle spreading over her stomach. Her hand covered a bloody wound, and that's when he realized that a bullet had struck her.

"No! No, God, please!" he yelled as he instantly placed his hand over her wound, trying to apply pressure to stop the gushing blood.

"I'm okay . . . I'm okay," she whispered as she breathed slowly and deeply. "The baby . . . the baby." She began to cry.

"Oh my God. I have to get you to the hospital." Basil's heart dropped at the sight of the blood spilling from Mo's midsection. "Don't worry. It's going to be okay!" Basil said as his voice cracked and his bottom lip began to quiver. He sped toward the nearest hospital. He was shaking as he navigated the car through the streets, going north of one hundred miles per hour. Mo continued to breathe heavily as she cried, thinking only about her unborn baby. Basil clenched his jaws together tightly as he tried to keep his composure. He felt tears forming but had to stay calm for Moriah. He couldn't let her see him rattled. He knew he had to keep her calm, so in return he had to keep a cool head.

"Remember the first day I met you?" Basil said as he looked forward, trying not to let Mo see the tears welling up in his eyes.

"Yeah, you were at my dad's barbecue," Moriah said in between grimaces.

"That's right. You were sitting with your girls, looking like a bag of money," Basil said, smiling while a tear slid down his cheek. "You know what? I knew you were my girl the minute I laid my eyes on you. I already knew. It was something about you, Mo. I don't know exactly what it was, but I knew I wanted to be a part of it." Basil let out a nervous laugh. He wiped a tear from his eye. "Remember those big earrings you had on?" he asked.

There was a silence in the car. An eerie silence that Basil would never forget . . .

The double doors that led to Hurley Medical Center's emergency room unit flew open. In came a well-dressed, tall, dark man. He had a shiny bald head and a salt-and-pepper goatee that displayed his maturity. A look of concern and uncertainty was on his face. His gator-skinned Stacy Adams shoes clicked along the hospital's floor rapidly, echoing through the hall's corridor. He was accompanied by two other men, well-built and wearing expensive suits. The man leading the way was none other than Kane Garrett, the man who had controlled the city for years. He also was Basil's mentor and supplier for the streets . . . the place that had no king, only a position that was always available for the taking.

Kane had gotten a call from Basil telling him to hurry to the hospital. Basil told him that Mo had been in an accident. He didn't mention that she had been shot. Instantly, Kane assumed that Mo had been in some type of car wreck. He'd worked so hard to keep his only child from the streets that he was sure she would never feel the wrath of his sins or past demons.

Kane looked toward the waiting room and saw Basil sitting there with his face buried in his palms. As soon as Basil heard the footsteps, he looked up and saw his mentor. Basil instantly rose and walked over to Kane. Kane saw the pain in Basil's face and the water in his eyes.

"What's going on, Youngblood? Where's my baby?" Kane asked as he embraced his protégé. Basil buried his head in Kane's chest, trying to find the words to explain that Moriah had been shot. She was in the back fighting for her life and Basil felt that it was his fault. Basil was a broken man.

"The baby . . . ," Basil whispered as he shook his head in anguish. He was so confused and lost in the moment that he didn't think of the fact of the matter: he had never told Kane that he had a relationship with his only daughter.

"Baby? What baby? And where is my daughter?" Kane said in confusion as his eyes scanned the room frantically, trying to grasp the situation. Everything was happening so fast and chaos was in the air. He didn't know what was going on, except that something was wrong with Mo. He needed answers. All the while, a grown man was crying on his chest. Who happened to be one of the strongest, stand-up guys he knew. Kane knew it had to be bad. Just as he was about to open his mouth and say something, the doctor came from the surgery room. Basil turned around and stood next to Kane as he waited for an update on Mo.

The doctor was a middle-aged white man with a slim build. He wore a mask and his scrubs were covered in maroon-colored spatter. Blood was everywhere. He had bloody gloves on and was slowly removing them as he approached the men. He shook his head from side to side in disappointment as he stood in front of Kane and Basil.

The look in the doctor's eyes told it all before he could even open his mouth. Kane looked at the doctor move his lips, but it seemed as if the room were completely silent.

"Sir . . . sir," the doctor said, snapping Kane out of his brief mental hiatus. "I'm sorry, there is nothing I could do to save her."

Basil dropped to his knees and stared into space as if he had zoned out. He had just lost the only woman whom he had ever loved. Kane, on the other hand, couldn't believe what he was hearing.

"Wait. What? Where is my baby?" he asked as his voice began to crack.

"I'm sorry, the bullet struck her liver . . ." The doctor calmly explained what had happened, as he could feel the father's pain.

"Bullet?" Kane asked as his shoulders sunk in and his perfect posture began to crumble. His eyes instantly began to water, as the news was like a dart through his heart. "Wait. What bullet?" Kane looked around, trying to find the answers from someone. His two henchmen just bowed their heads, trying to avoid eye contact with their boss. They couldn't relate to his pain and didn't know what to say. He placed his hand on Basil's shoulder and looked down at him.

"Basil? Tell me something. My . . . my baby was shot?" he

asked as a tear slipped down his face and landed in his salt-and-pepper beard. Basil slowly stood up, his shoulder shaking with the force of his tears.

"I'm sorry for your loss," the doctor said quickly, just before he turned around and exited the waiting room.

Kane's eyes never left Basil. He didn't understand. He was totally lost. The love of his life, the seed of his loins . . . she was gone. "What happened to my daughter!" Kane cried out so loudly that the words echoed through the entire first floor of the hospital. Basil just cried, not knowing what to say.

"Tell me!" Kane roared as he grabbed Basil around his neck and squeezed with all his might. Basil couldn't do anything but cry. Kane eyes were bloodshot, and he was full of rage and sadness. Basil didn't fight back; he felt as if it was his fault as well. Kane's grip was so tight and firm, it was cutting off Basil's air supply. Kane's tears flowed as the two men stared into each other's eyes. Both were lost . . . both of their worlds had been shaken. They had lost their girl. Kane's head henchman, Fat Rat, grabbed Kane by the arm. He had earned the nickname because of his short stature and stocky build. Fat Rat clenched Kane's arm and whispered to his friend.

"Come on, let him go, Kane . . . let him go," he said calmly, as he knew that Kane was about to kill Basil. Basil acted as if he wanted to die and didn't put up a fight. He was younger than Kane by twenty years and also much stronger and taller. However, the guilt paralyzed Basil and he took the disrespect. The only thing he could think about was Mo lying slumped in his passenger seat.

Kane clenched his jaws together and looked into Basil's eyes, the whites of which were slowing turning red. He released Basil, and he dropped to the floor, coughing and gasping. Kane thought about his daughter and the blood on the doctor; was that of his own bloodline? Fury and grief swept over Kane. He grabbed the gun from Fat Rat's waist and pointed it at Basil's head. *Boom!* A single shot rang out, sounding like an explosion from a cannon. Basil's entire life flashed before his eyes and he went back to his earliest memory. *I guess what they say is true,* he thought; *before death, you witness your entire life in a flash.* Basil's life had begun in the same place that he had conquered. Inside of the Regency projects . . . the most deadly place in Flint, Michigan.

CHAPTER ONE

Back in the Day

"Okay, listen to me close. Okay, baby?" Frenchie said as she closed the top of her silk robe. She looked down at her young son, who looked up at her, confused about what she was asking him to do. She walked over to him and knelt down so she was looking him in the eyes. She grabbed his right hand and flipped it, palm up. She placed a neatly folded fifty-dollar bill in his hand.

"I want you to take this down to Nephew's house and . . ." Frenchie dropped her head in shame. She took a deep breath and continued, "Give him this. He is going to put something in your hand for me. Okay?" Tears began to form in her eyes. She was ashamed of what she was sending her naïve little boy to do.

"Okay, Mama," Basil said. His young mind couldn't wrap itself around that he had to go cop drugs for his crack-addicted mother. She owed so many dealers on the block, she couldn't

show her face anymore. She had managed to run up a tab with any
dope boy willing to give her credit. To avoid a beating or maybe
something worse, she had to send Basil to the wolves. Frenchie
couldn't risk going out and being caught by one of her dealers.

"When he puts Mama's package in your hand, you best not
open your hand until you get home. Got that?" she said, pointing her finger directly into his face.

"Yeah, I got it, Ma," Basil said as a wave of fear overcame
him. He was too naive to understand that his mother had just
done the hardest thing that she'd ever had to do in her life. She
chosen her desire to smoke crack over the well-being of her only
child. Basil didn't notice the tears in her eyes. He only noticed
her stern voice and the finger that was being pointed in his face.
He knew when Frenchie did that, she meant business.

Moments later Basil walked through the projects on the
south side of Flint, making his way through the concrete jungle.
The hot summer evening made the air moist, and the streetlights were just flicking on as day settled into dusk. He heard the
vulgar conversation of the winos who stood under the streetlights, and the chatter of the working girls who hid in the cran-
nies of the darkness, waiting for oncoming cars to approach.

"What you doing out here, li'l nigga?" he heard a hooker
yell out, but he ignored her and kept pushing, heading toward
Nephew's unit at the back of the projects. The boom of the
sound systems blasting out of jeeps and the horns blowing were
chaotic around Basil. The deeper he went into the projects,
the darker it got. The streetlights had been shot out, and it seemed
as if the street noises were growing dimmer and dimmer. His

heart was beating so fast that it felt like two baboons were trying to escape his chest cavity. The fear began to creep in slowly. Basil held his head high and continued to make his way. He saw men standing in the shadows, waiting for a play to make a sell. Basil approached Nephew's building, and the flickering light from a lamppost provided the only illumination. A bum was sitting on a chair by the door, singing an old gospel tune with a half-full bottle of malt liquor in his hand. Somehow, the song sent chills through Basil's body as the broken harmony serenaded the air.

"Wade in the water . . . wade in the water now, children," the old man crooned as his too-big clothes hung off of him and the smell of liquor reeked from his body. Basil cringed, flinching as he brushed past him. He finally made his way into the unit, and the smell of urine and filth invaded his nostrils. He quickly headed to the rear, where Nephew resided. He stared at the two doors before him, both being Nephew's spot. Nephew had somehow gotten a wall knocked down, turning two midsize apartments into one large suite. Nephew was the head man in the projects and well respected. He was a hustler in every sense of the word. He sold weight but he also broke his weight down and sold rock for rock. No money was too little for him and he was loved by everyone because of his humility. Nephew really was a man of the people and that's why he didn't feel threatened by living in the middle of his trap.

Basil knocked on the door and he could hear someone approaching from the other side. Seconds later the scrape of deadbolts being unlocked sounded. The door slowly opened and Basil looked at the man that the streets called Nephew. He'd taken on the name because of his position as a young hustler; all of the OGs called him their nephew, and the name just stuck. He was light brown with a good grade of hair. He stood about five-ten and was of medium build. The smell of marijuana and the smooth sounds of Sade hit all of Basil's senses at once. He looked up at Nephew and was mesmerized, as he always was by him. Nephew was the coolest guy in Basil's book. Nephew looked down at Basil and had a look of disappointment on his face when he realized that Frenchie had once again sent her son to cop on her behalf. Nephew quickly shook off the notion of guilt and smiled with his pearly white teeth.

"My li'l guy." He reached down and gave Basil a pound. "Come on," he said as he looked around and then stepped to the side to let Basil in.

As soon as Basil walked in he noticed the red carpet on the floor. Nephew must have just had it installed because it looked and smelled new. Basil looked around in amazement. He'd never actually stepped inside of Nephew's apartment. Basil always stayed at the front door while interacting with him, but now he was walking into Nephew's world. Basil looked over at the couch and noticed two women tangled wildly together, both passed out. Their huge sets of breasts were on full display. One girl was completely naked and the other girl had on a dress that was pulled down to her waist. Basil's eyes then shot to a table where a huge mound of powder was also on full display. Basil didn't know what it was, but he would soon find out.

"What's up, li'l man? Frenchie sent you around here again?" Nephew asked as he walked past Basil.

"Yeah," Basil said, almost in a whisper.

Nephew made his way over to a small golden Buddha statue. He reached down and took the head off, which opened up like a candy jar. That's where he kept his crack cocaine. He always felt bad when he served little Basil, knowing that it was wrong, but his hunger for money always prevailed. He looked over to Basil, and that's when Basil opened his hand and exposed the fifty-dollar bill. Nephew pulled out two grams and wrapped them in a plastic sandwich bag and tied a knot, all in one swift motion. He then walked over to Basil and took the fifty dollars and placed the rock in his palm. Basil never looked down, just as his mother requested, and he gripped the bag tightly, knowing that Frenchie would kill him if he lost her package. Basil turned to walk out of the door and Nephew called after him.

"Li'l B!"

"Yeah," Basil said timidly as he turned around.

"You'll understand when you get older. Cash rules everything," Nephew said, feeling guilty and understanding that he had to explain his greed to the youngster. Basil nodded his head as if he understood, but his adolescent mind couldn't grasp the ideology. Basil disappeared into the dark hallway and made his way back home to deliver crack to his mother.

Frenchie impatiently peeked through the blinds, trying to see if Basil was coming. Her looks were still intact and her light, bright complexion seemed as if it were kissed by the sun. She wore a silk robe and rollers were in her hair as she counted the moments until she got her blast. Frenchie was a single mother and tried her best to provide for her son, but her habit repeatedly kept her from being a good mother. What started as a social hobby had slowly turned into a full-blown crack addiction. Crack cocaine was a new drug, and most people felt it was the "new thing" and didn't know it would single-handedly ruin an entire generation. She kept thinking about sending her son to cop for her and the sadness piled on heavily. The remorse only made her crave the drug more. She needed something to mask the guilt and pain. She saw Basil approaching her unit and she began to rub her hands together frantically, anticipating the blast of crack she was about to inhale. As soon as Basil walked through the door, Frenchie rushed to him and it seemed as if she were high already. The pure anticipation of smoking had her high.

"Okay, baby. Give Mama her package," Frenchie said as she reached into her robe's pocket and began to feel for her glass shooter, a pipe that she used to smoke her drugs. Basil slowly opened his hand, and for the first time he looked down and saw what it held. The beige rock that sat in his hand would change his life forever. Frenchie quickly snatched the baggie and closed it in her hand quickly, as if trying to hide it from Basil's eyes. However, the damage was already done.

Frenchie hurried to the bathroom to board a first-class flight to cloud nine . . . leaving Basil standing there, wondering what he had just helped her do.

After that, Basil scored for his mother all the time. She was a prisoner in her own home. Frenchie would never leave unless it was nighttime or she was in disguise, so as not to run into the dope boys whom she owed.

One morning, at the first of the month, Frenchie received a government-issued check. She was ready to score again. So she prepared Basil for the usual routine: she gave him money so he could go pay a visit to Nephew. It was about noon when Basil headed out for Nephew's unit, scorching as the sun beamed down. As soon as Basil got a couple steps, he saw a young hustler in a black hoodie approaching. As he got closer, Basil instantly knew who it was, a man by the name of Dog. Dog was tall, slim, and black as tar. He was from down South, so he had an accent and slurred his words with that Southern drawl. He had lazy eyes that made him always seem high. His look alone was scary, especially to a young boy.

"Aye, you! Yo' mama in there?" he asked aggressively as he approached Basil.

"Nah, she just left," Basil lied as he gripped the money tightly in his palm.

"Stop lying, little punk. I been standing against that light pole for about two hours," he said as he pointed to the pole about one hundred feet behind him. Basil was at a loss for words; he didn't know what to say. He looked up at Dog, who seemed to be seven feet tall, as Dog hovered over him and looked down menacingly.

"She's gone," Basil said as he balled up his fist tighter and returned the stare, clenching his jaw. Without warning, Dog's fist came down hard across Basil's face, causing him to crumple to the ground.

"Tell yo' crackhead-ass mama that I want my money. If she don't pay me my money, I'mma smack yo' ass every single time I see you," Dog barked as he looked down at Basil. Basil wanted to cry but he didn't want to show fear. He stood right back up while holding his mouth. Blood was leaking from his lip and his adrenaline was pumping. He stood firm with his fist balled up while looking up at Dog.

"Oh, you got heart, li'l nigga?" Dog said as he smiled at Basil's bravery. Basil wanted to fight Dog so bad, but he knew that he was no match. He was afraid. However, he didn't let it show as he stood firm with his chin up and chest poked out. Basil's eyes began to water as he felt a pulse in his bottom lip. He had never been hit so hard. Dog smiled, and it was obvious that he was having a great time bullying Basil.

"Like I said, tell that bitch I said I want my money," Dog said as he walked away and took his position leaning against the light post. Basil dropped a tear of embarrassment and anger. He quickly wiped it away and headed to Nephew's unit with hatred in his heart for Dog. He began to swing at the air as if he were hitting Dog. *I can't wait until I get older,* he thought as he continued to walk. At that moment, he finally understood fully why his mother couldn't show her face in the projects. She was trying to avoid what had just been bestowed on him by Dog. As Basil got closer to Nephew's unit, he noticed an all-black shiny car sitting in front of it. The car was like nothing Basil had seen before. He didn't know it, but he was looking at a Rolls-Royce. The wheels were shiny and it seemed as if sparkles were bouncing off of the car. Basil stood in awe as he gazed at the foreign spaceship before him. Kids began to gather around to admire this car that sat in their projects.

"Man, this is Kane's car!" one of the kids bragged as he placed his hands on the window and tried to peek inside through the dark tint. Another kid leaned against the car and posed as if he were in a rap video. "When I get on, I'mma cop me a joint like this. I'm gon' be the biggest dope man the Regency's ever seen, bruh," he said proudly while doing his best d-boy stance. Just as Basil approached the crowd, the doors to the unit flew open. A shorter man came out first, carrying a duffle bag, and the next man was Kane Garrett. He wore a three-piece suit and had long, thick sideburns that led into his thick beard. Everyone marveled at him, and it seemed as if they held their breath to focus solely on Kane. He strolled over to his car, but not before his right-hand man opened the door for him. All of the kids stepped back from the car and watched closely. Kane reached into his pocket and pulled out a knot of money that was as thick as a roll of toilet paper. He peeled off hundred-dollar bills and began handing them out to the kids, causing a complete frenzy. Everyone ran up to Kane, trying to get their cut, but not Basil. He played the back and just watched. After Kane rationed out the bills, he looked over at Basil and walked toward him. He looked down and slyly said, "What's up, li'l man?" then slid a crisp one-hundred-dollar bill in Basil's top pocket. He got into his car and his henchman closed the door for him. It was smooth as clockwork and just like that he was gone. Basil smiled and admired the man who had just pulled off. That was the first time he met Kane Garrett.

Basil left the crowd and headed to Nephew's spot. He knocked on the door and moments later Nephew answered. As always, he had a smile on his face when he saw his young friend at the door. Nephew stepped to the side and let Basil in.

"What's the word, B?" Nephew said as he walked over to his Buddha statue, where he always kept his stash.

"What's up, Nephew," Basil answered as he opened his hand, exposing the two crinkled-up fifty-dollar bills that Frenchie had given him. It was the first of the month and Frenchie was planning on getting super high with the government's money. Nephew grabbed a couple grams out of the Buddha statue and walked over to Basil.

"Listen, I'm going to put you on game," Nephew said as he looked down at Basil. "I'm going to show you how to make some money. Your ma have friends come over that smoke this shit, right?" Nephew asked, stood over him and smiled, putting a plan together on the fly.

Basil shamefully nodded his head, admitting to what he saw on a nightly basis. Nephew had seen Basil almost every day, copping for his mother or one of her friends, and decided to put him on.

"Okay. Dig this. I'mma show you how to make money. Instead of coming to me when your mother wants some yay . . . you can serve her," Nephew instructed.

"Huh?" Basil said in confusion, not fully understanding what Nephew was offering.

"Yay. Rock. Crack," Nephew explained as he held up the big rock of cooked-up cocaine. "You can serve her," he repeated as he dropped an eight ball in Basil's lap. "That's three grams. I will cut it up for you into twenties. Every rock cost twenty dollars. Got that?"

"Every rock cost twenty dollars?" Basil repeated as he picked up the bag and examined it.

"That's right. Every rock . . . twenty dollars. You take five and bring me back fifteen. Every sell, you make money and I make money."

"I guess I can do that," Basil said, still slightly confused about what was going on.

"I know it seems hard, li'l nigga. But you will get the hang of it in no time," Nephew said confidently. "You saw Kane out there?"

"Yeah, he had that dope ride. It was all that," Basil said, grinning at the thought.

"Right. Well, I'm going to get me one by the end of the summer," Nephew said as he crossed his arms and smiled as well.

"For real?" Basil said as he lit up like a lightbulb. "Can I ride with you?" he asked excitedly.

"No doubt, li'l man! You are going to be the first one I pick up."

"Word!" Basil exclaimed.

"But, do you know how I'mma get one?" Nephew asked as the smile slowly crept off his face and he grew a stern, more serious look.

"How?" Basil asked.

"By selling that," Nephew said as he pointed at the crack. At that moment, things got a bit clearer for Basil. He picked the crack up and looked at it as if it were gold. That's when he began to equate money with selling drugs. The comprehension of hustling began to sink in.

"Okay. I can do it," Basil said confidently.

"Let's get to work, then." Nephew took a seat next to Basil and reached under the lush couch, then pulled out a shoebox lid with a couple of razors in it. He took the eight ball and began to bust it down, creating pieces. Basil watched as Nephew showed him how to bust it without making it crumble. They sat there and talked for hours, and Basil questioned Nephew as if Nephew were a professor in a college auditorium. Basil was getting a crash course in selling crack, and he was about to grow up rather quickly, with the help of Nephew.

As they were wrapping up and Nephew was sending Basil back home with the product, he noticed Basil's lip. "What happened to your lip?" Nephew inquired.

"It's nothing. Dog just roughed me up," Basil said as he dropped his head in embarrassment.

"Dog?" Nephew asked, instantly becoming irritated. He didn't like Dog in the slightest.

"Yeah, he was looking for my ma. He slapped me . . . but I got right back up, though," Basil said as he poked out his chest.

"Okay. I'mma have a talk with Dog, a'ight?" Nephew said.

"Okay."

Nephew was burning on the inside. Dog was an out-of-towner who'd gotten comfortable in Nephew's territory. The only reason Nephew hadn't approached him about the incident was because Dog was one of Kane's workers. Both of their plugs was

Kane, and Nephew didn't want to cause any friction. However, the news that Dog had put his hands on Basil had him heated. Dog was a grown man, and bullying a child was a no-no in Nephew's book.

"I shoulda called the police on him," Basil added, as he thought about how hard he'd got slapped.

"What the fuck you just say?" Nephew asked as he stood up and frowned. Basil instantly grew confused. He didn't understand what he'd done wrong.

"I said, I shoulda called..." Basil stammered as Nephew stared at him with piercing eyes.

"That's what I thought you said. Listen up and listen close, because I'm only going to tell you this once. We never call the police under any circumstances—you hear me?" Nephew scolded as he reached down to Basil and grabbed him by the collar. "We hold court in the streets and never talk to the police about anything. Right or wrong, the police business is never street business. You got that?" Nephew said. He wanted to be loud and clear on the rules of the game, and wanted to make sure Basil didn't get them twisted. In the life they were in, police were the enemy and never to be used as a tool, help, or a scapegoat.

Basil nodded his head and Nephew released his grip. Basil's heart was pounding and he knew from that day forward that the police weren't his friend; Nephew had made sure of that.

"Now go on and get out of here. I'll handle Dog for you," Nephew said as he fixed Basil's collar and playfully hit him in the back of the head. Basil quickly exited and returned home to make his first sell ... to his own mother.

It was like Nephew had woken up something deeply rooted inside of Basil. From that day forward, Basil worked under Nephew and became a hustler.

Basil continued to make crack runs for his mother, but instead of walking to Nephew's unit, he would take from his own stash. He would then take a spin around the block and return to serve his mother and her friends. This became a frequent ritual, and Basil got better and better at it. At first Nephew had to give Basil pre-cut rocks, but after a time Basil began to cut his own and could tell the rocks' weight by eyeing them. He began to get eight balls from Nephew, which was three and a half grams. Basil graduated quickly, became more advanced.

Basil used Lil Noah as his helper and began to give him the same deals as Nephew had initially given him. Lil Noah was a longtime neighbor of Basil's who was a few years younger than him. Lil Noah looked up to Basil and had dealt with a parent on drugs as well. They were two peas in a pod and cut from the very same cloth. Basil's clientele expanded from his mother and her friends, to Noah's mother and her friends, to his whole unit. Basil grew up fast and was learning the ins and outs of a life of hustling. He wasn't making too much noise in the drug game, but everyone knew that he would be the man when he came of age. It was all in his demeanor. He just had to wait his turn.

"Please stop! Please!"

A loud commotion woke Basil from his sleep, scaring him. He heard his mother yelling and crying. It was coming from the front room of their small apartment. His heart beat rapidly as he stood up and wiped the sleep from his eyes. He rushed into the front room to see a sight that would haunt his thoughts for a lifetime. Dog was standing over his crying mother with a steel pipe, crashing it down on her hip repeatedly as she screamed for help. Dog looked like a monster as he grinned sinisterly and sweat beads dripped from his forehead.

"You think I'm playing about my fucking money?" he asked just before he struck Frenchie on her hip again with brutal force. Dog grunted, indicating he was using all of his force to punish the poor lady. It was a gruesome sight. Spit flew out of Dog's mouth as he barked at her about his money. Frenchie screamed in pain as she gripped her maroon-colored, bruised hip and upper leg. Basil instantly rushed over and covered his mother as he began to cry with her. He tried to protect her from another violent hit.

"And what the fuck you doing?" Dog asked as he raised the pipe again while looking down at Basil, trying to protect his mother. Without hesitation, Dog crashed the pipe down on Basil's back, causing him to scream out in pain. Basil clenched up in agony.

"Please, no! I will pay you your money!" Frenchie screamed in between her cries. Dog tried to answer, but he was too out of breath to respond. Frenchie looked at her son, who was in excruciating pain, and the guilt came crashing down on her. She knew it had been all her fault, bringing this pain into her family. She whispered in Basil's ear, "Run. Get out of here."

There was no doubt in her mind that Dog would kill them both. Dog was furious, and at that point, Frenchie only wanted to get Basil out of harm's away. Basil got up while holding his back in pain. He then darted for the door, and out of instinct, Dog gave chase. Basil's heart was racing and his back ached with every stride. He heard Dog behind him and he tried to speed up to evade the beating. However, it was to no avail. Dog grabbed Basil by the back of his collar and pulled him to the ground with ease. They were now outside for everyone to see. Dog was high on coke and didn't care who was watching. He wanted to make a statement in front of them all. He wanted the entire projects to know: don't fuck with Dog's money.

Dog looked down at Basil and gave him a swift kick to the midsection, causing Basil to curl up like a lawn chair. A small whimper came from Basil as he gripped his stomach in pain. Dog held the steel pipe that he had gotten from the side of the building earlier. He raised it in the air as if it were a sword and looked around as a couple people began to gather. Neither said anything out of fear that they would be next. Dog gave another kick to Basil, this time in his backside. His size-thirteen Timberland boots felt like hammers. Basil began to cry. He didn't let out a sound, but the tears fell freely.

"This is what happens when muthafuckas don't pay Dog," Dog said, talking about himself in the third person. He raised the steel pipe again to strike Basil, but was surprised when he felt someone grab the pipe. Dog turned around, enraged, not believing someone had the nerve to butt into his business. However, when he saw who it was, his temperature changed immediately. Dog looked into the eyes of his supplier, his boss, and the man who ran the entire city. It was Kane Garrett. Kane had a look in his eyes that Dog had never seen before. Dog looked around and saw Kane's open car door and his henchman Fat Rat, standing with his arms crossed at the rear of the car, watching his every move.

Kane had come to the projects to handle some unfinished business and pick up money when he saw a crowd forming and the pandemonium. When he saw the child on the ground, he knew he had to step in. Kane, not the type to get his hands dirty, usually wouldn't have gotten involved. However, his morals wouldn't let him pass by without stepping in. Kane's eyes were piercing and he had a menacing scowl on his face. He said nothing, but his eyes told Dog everything that he needed to know. Just as Dog was about to say something, Frenchie appeared, crying her heart out.

"Basil!" she yelled as she limped toward her son. She helped him off the ground the best she could and held him in her arms as she continued to cry. She kept whispering that she was sorry.

"What's going on here?" Kane asked as he tossed the pole to the side. He then straightened the collar to his well-tailored suit and took a wide stance as he crossed his arms in front of him. His diamond Rolex was on full display and sparkled in the sun.

"This bitch owes me money and I had to show a little muscle to get things handled," Dog said; he was noticeably calmer than before. Kane looked at Dog without saying anything and analyzed the situation. He then calmly stepped toe to toe with Dog with his jaw clenched and a stern look on his face. He said something to Dog that made Dog's head drop. Kane spoke so quietly, no one could hear him except Dog. Kane stepped back and waited for Dog to leave. Dog's head dropped further as he made his exit through the crowd.

Kane walked over to Frenchie and Basil. He reached into his pocket and pulled out a wad of money that was neatly folded in a diamond-encrusted money clip. He looked down at Basil and smiled, displaying his pearly white, straight teeth.

"What happened is not to be repeated or talked about after today," Kane said kindly. He peeled off ten one-hundred-dollar bills and placed them in Frenchie's hand. Kane looked at her bruised leg, which peeked out of her robe, and quickly looked away. The sight was too much for him. Frenchie looked down at the money in her hand with tears in her eyes. Just as she raised her head to thank Kane, he turned and headed to the car. Fat Rat opened the backseat door for him and he slid in smoothly. Kane was a gangster, effortlessly. Everyone watched as the car took off, in awe, knowing that they had just seen a boss at work.

Frenchie and Basil dropped their heads in embarrassment. They were humiliated in front of their entire community and neither of them had the nerve to look up as they made their way back to their unit. Basil helped his mother as she grunted with every step. They never mentioned what had happened. It was like an unspoken rule between them, and it drew them closer.

CHAPTER TWO

It's family over everything. Remember that?

—KANE GARRETT

The next couple of days, Basil was sore from Dog's thrashing and hatred built up in his heart. Basil wanted to kill the man for what he had done to his mother. It seemed as if his every thought was about Dog and how to get back at him. It almost became an insatiable hunger, to get back at Dog. Every single time he saw his mother limp, it reminded Basil of the brutal attack. Thinking of revenge with Dog almost became an obsession with him. One day while Basil was sitting in his room, an idea struck him like lightning, and he had a plan. He remembered that Nephew kept a small-caliber gun under his couch pillow, right in the living room. Basil always saw the handle hanging out and felt it when he sat in the spot. Basil needed to get to that pistol so he could shoot Dog. That way Dog could never hurt him or his mother again.

Basil recalled how Nephew mentioned that he would be in Detroit at the casino all weekend. Basil thought about how

Nephew kept a spare key right under the doormat that opened his apartment. Basil needed to get to that gun and this was the perfect opportunity. He would slip in, get the gun, and handle his business with Dog. Basil planned to return the gun before Nephew came home. It was the perfect plan.

Basil made his way to Nephew's unit, mumbling to himself about how he would shoot Dog right in between the eyes for what he had done. In Basil's young mind, murder wasn't fully understood. All that he knew was that he wanted to cause hardship to Dog and make sure that his mother would never get hurt again by him.

Basil thought, the key was in Nephew's hiding spot. Basil got the key and headed to the apartment. His heart pounded as he cracked the lock and slowly opened the door. He crept into Nephew's spot, then hurried to the couch and got on his knees. He reached under the couch pillows until he felt the cold steel of the small-caliber gun. Basil quickly pulled out the gun and looked at it in awe. The shiny chrome and heaviness of the gun pleased him as he studied it closely. He pointed it and squinted his eye as if he were about to shoot it. He imagined Dog being on the other side of the gun and it nudged him to complete his mission. He tucked the gun into his waistband and exited out the door. He was headed to Dog's unit and nothing was going to stop him from doing what he planned on doing.

Basil walked to the unit with murder on his mind. His young friend Lil Noah headed toward Basil playfully. Lil Noah was shorter than the other boys his age and had known Basil since they were toddlers.

"What's up, Basil? Man, everybody is talking about how Kane had your back! That nigga the boss!" Lil Noah said proudly as he walked alongside Basil.

"Go home, Lil Noah," Basil said without even turning to look at him.

"Man, put me on with Kane. I'm trying to get on," Noah said as he walked with a diddy bop. He wanted everyone to see him walk with Basil so he could get some props later. "You always get put on. First Nephew, now Kane," Noah boasted. Basil didn't know it but all of the young boys admired him because of his connection with Nephew. What they didn't realize was that Basil was cut from a different cloth. He wasn't loud, playful, or even child-like. That's what put him in position with Nephew. Even though Basil wasn't making any real money, his legend was growing with his peers and he never even knew it. That was because he didn't associate with them in the slightest. Lil Noah was his only friend and Basil liked it like that. He wasn't trusting, and his circle of friends or lack thereof reflected that.

"Go home!" Basil said sternly as he balled his fists. Basil stopped and looked at Lil Noah intensely, letting him know he was not playing around. Lil Noah smiled and put his hands up.

"Okay, Basil. Sheesh," he said, still smiling.

"I'll come talk to you later," Basil said as he lowered his voice, realizing that he was lashing out against his only friend.

"Cool," Lil Noah said as he walked away. Lil Noah was waiting for his chance to get on, and he knew Basil would one day be his way out of the hood.

Basil refocused on the task at hand. He headed to Dog's

unit but stopped in his tracks when he saw a big moving truck in the front.

Dog stood there smoking a blunt as he watched the movers move his furniture into the truck. Basil thought about walking up on Dog and shooting him right in the face. However, there were too many people outside.

"Damn!" Basil said under his breath as he watched Dog smoked the blunt, carefree, while surrounded by a couple of guys laughing. Basil put his hand under his shirt and felt the gun. His fingers began to itch; he wanted to take it out and handle his business so badly. "I hate you, Dog," Basil whispered as a single tear dropped and he clenched his teeth so tightly that the muscles in his jaws began to show. Dog, in the middle of his laughter, looked over at Basil. Dog said something to his boys and pointed at Basil. Basil couldn't hear what he said but he knew it couldn't be anything good. Dog shook his head and pointed his middle finger at Basil and returned to his conversation. Basil didn't know, but Dog's stunt had got him shunned out of the projects, which Kane controlled. Kane had given him a week to get out. Dog was upset and wanted to protest, but he knew better than to go against the grain with Kane. It was all Basil's fault. If Basil hadn't run out of the unit when Dog was beating him, then Kane would have never known.

Basil gave up on his plan and turned around, vowing to catch Dog slipping one day. He headed over to Nephew's unit to put the gun back under the couch pillow. Basil regretted not shooting Dog, but it was just too risky. Visions of his mother being brutally beaten continued to haunt his thoughts. Basil had pure hatred for Dog. His moving away wasn't enough; Basil wanted to kill the man. Dog had unknowingly taught Basil something that would forever be engraved inside his heart. Dog had taught Basil how to hate.

Basil forced everything out of his mind as he walked back to Nephew's unit. It was as if he was in a daze. His eyes were staring at nothing in particular but he never blinked, not even once. When he got to the unit, he snapped out of it, and a wave of comfort overcame him as he realized that Dog wouldn't be around to hit on his mother again.

Basil crept into the apartment. Just as he put the gun back, he heard someone at the door, jingling keys. Basil instantly began to panic. He grew short of breath and his hands began to shake uncontrollably. He knew if Nephew caught him inside of his apartment without permission, he would be in deep trouble. Without thinking, Basil hopped behind the couch, just in the nick of time. He peeked in between the end table and the couch, and watched what was to unfold. Nephew came in, followed by two other men. Basil immediately recognized them: Kane and Fat Rat.

Basil tried to slow his breathing and placed his hand over his mouth. He was shaking like a leaf, hoping that he wouldn't be discovered. It wasn't long before the conversation began. Basil listened closely.

"This must have been real important. I was in Detroit on a hot streak," Nephew said with obvious nervousness in his voice.

"Have a seat, Nephew," Kane said calmly, as if this were his home rather than Nephew's.

"What's up, Kane?" Nephew asked as he looked at Kane and then Fat Rat.

"You know what we are here for," Kane stated boldly. Just as the last word slipped out of Kane's mouth Fat Rat slowly pulled out an all-black .45-caliber gun. He wore a black leather glove on the hand that held the gun.

"Wait! Kane, it's not what you think!" Nephew said.

"It's family over everything. Remember that?" Kane said. Still poised and calm, he chuckled. "I have the feds on me, and because of you. All because of your disloyalty. They can't touch me, though. They probably going to hit me with tax evasion, right, Rat?" Kane said playfully as he looked to his right at Fat Rat. Fat Rat nodded his head in agreement, without cracking a smile in the slightest.

"Yeah, that ain't nothing, though. We gon' walk that down with ease," Fat Rat said confidently as he pointed his gun at Nephew's head.

"Wait, Kane. Just hear me out!" Nephew pleaded and held his hands in front of him.

"There is nothing more to talk about, my G. You broke the rules and now you have to pay," Kane said. He spun on his heels and headed for the exit. The silencer on the tip of the gun muffled the sound of the gunshots, but they were still loud as Fat Rat emptied one bullet into Nephew's head and then another two into his chest, rocking him to sleep forever.

Basil jumped in terror and shrieked. Fat Rat instantly pointed the gun toward the couch, and Kane turned around and looked in the crack between the couch and the table. He and Basil locked eyes. Basil froze in fear as he stared at the man with all of the power. Kane smiled and looked away.

"Come on, Rat. Let's go. There is no one in here," Kane said as he opened the door. Fat Rat looked at Kane as if he were crazy. Kane repeated himself, this time with more conviction.

"Fat Rat! Let's go!"

Fat Rat complied and followed him out of the door. Once the door was closed, Basil emerged from the back of the couch and looked at the corpse in disbelief. He had never seen a dead body before and his limbs shook uncontrollably. The smell of feces filled the air and began to stink up the room. Basil didn't know that when someone died their muscles relaxed and frequently a last bowel movement ensued.

"Nephew . . . Nephew," Basil whispered harshly, hoping that Nephew would respond. But it was too late. Nephew was long gone. Basil didn't know what to do. His instincts kicked in and he went straight for the Buddha statue. He began to stuff all of the drugs into his pockets that Nephew had stashed there. He then rushed to the back of the apartment and went for Nephew's shoebox that he kept all of his money in. There was a little over thirty thousand dollars in cash in it. He scooped that into his pockets and headed out the door. He couldn't believe what had just happened to Nephew. Basil's world was turned upside down. It seemed like he had grown up in one week's time. He had just gone through events that would change his life forever.

CHAPTER THREE

Never be Queen for a Day.

—FRENCHIE

Cops knocked on Frenchie's door at nine the next morning. She was already up, watching the news as the reporters talked about the homicide that had occurred in her apartment complex just a day before. She shook her head in disgust. She had been copping crack from Nephew for years and felt bad for how this had gone down. She closed her robe and went to the door to see who was banging so loudly.

"Who the fuck is banging like the mu'fuckin police?" she asked as she snatched the door open with a heavy attitude. To her surprise, it was the police. Two middle-aged white men in suits and with badges hanging from their necks. Both of them had potbellies and buzz cuts.

"Hello, ma'am. We are with the Flint Police Department. I'm Detective Green and this is my partner, Detective Wilson.

We need to speak with your son about a homicide that happened yesterday," the taller officer said.

"Homicide? My baby doesn't know anything about no homicide," Frenchie snapped as she rolled her eyes at the officer.

"Listen, we just want to talk to him. That's all," the shorter officer added.

"Fuck that. Y'all don't need to talk to my baby about shit. He doesn't have any kick-it for neither of you," Frenchie said confidently as she began to close the door. Just before the door closed, one of the officers put his foot inside, stopping it.

"Look, we can do this the easy way or the hard way. I only need thirty minutes to get a warrant to come in and get him. He is not in any trouble, we just want to ask him some questions. We know he used to be Nephew's runner. Just a few questions, that's all."

Frenchie thought about putting up a fight, but then she thought about the drug pipes and things she had around the house. She didn't want Child Protective Services to get involved, so she opened the door while rolling her eyes.

"Five minutes!" she spat as she stepped to the side.

"Five minutes. That's all we need, ma'am," the shorter officer said. The two walked past her and went to sit on her couch.

"Uh uh. Don't sit on my couch. You won't be here long enough to get comfortable," she said, stopping the officers in mid-squat. "Basil! Get in here!" Frenchie yelled back into the apartment. Seconds later, Basil emerged.

"Yes, ma'am," Basil said as he stepped into the living room, surprised to see the two unfamiliar white men.

"These two men said they need to ask you some questions," Frenchie said.

"Hello, Basil. I'm Officer Green and this is my partner. We need to ask you about Nephew," one of the men said as he reached into his back pocket and pulled out a small notebook. Basil remained quiet as he stood before the two officers.

"When is the last time you saw Nephew?" the other officer asked. Basil simply shrugged his shoulders.

"I don't know . . . a couple days ago, maybe," Basil said without emotion.

"We were told you were seen coming out of his apartment yesterday," the man added.

"Nah, wasn't me. I don't know what the fuck y'all talking about," Basil said, not caring if he cursed at the police.

"Are you sure about that?" the other officer asked.

"Yeah, I'm sure," Basil said as he crossed his arms.

"So you weren't at his apartment yesterday?"

"Nope," Basil responded.

"Listen, you can tell us if you saw something. We are here to help you, not hurt you," one of the officers said as he kneeled down to get eye level with Basil.

"Like I said, I didn't see anything. Nephew was my big homie. He used to give me lunch money, so I went over sometimes. I don't have anything else to tell you," Basil said as he looked over at his mother, who wore a slight grin. "Can I go to my room, Ma?" Basil asked.

"You sure can, baby. Officers, your five minutes is up," Frenchie said as she limped over to her door and opened it. She stepped to the side to let them have a straight path out of her apartment. The officers headed out, obviously mad.

"We will be in contact," Green said as he went past Frenchie. Before he could say anything else, Frenchie had slammed the door behind them. Where she and Basil were from, they hated the cops and it wasn't a secret. Basil faded back into his room and took a deep breath. He knew that he couldn't talk to the cops. Even though Nephew was his man . . . he couldn't break the rules. Frenchie walked over to her son, looking him directly in the eye. She was trembling, but she had hidden it well in front of the police. It was as if she was releasing the anxiety now that they had left, and felt her true emotions coursing throughout her body; she was petrified. Any cooperation with the police was a no-go; there was a big disconnect between the people of the projects and law enforcement. The mere presence of the police sent chills throughout the toughest gangsters, but Frenchie couldn't be prouder of her young son for standing up like a true man. She laid her head on his small chest and hugged him tightly as she rocked back and forth.

"You did good, baby. Never be Queen for a Day," she said. The term was used for a snitch, and Basil had just shown he knew her meaning well.

In the following weeks, Kane was in the news, the local papers, and the talk of the town. He was being indicted for conducting a criminal enterprise, racketeering, and money laundering. The media were in a frenzy. Half were describing Kane as a drug kingpin who thumbed his nose at the law, and the other half called him a pillar of the community and an esteemed businessman. His local grocery stores helped him with his front. However, the streets knew the truth. Kane had consistently flooded Flint with cocaine for years.

The black market took a big hit when Kane was going through the trial. No one had any product. Dog was gone, Nephew was gone, and Kane was under the watchful eyes of the law. However, Basil slow-rolled the coke he'd found in Nephew's apartment and became the go-to guy. He was coming into his own and eventually would take over the Regency projects. The coke he found in Nephew's apartment lasted him all summer and he eventually found another connection by the name of Boone, on the north end of town. In three months' time, Basil became a full-fledged hustler. He was the youngest in charge of the market and was gaining respect.

While Basil was emerging, Kane was fighting his case in court and eventually beat everything except the money laundering charge, which resulted in a tax evasion charge. The money he had acquired did not add up to his bank account, so he had to pay. Seven years, to be exact.

CHAPTER FOUR

Seven Years Later

The anticipation built as bystanders and spectators awaited the arrival of Kane Garrett, the newest professor at Michigan State University. Three black SUVs pulled in front of the lecture hall, and cameras flashed and news reporters gathered around the trucks trying to get pictures of the former drug kingpin who had beat the system. Everyone in the state knew what Kane had done, but no prosecutors could nail him. All of the charges, of conducting a drug enterprise, conspiracy, and money laundering, never stuck to Kane and the prosecution had to settle for a tax evasion charge. Kane owned half of the property in Flint and a small mistake was made in filing his taxes. That was the only reason he stepped foot in prison seven years earlier. However, this only added to his legend and made him more polarizing and infamous. Instead of shunning him, the community embraced him even more and his legend grew each day he was gone away. Local politicians and even news stations stood behind him and called for his release, stating that he was a pillar of the community and not a criminal. While he was out, Kane spread money throughout the city freely and was a fair business-man. These good deeds came back and helped him when he needed it the most. This forty-five-year-old king had the city on his back.

Kane stepped out of the truck and as soon as his black wing-tip gators hit the pavement the chatter among the crowd became complete mayhem. Reporters gaveled at the tall, dark man with a million-dollar smile. His bald head shone in the light, and his stride was graceful and confident. His crew quickly formed around him as they made their way through the crowd and to-ward the entrance of the hall. Microphones were everywhere and pointed at Kane as he smiled and seemed unbothered. Most reporters were asking him how an ex-con had landed a professor's job at one of the highest-paying universities in the country. It didn't hurt that the dean of the college was a former Flint politi-cian and childhood friend of Kane. Speculation was running rampant. However, no one could contest that Kane was a master of business, or that he had a PhD. He was fully capable and qual-ified for the job. As he maneuvered through the crowd, it began to part like the Red Sea. As he made his way up the steps, Kane saw a familiar face posted against the wall. He made eye contact with the young man and then quickly focused back on the report-ers hounding him.

Basil, wearing a black hoodie, leaned against the building and watched all of the chaos. He chuckled to himself, looking at the circus that was the first day of his senior year in college. He was studying business, and just by chance, he was going to be in the class of the man he had heard so much about his whole life. Basil felt nervous because all of the police were around for crowd control. What made him so uptight was the fact that he had sixty thousand dollars in his book bag from a sell he had made about thirty minutes earlier. He didn't have time to drop the money off at his spot, so he had to bring it with him. He didn't trust leaving it in his car so he had to do what made sense. Basil slipped through the side door, avoiding all of the ruckus, so that he could attend class. Little did he know, he would get much more than business lectures. He was about to receive the game and the rules that came with it.

No cameras, phones, or journalists were allowed in the lecture hall, so it was an intimate setting as Kane Garrett stood before ninety-five students front and center. The doors were locked and black construction paper covered the glass openings, so that no one could peek in. Kane requested this, so there would be no distractions and his lessons could be as impactful as possible. Kane looked at all of the young faces while smiling. His right-hand man, Fat Rat, stood by the door as if he was standing guard. The students were nervous and excited at the same time. They had never taken a class anything like what they were experiencing now.

Basil sat in the last row with his hoodie on as usual, trying to keep a low profile as he always did. He had managed to juggle a street hustle during three years of college and maintain a 3.0.

Not bad for a fatherless black kid out of Flint. He felt his phone buzz in his pocket and immediately grabbed it. He looked down and saw a message from Lil Noah. It simply read, "Half-Time." Basil smiled and put away his phone, knowing he had a sale for a halfbrick waiting for him. "Half-time" was street lingo for a half kilo and Basil was the plug. He focused back on Kane and paid close attention. Basil was particularly interested because Kane was from his neighborhood and was everything Basil wanted to be.

CHAPTER FIVE

Now, the million-dollar question is ... who has my money?

—KANE GARRETT

The entire Regency projects were live. That particular day was a great day for the neighborhood. It was a hot summer day, and the smell of charcoal and barbecue filled the air as music from loudspeakers resonated throughout the entire projects. A local band played on a stage set dead in the middle of the projects. It was a block party like no other. The projects stood still for a couple hours to celebrate. It was the homecoming of Kane Garrett and everyone was waiting for him in anticipation. The street executive was finally coming home.

In his prime, Kane made sure everyone ate and spread the wealth when he was in the drug game. Although he moved drugs throughout the projects, he gave back to the community. His businesses provided jobs and his humility made him approachable. In the land of no hope, he gave it. Within that small community he was king and everyone was elated to have him back. When Kane was out, the Regency projects got money and there wasn't another place in Flint that did numbers like their hood.

Basil played the cut and sat on the stoop with Lil Noah, watching the festivities from afar. He wasn't in the mix but he was close enough to see what was happening. He watched as three tinted black SUVs pulled up. Out came Kane Garrett and his entourage. Instantly, the roar of the crowd was colossal. Kane stepped out, dressed casual in slacks and a fitted polo shirt. A presidential Rolex was his only piece of jewelry. However, that one piece spoke volumes.

He began shaking hands and kissing babies as if he were a politician. All eyes were on him. People didn't pay attention to who stepped out of the second truck, but Basil did. A beautiful fair-skinned young lady stepped out. She looked exotic with her neatly twisted dreads and cat eyes. She had her locks pulled back into a ponytail and big bamboo earrings on. She was accompanied by two other girls but Basil could focus only on her. She was the most beautiful woman he had ever seen. She had a slim frame, but her ass was plump as if there were two melons inside the back of her sundress. With every stride, her plumpness peeked through the thin sundress material. Her extremely full lips and cat-shaped eyes gave her the look of an Egyptian goddess. Basil stared in admiration as she followed closely behind Kane as he maneuvered through the crowd. The crowd parted like the Red Sea as his crew made their way. They all walked over to a nearby picnic table and soon Kane's goons surrounded them and stood as if they were guarding the pope. Kane moved like a boss and there was no denying it.

"Yo, who is that?" Basil said, his eyes focused on the mystery woman.

"Yo, that Kane's daughter, Moriah. I went to high school with her. That bitch got picked up and dropped off at school in limos. Every fucking day, my nigga . . . every day," Lil Noah said as he rubbed his hands together and looked in Moriah's direction.

"Word?" Basil asked in a low tone.

"Straight up," Lil Noah said as he nodded his head in confirmation. He continued, "She ain't giving up that pussy either. She used to chop niggas instantly when they tried to get with her. She wasn't giving up no play. The bitch stuck up if you ask me." Basil just nodded his head while listening. He had tuned Lil Noah out already. He was locked in on Moriah and her unique look. Her natural look was so pleasing to him. The Afrocentric aura, along with her olive skin, was mesmerizing.

Kane sat back and felt the energy of his people. He bobbed his head to the music, enjoying himself. He looked over at his only child, his baby girl, Moriah. She was only twelve when he went to jail and it seemed like yesterday that she had pigtails. However, now she was a full-grown woman and had begun to look like her mother more and more each day. Kane looked over the crowd and then to his right-hand man, Fat Rat. He was a stone-cold killer, nothing more, nothing less. He had been running with Kane since they were teenagers. His only job was to watch Kane's back and he did that with precision and loyalty. He faded off the scene during Kane's imprisonment, but had returned to form the exact day Kane was released. Kane leaned over and whispered to one of his henchmen, telling him to keep an eye on his daughter. He signaled for Fat Rat to follow him and he slipped into one of the units. They faded into the building and stepped inside apartment 101. It was Kane's apartment, which he'd had for over twenty years. He held all of his meetings there. The spacious, empty studio-style apartment had hardwood floors and a certain coldness to it. He never kept any money or drugs in there, just a big round table and chairs. It was a special hideout where he always held court. He and Fat Rat stepped in the room, which had five gentlemen in it. They all waited patiently at the table to get back to business. All of them were old heads who controlled the drug flow throughout the city, one guy for each side of the city, and they all were Kane's guys. He supplied them for years and when he went to jail, their business suffered. Kane never gave away his connect so the flow stopped when he stopped.

"Good evening, fellas. Good to see everyone," Kane said as Fat Rat took a position next to the door and leaned against the wall. Kane slowly circled the table and placed his hand on a gentlemen's shoulder and smiled.

"Good to see you, Stevie D," Kane said to the smooth high-yellow man with a Dob hat. A red feather stuck out from the hat, which and was slightly tilted to the side, and a toothpick dangled from the right side of the man's mouth.

"Welcome home, Kane," Stevie said as he gave him a handshake and a smile. Kane smiled and nodded as he made his way around the table. He exchanged nods with everyone else at the table and got right down to business.

"Let's be clear. I am officially out of the game for good. But before I went in, I hit each one of you with fifty bricks consignment," Kane said as he continued to slowly circle the table. He held his hands behind his back and spoke calmly while addressing his old workers. "Just because I went away for a bit, that doesn't mean that that debt isn't owed to me. Everyone thought I was going to be gone for life. Everyone counted me out. People forgot about me. No one wrote me, checked on my daughter, or came to visit. No one except Stevie D," Kane said as he shot a quick look at Stevie.

"Yo, Kane," one of the men tried to begin, but Kane quickly raised his hands, signaling for him to cease all talk.

"Like I said, before I was interrupted, Stevie D was the only person who came to see about me. I can deal with that. I know how the game goes. Out of sight, out of mind, right?" Kane asked rhetorically as he displayed his famous smile, while still circling the table with his hands behind his back. "Fifty bricks at twenty thousand apiece. What's that, Rat?" Kane said, looking over at Fat Rat.

"One million," Fat Rat said definitively.

"One million dollars! Apiece!" Kane stated as he stopped at the head of the table and rested both of his hands on the oak wood. He leaned forward and said in a lower tone, "Now, the million-dollar question is . . . who has my money?"

The room grew silent and it almost seemed as if it grew colder as the words resonated in the men's heads. Kane's stern stare was menacing, and what usually were kind eyes and a great smile were now monstrous. Kane wasn't playing any games at this point. Stevie D was the first to address the question. He reached under the table and pulled out a briefcase. He placed it on top of the table and slid it across to just in front of Kane, who placed his hand on it and popped open the latch. Inside there were nothing but Franklin faces.

"There you go. It's all there. I've been sitting on that for six years," Stevie said.

"My man," Kane said as he smiled at Stevie. Fat Rat quickly came and removed the briefcase from the table and took his position back at the door. The room grew silent once more, and it was obvious that no one else had the money to pay Kane.

"Fred, you have my money?" Kane asked as he looked over at the stocky dark man that sat at the table.

"Shit hard out here, bruh. I—" Before he could finish his sentence, Fat Rat crept behind him and raised a .40-caliber pistol with a silencer tip. He pressed the barrel to the back of the man's head. *Boom!* He sent a single bullet through the back of Fred's head. Blood splattered all over the oak table, and everyone except Fat Rat and Kane flinched. Fred's body was slumped on the table as blood oozed from his mouth, and his eyes stared into space.

Kane smiled as he saw the terror in his former workers' eyes.

"Now, I ask again. Who has my money?" Kane said as he began to circle the table once again.

"I will have it. Give me a month," another guy said with a trembling voice, terrified to say anything in the vein of not having Kane's money.

"That's more like it, my friend." Kane said as he placed his hand on the man's shoulder, making him flinch to the touch. Kane continued, "Rat, Stevie D. Let's go enjoy some barbecue. I want the rest of you guys to have my money in one . . . no, two months. Kane is home. Clean this mess up and come out and enjoy the festivities."

Kane headed toward the door, leaving the room full of fear. Three men were left, two alive and one dead. The king was home and he was making it known. He was coming for everything he was owed, nothing more and nothing less.

When Kane, Stevie, and Fat Rat got into the hallway, Fat Rat began smirking. "Kane, why didn't you let it be known that he was a rat?" Fat Rat asked, referring to the federal informant that he had just killed. Fred had turned state when he got caught with weight about a year earlier. Kane smiled back and slyly slid his hands in his pockets.

"I had to make them sweat," Kane said, causing all of them to burst into laughter. Kane was strategic like that. He always played life like chess. He had to kill Fred regardless, so he figured he could kill two birds with one stone. He could press the issue about his owed money and also knock off Fred. It was simply genius.

They began to hear the music from the band outside and they returned to the crowd as if nothing had happened. "Feels good to have you home, Kane," Fat Rat said as he patted Kane on his back.

"Feels good to be home," Kane answered as he watched his people dancing, having a good time in his honor. He had been anticipating this day for seven years and it had finally come. The king had returned to his throne. But this time he would take over in the dark. He would never make the mistake of being in the limelight again. Prison didn't rehabilitate Kane. It only made him more strategic. The PhD in business that he had acquired while inside also helped him. Not to be a better businessman, but to be a better drug kingpin. The game would never be the same.

No one knew, but Kane was nearly broke. He wasn't broke in the eyes of a working man, but a man of Kane's status needed millions. The seven-year drought had disrupted his cash flow and the government stripped everything from him. His ten-million-dollar tax bill and all of the liens had him low on funds. He'd had just enough stashed so that his daughter wouldn't feel the blow while he was away. He took care of her aunt that raised her while he was away handsomely, but that cash was low and he needed to get back in position. Kane knew that he was under surveillance and the watchful eye of the law, so he had to move smarter, wiser, and farther under the radar. He created a plan in prison and it would soon be known as his blueprint to criminology. He just needed to find a protégé to complete his plan. If Kane put the right pieces in place, he could then apply his well-thought-out "street" business plan.

CHAPTER SIX

Never chase two rabbits . . . because you'll end up losing both.

—KANE GARRETT

Basil had slipped away from the celebration and headed to his low-key spot on the west side of Flint. Only two people knew about this particular spot: Basil and the person waiting on the inside for him. He slipped the key into the keyhole and unlocked the door. He heard the sounds of Pac serenading the air, and the smell of vanilla incense filled his nostrils. He walked into the spacious apartment that he had occupied half of the time with his girlfriend, Vivian. Vivian was straight from the hood and feisty was an understatement. A real around-the-way girl with street savvy. Basil walked into the spot and immediately called for her.

"Viv!" he yelled as he sat down on the couch. He also sat the book bag on the coffee table. Moments later Vivian came in. She wore small boy shorts that barely held her butt cheeks in.

The bottom of her enormous ass hung outside of the shorts and looked like two caramel teardrops. Every step made a thud, and her thick legs and heavy bottom side were on full display.

"Hey daddy," she said as she walked in and grabbed the book bag and peeked in.

"Hey ma. Count up," Basil said, getting straight to the point. He always made Viv double-count, rubber-band, and stash his money after every good day. She kept all of his money, put up for him, and weighed his product faithfully. Basil taught her to rubber-band the ten-thousand stacks with colorful rubber bands and the twenty-five-thousand stacks with regular beige bands. That way he could count them by eye and quickly. It was a system they had and she was the only one he trusted with his drug money. He met her through his connect Boone. Being that she was Boone's cousin, Basil had seen her when he used to go and cop from Boone. She used to cook up his dope for her cousin at his crack spot. Basil caught her in the mall one day and a simple conversation led to him dicking her down in her apartment and she never let him out of her grasp since. Basil watched as the ghetto black Barbie strutted past him, swinging her hips from side to side. The weight shifted from left to right, her ass jiggling on every stride. Her caramel complexion and dark silky hair made her look unique. She wore a neat ponytail pulled tightly and her hair flowed down her back. She was a stallion. Her thighs were thick and her waist was trim, giving her a perfect hourglass shape. Basil's eyes were glued as she put on a show. She knew Basil was on his way with the bag and she wanted to entice him, hoping that he might give a little hush money.

She bent over in front of him, knowing that her hanging fat vagina lips were viewable from the back side. She had it trimmed like he liked, not bald . . . but not a hairy jungle either. Out of habit, Basil smacked her ass, making a large echo sound throughout the apartment. On cue, she began to wobble it just as his hand lifted off of her plump cheek. She loved the way the sting felt.

"Damn, ma," Basil said under his breath as he watched the show she was putting on for him. "Gon' with that. I know what you trying to do," Basil said, slightly smirking.

"I don't know what you're talking about," she answered mischievously. Viv pulled out a rubber band full of bills, thumbed through them, and turned around. The way he made money in the streets turned her on every time. She slowly straddled Basil, putting her weight on him. Basil instinctively placed both of his hands on her rear and he could feel the heat coming from her pelvic area. She playfully flipped through the bills and licked her full, slightly oversize lips. "So, how much I get off this batch?" she asked as she slowly grinded in his lap, trying to awaken his manhood.

"We don't talk about money, ma. You hold me down and I will do the same," Basil said in his always low voice. He grinned as he lightly lifted up, poking her with his tool.

She began to feel him rise through his sweatpants and smiled, knowing she had him right where she wanted him. She felt herself beginning to get moist in between her legs and slowly grinded him some more. She tossed the money to the side and began to French-kiss Basil. She moaned softly and started rubbing her breasts through her shirt. They were big, round, and supple. She didn't have on a bra, so her erect nipples became noticeable through her T-shirt. They stuck out like two bullets. As Basil continued to kiss her, he gently squeezed her backside and had more than a handful. She reached down and pulled out his nine-inch, thick tool, swiftly sliding it inside of her without hesitation. Her boy shorts were moved to the side, giving him easy admission to her warmth. She was soaking wet in anticipation. The seat of her shorts were drenched.

"Ooh," she crooned as he slid deep inside of her. Her tight womb was extremely wet, and wet noises filled the air as she began to grind on him, sitting down on him while taking him all in. Basil was rock hard and he had reached his full potential as his pole stood up straight like a tower. She slid up and down on his shaft as she threw her head back in pure pleasure and pain. Basil gently sucked on her left nipple and squeezed her ass cheeks as they bounced down on his lap, clapping thunderously with each landing. Basil admired her body as she rode him like a jockey on a stallion. Her breasts bounced in the air as sweat beads began to drip down her torso, driving Basil wild. All of a sudden, she jumped off of Basil. She then turned around and sat back down on him, positioning herself in a reverse cowgirl. She placed her hands on the floor and began to work her ass in a slow, snake-like motion. Basil looked down at what was happening and bit his bottom lip as she made his rod disappear and reappear repeatedly. Her wetness began to drip onto his lap and it only added to the mind-blowing experience. Basil felt himself about to explode as he grabbed her waist and helped her slam down onto him. He knew he would release himself at any second, but he wasn't done just yet. He stopped her, slid out of her, and pushed her off of him. He then stood up and tossed her onto the couch. He parted her legs and took a peek down. Her juicy lips were glazed and her erect clitoris was pulsating. Her lovebox was on full display as the shorts were stretched and wildly pulled to the side. He quickly pulled his shirt over his head and off of his body, revealing his ripped chest and flat stomach. He grabbed both of her legs and gently pushed them back to the point where both of her feet were over her head. He slowly slid inside of her and began to grind in hard, slow, circular motions. She moaned in pleasure as Basil grinded inside of her. She begged for more and Basil gave it to her just like she requested. He looked down at her and her eyes were closed as she flicked her tongue like a snake, imagining she was eating another woman's lovebox. The look alone drove Basil wild.

Basil loved the way Viv made love. Maybe it was the fact that she was ten years his senior that drove him wild. Experience was her best teacher. She was an all-out freak and Basil loved that side to her. He didn't love her, but she was the only girl he trusted and he knew that she was loyal. She was his ride-or-die chick and the thought of that made him climax. He grunted and pulled out as he stroked himself. Without hesitation, Viv sat up and began to give him fellatio, moaning at the same time, catching everything that he let out. Vivian was amazing.

Basil's legs got weak as he gripped the back of Vivian's head and threw his own head back in complete bliss. He fell onto the couch and breathed heavily with his eyes closed. She got up and walked away toward the bathroom. Basil peeked as her fat cheeks wobbled as she walked. He shook his head in awe and took a deep breath. She returned to him with a warm towel as she cleaned him as he rested.

"I heard the projects was live today. Kane came home, huh?" Viv said, referring to the biggest news in the city.

"Yeah. He brought the city out," Basil replied.

"I know it's about to be on now," Viv said, smiling.

"What you mean?" Basil asked as he slightly frowned.

"You know . . . with Nephew being your big homie before he died. Everybody saying you're next in line to be the man."

"Everybody like who?" Basil asked, hating that Viv was discussing street business with him.

"Everybody's talking. They say Kane about to connect you to the plug like he did Nephew."

Basil shook his head in disgust, knowing that she had gotten the news from her cousin Boone. "You need to stop listening to everyone else. They just talking," Basil replied as he stood up and disappeared into the back of the apartment. Basil began to think about what he'd witnessed and never told anyone. He always wondered what the real reason was behind Kane killing his big homie. He would soon find out, once he got deeper into the game.

"Which leads me to my next rule of thumb that any businessman, or—woman, should live by. Never chase two rabbits . . . because you'll end up losing both," Kane said as he paced the front of the lecture hall with both of his hands in his pockets.

His sleeves were rolled up and he had on Ferragamo slacks and loafers. He had taken off his Italian-cut suit jacket, which was his daily uniform. He had finally grown accustomed to being a professor. The hype had died down and there were no longer reporters and cameras outside the classroom. There was only him and his students as he imputed his knowledge on business and how to maneuver among vultures. They were six weeks into the semester and Kane was getting into the meat of his teachings. He tended to break down his business lessons as if they were street deals. This technique drew Basil in and he understood a tad bit more than the other students. Kane was giving them the laws of the street and they didn't even know it; but Basil did.

Kane looked at his watch. "That's our time for today. I will see everyone next Thursday. Have a great weekend," he said just before he retired to his desk as the students began to file out of the class. As usual Basil was in the back of the lecture hall with a hoodie on. He was one of the last ones to exit and had his head down as he headed toward the door.

"Mr. Branch," Kane said smoothly as he sat with his hands crossed. Basil immediately raised his head and looked over at Kane. "I need to have a word with you," Kane added. Basil paused for a second, taken aback by the request.

Does he remember me? I wonder what he wants, Basil thought as he tossed his book bag over his left shoulder. He looked around and slowly headed over to Kane, who patiently waited for everyone to exit before he began speaking.

"Do you remember me?" Kane asked, after making sure everyone was out of the class. Kane nodded to his right-hand man, Fat Rat, signaling him to close the door. Basil also looked around and took his time before answering.

"Yeah, I remember," Basil admitted as he repositioned his book bag on his shoulders. Kane slowly began to walk toward Basil and eventually was standing toe to toe with him.

"I respect what you did back then. You didn't break the rules," Kane said as he pointed at Basil's chest.

"Wasn't my business. I'm no rat," Basil said, looking straight into Kane's eyes.

"No doubt. If you ever need—" Kane began, giving him his famous smile. However, Basil cut him off.

"Listen, I don't want anything from you. I didn't do it for you. I did it for me and my morals. I don't fuck with the police. Obviously, y'all had a problem and that problem wasn't my business. Feel me?" Basil asked.

"I hear you. But let me tell you this. Nephew was my guy. I had love for him. However, in that game I was in . . . there was rules. Rules that aren't meant to be broken without consequence. Nephew broke those rules. So I had to handle my business."

"I don't have anything to do with that," Basil said, trying to stay clear of any drama. He was there for an education, nothing more, nothing less. "Have a nice day, Mr. Garrett," Basil said before he nodded in respect and headed toward the exit.

"Mr. Branch. Nephew used to serve your mother, right? Was he really looking out for you or was he using you as a pawn?"

Basil stopped in his tracks but didn't turn around. His right hand was on the doorknob, but he didn't turn it. It was as if he were frozen. He thought long and hard about what Kane had just said. He'd never looked at it in that light. The thing that haunted his soul his whole life was his mother's addiction. For some reason, he never thought about the role that Nephew had played in her addiction, which would turn out to be one of the biggest downfalls in her life. Although he sold drugs himself, the damage that addiction had done to his mother was unforgettable.

"Now my next question is, do you want to be a pawn or a king?" Kane asked. Basil turned and looked at him.

"I want to be king," Basil said, nodding his head. He knew what time it was and what Kane was referring to.

"Let me show you how. You up for a quick trip?" Kane asked as he rubbed his hands together, devising a plan in his mind. Basil couldn't help but smile. The smile was contagious. Kane cracked a smile and then Fat Rat. It seemed as if all of them knew money was about to be made.

"Ha-ha, I knew we had one," Fat Rat said as he began to slowly clap and walk toward Basil. Fat Rat threw his arm around Basil and shook him a tad. They all shared a small chuckle as Basil took his hand off the door handle. It was the beginning of a union that would shake the city up for some time.

CHAPTER SEVEN

The only color that matters is green. Remember that.
There is no racism, just classism.

—KANE GARRETT

Basil stared out of the jet's window admiring the fluffy, cocaine-colored clouds. The smooth sounds of the Isley Brothers played on the jet's speaker system and the cold air from the air-conditioning filled the cabin. The gigantic leather seats almost seemed to swallow Basil as he positioned himself comfortably. He looked over at Kane, who was smoking an oversize Cuban cigar while focusing on *The Wall Street Journal*. Kane had his left leg crossed over his other leg, displaying Armani socks with perfectly tailored pants. His head was low, and he wore his wood-grain-framed Cartier reading glasses, which sat on the tip of his nose. Basil looked over at Fat Rat, who had his head buried in a pillow while leaning against the jet's window. Basil was in a state of disbelief. He was on a private jet with the biggest boss his city had ever seen. The city's most honored and protected boss. The fact that Fat Rat was asleep, Basil knew, meant that he was trusted, and he sat back and smiled, thinking about the endless possibilities. Without even looking up, Kane spoke.

"This is only the beginning, son. Get some rest, you're going to need it," he said calmly, as if he were reading Basil's mind. Basil looked over in shock as Kane's words spoke directly to his thoughts. Basil smiled and shook his head, impressed as he enjoyed the tunes and the smooth ambience. He looked at the pilot, who wore casual clothes, and instantly knew he was in the company of the highest level of drug dealing. They were just entering the state of Florida and their next stop was Miami . . . Dade County, to be exact.

Later that evening, they checked into a small luxury resort just off the ocean. Basil looked out of his window and the view was amazing. Palm trees, blue water, and warm, humid air. It wasn't anything like back home and Basil was taking it all in. He heard a knock at the door and quickly focused his attention on it. He walked over to the door and opened it. Fat Rat stood on the opposite side, wearing all white linen and a straw fedora.

"Meet us downstairs in fifteen, Youngblood," Fat Rat said without any facial expression, cutting straight to the point. "Another thing. Keep this close to you at all times." He tossed Basil a small burner phone. Basil caught the phone and examined it, wondering what it was for. "This is a line that's to be used for communication with Kane and only for Kane. Got it?" Fat Rat asked.

"Cool," Basil said while still looking down at the outdated phone, and just like that Fat Rat left him standing in the doorway.

Minutes later, Basil was down in the lobby and saw a man in a suit standing by the entrance door. He waved Basil over and opened the door for him. Basil saw an all-black Lincoln parked up front. The doorman opened the car door for him and Basil smiled. He never had been given the five-star treatment before. He was a hustler, a street nigga. He had never been outside of Michigan and this experience was foreign to him.

"Thanks, G," Basil said as he reached into his pocket and pulled out a wad of money to tip the man.

"Ah, ah, ah," Kane said as he sat inside of the Lincoln, stopping Basil as he attempted to slide the man a twenty-dollar bill. "Get in," Kane said smoothly and patted the seat next to him. Basil put his money away and slid in.

"Always let your muscle handle the money," Kane leaned over and whispered to Basil, giving him game. The doorman closed the door and stepped back. Almost immediately Fat Rat hand him a hundred-dollar bill as he walked up to the Lincoln. Fat Rat sat up front with the driver and they pulled away.

The first stop was to a brick building that had no sign in the front. Basil looked on, but remained quiet.

"I brought you to Miami to introduce you to a new way of life. I have been watching you closely, Basil. I know about your little operation and I like what you are doing. But you see . . . I want to step you into the big leagues. I'm getting too old for this game, so it's not for me anymore. Let me explain something to you. Selling coke doesn't have a retirement plan. I need to think about the future. I have all the resources and a master plan. A master plan that can make both you and I a lot of money," Kane said as he pulled a cigar from his suit jacket and lit it.

"I'm listening," Basil replied.

"I have one of the best cocaine plugs in North America. As you know, I did a little time. So that means the feds are watching me closely. I can't move around like I used to. I have to keep my hands clean. So I need an extension of myself, you understand?" Kane asked.

Basil slowly nodded his head.

"I need you to be that extension," Kane confirmed.

"I'm ready," Basil answered.

"Not yet. If you're going to get money . . ." Kane paused and took a puff of the cigar and blew the smoke into the air. "You have to look like money." Kane stepped out of the car and entered the building, which belonged to an old friend of Kane's: his Miami suit tailor.

Kane watched as the gray-haired man took Basil's measurements. Basil stood on a soapbox with his arms stretched out as the tailor sized him up. Kane and Fat Rat sat back and smiled with their arms crossed. The transformation had begun and they knew that if they groomed Basil correctly, that they would have a monster on their hands. It was rules to the game and if Basil could grasp them, he would be the new and improved Kane Garrett. Kane planned on teaching Basil how to move among vultures and not to make the same mistakes he did. He saw a huge opportunity to get to a position where he once was. Kane looked on as the tailor slid an Italian-cut blazer onto Basil's shoulders. A perfect fit for a young king. Basil smirked as he glanced in the gigantic mirror that was in front of him. He liked his new look and he finally understood the power of a suit. It was the beginning of something special.

Kane leaned over to and whispered something to Fat Rat and within seconds Fat Rat exited the building.

"I have something special for you. While Fat Rat goes and gets it, lets talk," Kane said as the tailor patted Basil on the back, signaling that he was done. Basil stepped off the soapbox feeling like a million bucks. The tailor exited and left them in the room alone to talk.

"You looking good, Youngblood," Kane said, flashing his smile.

"Thanks," Basil answered as he examined himself in the mirror, trying to get used to the feeling of having such snug-fitting attire. "Kind of tight," Basil added as he tugged down on the lapel of his suit.

"Trust me. It's just right. Bosses don't wear clothes hanging off their asses. You are dressed like a grown man. You can walk in any room and compete with that suit on. People believe there is still racism in this country. That's bullshit. The only color that matters is green. Remember that. There is no racism, just classism. With that suit you blend in with the elite class and that's half the battle. You have to get in to win," Kane said, dropping gems.

Basil listened closely and followed Kane over to the sitting area. They both sat on the leather couches and continued their conversation.

"I knew you were special. I saw it in your eyes as a young boy. I remember when I first saw you. I grabbed Dog off of you. Remember that?"

"How can I forget? I hate that mu'fucka still to this day," Basil said as his temperature noticeably changed. His jaws tightened and the sound of Dog's name brought rage to his heart.

"That still bothers you, huh?" Kane asked, noticing the pain in Basil's eyes.

"Yeah it does. Every time I see my mother's limp that he gave her, I see him beating her. Still to this day," Basil said as he dropped his head.

"Yeah, Dog wasn't a good guy. That's why I sent him away," Kane said. "How is your mother doing by the way?" Kane said as he placed his hand on Basil's shoulder.

"She's good. She's six years clean now," Basil said as he lifted his head and looked Kane in the eye.

"That's good. You should be proud of her," Kane answered. Just as he finished up his sentence, his phone buzzed on his hip. He answered the phone and listened to the person on the other end. Kane listened closely, hung up quickly, and smiled. He stood up and looked at Basil.

"I have a gift for you," Kane said.

They walked outside and there was an additional car parked out front. Fat Rat stood at the trunk, waiting for Kane and Basil to come out. Basil and Kane approached the car, and Kane tapped the trunk and smiled.

"The special shipment is inside?" Kane asked Fat Rat with a huge smile.

"Yes indeed. Just as you ordered," Fat Rat said as he crossed his hands in front of him.

"Good. Basil . . . step over here for a sec. I have something for you," Kane said. Basil stood in front of the trunk. Basil already knew what was inside and he couldn't wait to get his hands on some weight to put on the streets. *I'm about to flood that mu' fucka,* Basil thought, referring to his area back home.

Kane nodded at Fat Rat, signaling him to push the button to pop the trunk. Sure enough, Basil's gift was inside waiting. However, Basil couldn't prepare for what he was about to see. Basil focused on what was on the inside and what he saw totally took him off guard. It was a man in the trunk, hog-tied, and in a fetal position. Duct tape was across his mouth and he squirmed like a fish out of water, trying to release himself from the bondage. Basil stepped back in confusion.

"Don't step back. Look closer," Kane said calmly as he stepped to the side and let Basil get a better look. Basil hesitantly stepped forward and looked at the man's face.

"Dog . . . ," Basil whispered and moved toward the man who had haunted his dreams for years.

"I sent him down to Miami years ago to work under a partner of mine. This is my repayment to you for not ratting on me," Kane said as he reached into his waist and pulled out a chrome .45. He handed the gun to Basil. Basil took the gun and looked at it as if he'd never seen a gun before. He examined it and its shape as if it were a piece of art. He then focused back on Dog, who looked in his eyes and had total fear on his face. His muffled pleas fell on deaf ears while Basil was locked in on murdering him for all the pain he had caused his family.

"I never forgot about what you did to my mother. I want to give you something," Basil said.

"Hold up," Kane whispered as he put his hand on Basil's wrist. Kane then placed his hand on the trunk and lowered it, leaving only enough room for Basil's hand to fit in the trunk.

"Don't want to mess up a good suit," Kane said calmly as he flashed his perfect smile and glanced around to make sure the coast was clear. Kane then nodded his head so that Basil could proceed.

Without hesitation he pointed the gun to Dog's head and let off two rounds. The blast echoed and ripped through Dog's flesh. Dog stared aimlessly into space with his eyes wide open. Basil had never killed anyone, but that one was easy for him. He had thought about doing it for years, so he was prepared for it mentally. He handed the gun back to Kane and his hand was shaking. However, it wasn't shaking because of fear, it was shaking because of the fiery rage that burned inside of him. Kane took the gun and placed it into the small of his back. He then looked at his watch.

"Let's get out of here. We have a meeting to get to," Kane said. He closed the trunk, leaving the corpse inside. The tailor came out and got into the driver's side and pulled the car in his garage. The extra ten grand that Kane left him was for the disposal. Kane, Fat Rat, and Basil got into the Lincoln that was waiting and headed to their next destination. They were going to meet the plug and the head of the Cartel . . . Carter Diamond.

Marble floors were underneath their feet and the setting was dimly lit and relaxing. They sat inside a members-only cigar lounge on Miami's strip. It was a small nook, but lavish and exclusive. The smell of robust cigars and the faint sound of a Miles Davis classic filled the air. In their company was Carter Diamond, an old friend of Kane's who had moved to Miami and become large in the drug game. Basil sat back and watched as the three old friends caught up while sitting around a hand-crafted wooden table. Fat Rat, Kane, and Carter Diamond smoked cigars and talked about old times as Basil just sat back and watched. Kane had instructed Basil to stand guard by the door while he talked business. Kane told Basil to keep the gun that he had killed Dog with, so that's what he had for protection. After an hour of talking, Kane called Basil over. Fat Rat went and stood by the door, taking Basil's place. Basil noticed the organization and knew that he was dealing with a different type of street player than he was used to. There was no half stepping.

"Basil, have a seat. I want to introduce you to someone," Kane said as he leaned back and puffed a cigar. Basil did as asked and sat down. He looked across at the man and immediately knew he was of a certain age. His neatly trimmed, grayish five o' clock shadow was a dead giveaway. Basil looked at the man's pinky ring and saw a cluster of shiny diamonds, and they sparkled so vividly in the light. He sat with a firm posture and a confidence in his eyes that oozed power.

"I want you to meet an old friend. This is Carter Diamond," Kane said as he smiled and looked over at his friend.

"Nice to meet you, sir," Basil said as he gave the man across from him a nod.

"Likewise, young man. So you're Frenchie's boy, huh?" Carter Diamond said with a smile.

"Yes, sir," Basil said.

"I went to school with Frenchie back in the day," Carter mentioned. He was from Flint as well and was deeply rooted in the city. He continued, "So Kane tells me you the next guy out of our city."

"Yeah, that's what they say," Basil replied confidently. Kane and Carter both broke out into laughter at Basil's response.

"I like this guy," Carter said as he looked at Kane while pointing at Basil.

"I told you. He's solid," Kane said in between chuckles.

"Okay, let's do it. How many can you handle?" Carter asked Basil, getting straight to the business.

"How many can you front me?" Basil asked, getting right to business. Kane just sat back with his arms crossed, grinning. Knowing that he was creating a monster. Kane could have easily done the deal for him, but he wanted to use this meeting as a teaching moment for his understudy.

"You can have as many as you can stand. The ball is in your court. I need ten grand per unit and the rest is yours. Shit so pure you cut it three times and it will be the strongest shit in the Midwest," Carter assured him. An involuntary smile spread across Basil's face.

"Okay, I'll take ten," Basil said as he began to think about how he was about to flood the streets. Kane smiled and put his hand on Basil's and gently tapped it as if he were saying, *I'll take it from here.*

"Make that a hundred," Kane said calmly as he looked at Carter. Basil didn't understand the level that Carter was on and who he was dealing with. Kane knew it was nothing but Basil's inexperience, and that asking for ten bricks on consignment was insulting in the league that they were in, so he decided to help Basil a tad.

Before he could speak, Carter Diamond said, "One hundred bricks it is," as he stood and buttoned the two buttons on his suit jacket. He extended his hand to Basil. Basil stood and shook his hand, and like that Basil was connected with the Cartel and had a solid plug on an endless amount of cocaine.

"Before you guys take off, let's celebrate. I'm attending the mayor's brunch tomorrow. You guys should come with. Make a few connections maybe," Carter suggested.

"Sounds like a plan," Kane said as he stood and shook his childhood friend's hand. Carter shook Basil's hand as well and just like that; it was over. Basil was connected.

Kane and Basil walked out of the lounge as Kane threw his arm around his protégé. "Now it's time to learn the rules to this game. It's time to start our takeover," Kane whispered to Basil as he exited the spot.

Basil fixed his bow tie and looked around, feeling slightly out of place. He had never worn a tuxedo before and he kept wondering if he looked silly or not. He watched as Kane stood in a crowd alongside of Carter and Fat Rat. They all had flute glasses in their hands and traded war stories while reminiscing and laughing among each other. A live jazz band played on the stage; they too wore tuxedos, all except the lead female singer, who wore a stunning sparkling dress. She sang her rendition of Nina Simone's "Strange Fruit." It was the day of the mayor's annual brunch. This was an invite-only, small gathering held for the movers and shakers of Miami's business syndicate. Carter Diamond was the lead sponsor and the mayor's special guest. Basil studied how the people interacted with Carter, and if one didn't know any better, they would have mistaken him for the mayor. Basil stood against the wall. He felt out of place as he watched the snooty attendees mingle among each other. Just as Basil was about to call the waiter over to bring him another drink, a young man stood right next to him, and leaned on the wall.

"You must be Kane's guy," the Dominican-looking man said. He also wore a suit, but his suit was baggier than the other gentlemen's, making him stick out like a sore thumb. His long silky hair was pulled back into a tight ponytail and his neck tattoo was on full display. It read, "MECCA."

"Who wants to know?" Basil said as he looked around the room and intentionally not at the guy.

"Whoa . . . whoa. Slow down, playboy. I just saw yo' ass over here looking uncomfortable than a mu'fucka. I just thought you would want to take a smoke break. Feel me," he said as he looked around and then reached into his inner coat pocket, pulling out a neatly rolled joint. He dragged it underneath his nose and inhaled deeply, enjoying the strong weed aroma. Basil looked at him and the joint and didn't say anything for a few seconds. He then broke down and smiled.

"Man, anything to get away from these snooty mu'fuckas," Basil admitted. They shared a laugh and snuck out unnoticed. A few minutes later they were sitting in Mecca's Lamborghini sharing a joint. Mecca was parked on the side of the street, directly across from the venue. They watched the scenario as they shared the ganja. After the third joint and several mini-conversations, they had grown a rapport. Basil, not being a heavy smoker, was feeling higher than he ever had been.

"So, you Uncle Kane's soldier, huh?" Mecca said just before he took a deep pull on the joint. He held the smoke in his chest as he looked over at Basil and passed the joint. Basil unloosened his bow tie and grabbed the joint and took a puff. The snore-fest that was the mayor's ball called for a brief escape. Everyone there was twice his age, all except Mecca.

"Yeah, something like that. He's the big homie for sure," Basil said as he blew out a stream of smoke. The sun beamed down and the car was ice cold, as the strong air conditioner made it seem like a deep freezer. It was like heaven compared to the hot, muggy Miami weather.

"Unc always dolo. Well, excluding Fat Rat. But I never see that nigga with any young niggas. It was a surprise when he came down here with you. That nigga does not trust anyone. He just like my pops. I think that's why they get along so good," Mecca said as he placed the joint in between his lips and let it dangle freely. He reached around his head and yanked then popped the tight rubber band that pulled his hair in a ponytail. Instantly his long silky hair fell and he shook it so that it spread wildly onto his shoulders. Mecca had an abundance of tattoos on his neck and hands, and Basil examined them carefully. Mecca had an explosive personality and his demeanor was that of power and recklessness. Basil didn't know why, but he liked Mecca. Mecca was just a wild young boss that did it his way; a rebel, perhaps.

Mecca couldn't help it. He was what he was and no tuxedo could mask it. His wild look fit his personality perfectly. He reached down to his radio and the sound of Rick Ross slowly began to pump out of the bass-heavy speakers.

"I heard what you did to Dog," Mecca said with a smirk on his face. Basil was taken aback by his comment. He just mentioned the murder nonchalantly and Basil didn't know what to say. Mecca noticed Basil's reluctantance to respond. He playfully tapped Basil's chest and continued the conversation.

"Don't worry about that. I didn't like that nigga anyway. He was grimy and the only reason we let him eat round here is because Unc sent him down," Mecca assured him.

Basil remained silent and nodded his head, not wanting to incriminate himself in front of this guy he barely knew.

"Yo, is it always this hot? Damn," Basil said, changing the subject, as he looked at the thermostat on Mecca's dashboard, which read ninety-eight degrees.

"Every day, B. Every day," Mecca said proudly as he watched as a group of girls walked past. They wore small pieces of clothing that left nothing to the imagination. Their plump ass cheeks hung out of the bathing attire and their long hair blew in the wind. Mecca couldn't help himself. He rolled down his window and propped himself on its ledge so half of his body stuck outside of the luxury car.

"Yo, can I talk to y'all for a second?" Mecca yelled out. The girls looked back and were impressed by the spaceship-looking car. The sparkle in their eyes convinced Mecca that he would be bending one of them over doggy-style later that night. Basil sat in the car and watched as the girls came over to the car and talked to Mecca, giggling frequently as Mecca laid down his game.

In the meantime, Basil watched as two Haitian men approached the venue and something peculiar caught his eye. Both of the men wore trench coats in the dead middle of a scorching hot day. Their long dreads and sunglasses were as dark as their skin. They had tuxedos on and headed directly into the venue. Basil gripped his pistol and pulled it from his waist, and a million thoughts began to run through his mind.

Am I bugging? he asked himself as he contemplated if he should move on his notion. Something just didn't set right with him on what he saw. His whole future was based on a few people that were in that building. He knew he couldn't gamble with that. Basil stepped out of the car with his gun in hand.

"Ayo, where you going, fam? Bro, you high . . . chill," Mecca said as he looked at Basil creep across the street with his gun in his hand. Mecca quickly shooed away the girls and hopped out of the car, but not before grabbing his gun from under his seat. He caught up to Basil and trailed him as he smiled. Mecca loved the drama and his trigger finger began to itch. He lived for days like this, and he didn't know what was happening but he was all in. They crept into the front entrance, right behind the two Haitians.

Kane, Carter, and the mayor of Miami smoked cigars while on the balcony that overlooked the beach. The faint sound of jazz came from the ballroom behind them. The glass doors were shut tightly and provided enough privacy for them to openly discuss business.

"So, the next shipment will be in next Thursday. Are we covered?" Carter Diamond said, one hand in his pocket and the other holding a thick Cuban cigar.

"Absolutely, the coast will be clear and I have workers in place that will make sure your load gets on soil without any problem. Also a police escort will provide grand transportation to your drop-off spot," an elderly, deeply tanned white man said with a pearly white smile.

"Music to my ears," Kane replied as he reached into his inner jacket and pulled out a check. "By the way, here is a small donation to your wonderful charity," he added sarcastically. The mayor grabbed the check and nodded in amusement.

"Mr. Garrett, this is amazing. On behalf of my entire organization, we thank you," he said just before he winked at Kane. Carter followed up by reaching into his pocket and also donating a check to the charity. The mayor smiled and accepted it gladly as well. All of the men raised their cigars in a victory for all parties involved. Carter and Kane had just solidified the passage of a few tons of pure cocaine into the States. This was drug dealing at its highest level. The business that just got handled by a handshake on the balcony of a Miami hotel would trickle down and reach the grimiest places of the ghetto within a few weeks. That's what you called distribution at its finest. As Kane opened his mouth to speak about trying to establish a pipeline with some of the mayor's political friends in the Midwest, the double doors swung open and a slim chocolate-skinned waitress with an innocent face came through carrying a tray with three champagne flutes. She was a beautiful young lady who didn't look a day older than twenty. She avoided eye contact with them, which made her shyness more noticeable and her look adorable to the seasoned businessmen.

"Why, thank you, beautiful," Carter said with charm as he grabbed one of the flutes. He reached into his pocket and pulled out a diamond-encrusted money clip. He swiftly slid one of the hundred-dollar bills from his bankroll and placed it on the young lady's tray. The other two men followed suit, and the young lady bowed in respect and turned around to head back to the ballroom.

"I would like to make a toast," the mayor said as he raised his glass. Just as Kane and Carter raised their glasses, commotion erupted on the main floor and sounds of frightened screams erupted, sending the guests into a frenzy.

Basil peeked into the supply room and saw five women and four males tied up. It was a mix of waiters, security, and chefs. All of their mouths were duct-taped as well as their feet. They sat in a huddle as they cried and forced muffled moans. They were being held hostage for one reason: so that the Haitian mafia could take over their jobs to kill Carter Diamond. All of this had been done under the nose of the mayor. A well-orchestrated ambush was approaching. Basil couldn't believe his eyes as he crept toward the hostages with his gun up while placing his finger on his lip, signaling them to be quiet. Mecca was close behind with his gun also drawn. Basil whispered to them, "I will get you guys untied. Just be quiet and patient," as he closed the door, leaving them in the dark room once again.

Minutes before, Basil had trailed the Haitians to the kitchen and that's how he stumbled onto the staff. He knew that his intuition was right and now he had to stay calm and figure out how to get Kane out of the sticky situation. Basil and Mecca crept toward the main kitchen area and saw a group of men huddled and talking to one another. They all wore staff attire; most of them had dreadlocks and deeply dark skin, which are strong Haitian features. Basil heard someone coming so he ducked behind a tall food cart and remained quiet, and Mecca put his back against the wall, just around the corner of the kitchen.

Basil looked at Mecca and he was surprised because Mecca was smiling. It was as if he were a young boy in a candy shop. Mecca's trigger finger began to itch and he held his gun up, ready to pop off. Basil looked at him and thought, *This nigga is crazy for real.* Basil quickly shook off the thought and got ready to pop off himself. He nodded his head, signaling Mecca that it was go time. They swung around the corner in unison with their guns drawn and pointed at the Haitian men. They quickly approached the three men and relieved them of their guns, which were tucked inside their aprons.

"Look like we fucked up y'all plans, huh," Mecca said mockingly. Mecca pressed his gun aggressively to one man's forehead and looked at him intensely. Deep inside Mecca hoped that he would make a move so that he could blow his brains all over the kitchen's walls. The Haitian men put their hands up, surprised by their plan being detoured. They'd been moments away from airing out the whole building. The automatic assault rifles that were lying on the counter, wrapped in their overcoats, had been about to be put to use. The Haitian men traded words with one another in French.

"Yo, cut that shit out. How many of y'all in there?" Basil asked as he dug the barrel of his gun into one of the men's neck. The man looked at Basil and continued to speak in French.

"Speak English, mu'fucka!" Basil demanded. Mecca couldn't take it anymore and he pulled the trigger, sending a hollow-point bullet through one of the dread-heads' skull. Blood and brain matter splattered over his comrades' faces and panic filled the air. Mecca, on the other hand, was laughing uncontrollably as he got a rise out of seeing the man's body drop and fear fill his team. The sound of chaos came from the main ballroom. Mecca's face and white tuxedo were covered with blood. He grabbed one of the other Haitian hitmen around the neck and made it a tandem, sending another shot through his head. *Boom!* Even Basil was surprised by his brazen actions. Mecca was a diabolical gangster and he lived for moments and situations like the one that was occurring. It was right up his alley. Mecca grabbed the third Haitian by the back of the neck and squeezed with all of his might. The man's veins were forming in his head and neck as he remained silent. He breathed heavily and his jaws were clenched tightly. His two cousins had just been murdered right in front of him and his hatred for the Cartel grew even more.

"How many more of you?" Mecca asked as he pressed his forehead directly against the man's and smiled demonically. He dragged his gun slowly down the side of the Haitian's face as he played an evil mental game with the man. The sound of pandemonium from the frantic patrons was wafting in from the other room. However, Mecca acted as if it were only him and the Haitian left on the entire earth; he was locked in. It was an extreme rush for him and his adrenaline pumped, giving him a high that he chased daily. "I can't hear you, homeboy," Mecca said through his clenched teeth. Basil watched in shock, Mecca face-to-face with the man as if they were friends of twenty years, Mecca's exchange with him intimate . . . demonic almost. The man held on to his silence, and Mecca saw that he was stubborn and he wasn't going to get anything out of him. Mecca grew impatient and struck the man with the butt of his gun, causing him to crash to the floor. The man pressed his hand to the bloody gash on his forehead. Blood seeped through the Haitian's fingers as he moaned in agony and rocked back and forth. Mecca quickly snatched him up by his collar and directed him into the ballroom. Mecca dug his gun into the Haitian's back and guided him through the sea of frenzied people. The guests were looking confused and distraught, trying to figure out what was going on. A few people fled past Mecca and ran toward the exit. Basil followed close behind Mecca with his gun drawn. They both noticed a female exiting the balcony where Kane, Carter, and the mayor stood. Mecca immediately noted her Haitian facial features. Her smooth chocolate skin and high cheekbones were a dead giveaway.

"Grab that bitch," Mecca whispered to Basil as they approached her. Basil quickly grabbed her by her shirt collar, causing her to drop her tray and scream in terror. He pushed her back onto the balcony.

"What the hell is going on!" Carter Diamond said, thinking his son had done something reckless as usual.

"Tell him! Tell him who you are!" Mecca yelled as blood trickled down his own face from the men he had just murdered.

"What's going on, Carter? This is outrageous," the mayor said as his face turned plum red. Carter instantly began to understand what was going on and quickly went into action.

"Mr. Mayor, I think it's time for you to leave. I'll be in touch," he said as he patted his back. Kane, on key, stepped to the side, giving the mayor a path to exit. The mayor hurried out and the other members of the Cartel who were scattered throughout the room headed out to the balcony. Carter knew that he had to do what he was going to do quickly before the cops came, so he got straight down to business.

"Who sent you? Matee?" Carter asked calmly as he walked up to the Haitian man. Carter got no response, so he tilted his head and got closer. "Come on. You can tell me," Carter said as he playfully smacked the man's cheek twice. "Come on. Who sent you?" The Haitian man still didn't respond, so Carter wasted no time. "Yo, you strapped, Kane?" he asked while keeping his eyes focused on the Haitian.

"It's close by," Kane responded casually with a grin on his face. Kane then ran his hand down his goatee, and stuck two fingers in his mouth and whistled speedily. He promptly shot a look at Fat Rat. Fat Rat expeditiously pulled a gun from the inside of his blazer, cocked it, and handed it to Kane. Carter held his hand out and wiggled his fingers, waiting to feel the cold steel in the palm of his hands. Kane placed the gun in Carter's hand and in one swift motion, Carter put the gun to the Haitian's head and pulled the trigger. *Boom!* Brain matter splashed everywhere and the smell of blood was overpowering. The members of the Cartel jumped at the gunshot and watched as the Haitian's limp body dropped to Carter's feet. Kane was the only one that didn't flinch. It was as if they had done that little routine a million times before. It was business as usual.

As the man bled at his feet, he quickly focused his attention on the waitress, who was crying her eyes out. Her hands trembled as she tried to cover her mouth, attempting to muffle her cries.

"You know him, sweetheart?" Kane asked.

"Oh my God. No . . . no, I don't know him," she said as she continued to cry uncontrollably as she stared at the dead body on the ground. The Haitian's head was half blown off and the gruesome sight was almost too much to bear.

"It's okay . . . it's okay," Carter said comfortingly, as he stepped to her and kissed her forehead. "Everything is going to be all right. I promise." Carter cupped her face and looked at her

with his perfect smile. She nodded her head, and believed that
he was not posing any threat to her.

"Have a drink to calm yourself," Kane said as he grabbed
the drink that she had delivered them just a few minutes before.

"I don't drink," she said as she wiped the tears away.

"Go ahead, drink it," Carter said as he looked over to his
man Kane, who was now holding the drink to her quivering
lips. She shook her head no and quickly turned her head away
from the glass.

"Drink it!" Kane said in a harsh tone, making the young girl
flinch at the sound of his loud voice.

"Maybe she doesn't want to drink it because it's poisoned,"
Carter suggested. He swiftly raised the gun in his hand and
pressed the barrel to her forehead without hesitation.

"Drink it," he demanded without emotion. The girl held her
lips tightly, not wanting a drop of the champagne to get in her
system. The tears began to flow down her face even more and
it was evident who had sent her. Carter leaned over and again
kissed her on the forehead. He then stepped back and put a bullet through her chest without hesitation, sending her body flying
back like a ragdoll.

"Let's move out," Carter said as he stepped over her body and
out of the door. Basil watched in amazement as he saw a totally
new world . . . a totally new power. He was now forever connected
to the infamous Cartel.

CHAPTER EIGHT

Welcome to the Cartel.

—MECCA DIAMOND

The sound of the announcer pumped out of the speakers. The entire Cartel was in the VIP suite at the Miami Heat arena. They were all in attendance to watch the Heat play the Pistons. The extra-large suite was reserved for the most prestigious guests and Carter had season tickets for him and his entire team. The liquor was flowing and beautiful waitresses tended to the small group. Basil stood at the glass looking down at the court as he watched the crowd erupt at the sight of D. Wade's spectacular slam dunk.

"What's good, fam?" Mecca said as he approached Basil. He had two girls, one on each arm, and they both were stunning. One was ebony-colored with long legs and an ass like a horse's. She had a small waist but her curves were voluptuous and almost surreal. The other girl was a Caucasian redhead who had big perky breasts that seemed as if they were seconds away from bursting out of her small black dress.

"What up, fam?" Basil replied as he slapped hands with and embraced Mecca. Mecca then threw both of his arms around each girl's shoulder.

"I want you to meet Ginger and Kim. Pops sent them over," Mecca said smoothly as he looked over at the bar, where his father was standing holding a beer. Carter and Kane were both smiling as they watched Basil going through his initiation. Carter raised his glass and saluted Basil. Basil smiled and shook his head at the sentiment, then raised his glass as he thanked him nonverbally. The girls, almost on cue, left Mecca and instantly stood by Basil, one on each arm.

"Welcome to the Cartel," Mecca said playfully and he put his hand on Basil's shoulder and patted him. The two girls led Basil out of the VIP suite to the private suite next door. Basil could get used to this Miami living.

Meanwhile Kane and Carter talked at the bar as they surveyed the intimate gathering.

"Your guy saved my life yesterday," Carter admitted, just before he took a swallow of the beer.

"Yeah, Youngblood is very sharp. He's been like that since a young boy," Kane replied. "Just like his mom," Kane added thinking about how Frenchie used to be. She had so much promise before the drugs.

"Yeah, that's a shame, what happened to Frenchie," Carter said as he too thought about how Frenchie had been when they were younger. It was a distant memory but he remembered the good times. Carter quickly changed the subject and leaned in closer to Kane.

"Ah, I want to thank you for delivering those monthly envelopes to T for me. Even when you got locked up, you made sure your people got that to her. That's honorable," Carter said. Kane nodded. Carter had a love child with T that only a few people knew about. His connections with the Cartel prevented him from bringing his son into the light. His empire would crumble if his secret got out. He got his hometown girl pregnant just before he moved to Miami and didn't find out until years later, once his family was already established. As soon as Carter found out about his illegitimate son, he began sending money to him monthly and Kane was the pipeline that made it happen for him. Carter would be forever indebted to him for that.

"I took the liberty of adding twenty more units onto your guy's order. That's on me. If it wasn't for Basil's sharpness, I might not be here right now," Carter said in gratitude.

"Yeah, Youngblood was on his A game. Them Haitian mu'fuckas had the drop on you," Kane admitted.

"True indeed. Keep him around. He's going to be king one day. Might even take your spot," Carter said jokingly just before he finished off his drink. Kane chuckled, but deep inside he knew there was some truth there. Basil was a different breed. He was destined to be large in the drug game. He was too clever not to be. Kane knew that he was the new, improved version of himself and instead of jealousy, he felt proud. He was creating an "untouchable" with Basil.

Meanwhile in the next room, Basil was getting his mind blown. He sat on the comfortable leather couch with his pants down around his ankles. His head was thrown back and his eyes were closed as the sounds of slurping echoed throughout the suite. Two girls were at his feet, while on their knees. Both of them were giving him fellatio as they tag-teamed his slightly curved, dark pole. The ebony woman sucked on his balls while the other girl worked on his erect tool. Basil glanced down and saw the big perky breasts of both women. The large pink areolas of Ginger combined with the deep-chocolate-colored ones that sat at the tip of Kim's melons were a sight to see. They both had their dresses pulled down around their waists as they serviced Basil. Basil could get used to Miami. The city definitely embraced him. He continued to watch as the women tag-teamed him and he stood tall and firm as they began to moan loudly. He gently placed his hands on the backs of each of their heads as they slowly bobbed up and down. Tingles went up his spine as he felt an orgasm approaching. Basil clenched his ass cheeks and stiffened up his legs as his eyes began to roll back in his head. He had never experienced a sexual encounter like the one that was upon him. He had two of the most beautiful women that he had ever seen on their knees in front of him, blowing his mind.

"Ooh shit," Basil whispered as he began to pump, diving into Ginger's mouth with each thrust. He felt himself beginning to climax and his body tensed up as he pulled his tool out of the girl's mouth. He began to stroke himself and the two girls immediately got side by side and began to grope their breasts, giving him a place to release himself. Basil looked down and the sight alone sent him over the edge. He released himself on the two girls, and they gladly accepted everything he offered while moaning and touching each other. They began kissing one another, and Basil sat back and enjoyed the show while panting heavily from the exhilarating release he'd just experienced. "I love Miami," he whispered to himself as he sunk deeper into the couch.

CHAPTER NINE

Keep your enemies far. Not close . . . but far.

—KANE GARRETT

Basil and Kane wasted no time when they returned home. With the free bricks on top of their original order, they were able to drop prices even more than expected. Kane coached Basil as the takeover began. The first thing was for Basil to establish a team, and he went to his man Lil Noah first. Lil Noah had a group of hungry young fellows that followed him around and Basil immediately upgraded all of their positions in the streets. He put them on heavy, and in return they would handle any street beef or problems if they should ever arise. Lil Noah was loving the new position of power that Basil had put him in. The streets were not ready for what Basil was about to do. He also put Viv onto his new operation and she acted as a mule for his shipments from the Cartel. He sent her down to Miami monthly in a U-Haul with furniture and she always returned with bricks hidden in them. It was a smooth operation and well thought out.

"Corner the market and dominate. Why be a jack of all trades and a master of none?" Those were the words of Kane Garrett as he explained a popular technique in business. Instead of worrying about multiple markets and spreading your money into several investments, he taught that you should find your niche and dominate that particular arena. It made so much sense to Basil. So his first step was to take over his childhood neighborhood, which was the Regency projects.

Two weeks in Basil had positioned his team and prepared a hostile takeover. Instead of going against the community, he embraced them. He hired various older women in the complex to cook the coke, weigh, and bag up the product. Kane had explained to him that most hustlers made the mistake of hiring the young, around-the-way girls to bag the dope up, but in reality they were the last people you should employ. He instructed him to hire the elders in the complex, because they were usually the ones who called the police on drug activity. If Basil included them in the hustle, they would be fools to tell the authorities on themselves. So that's what Basil did. And that's when Basil really began to understand Kane's brilliance. He was a strategist and made him look at hustling from a business aspect.

Basil approached the respected members of the complex with an offer to give them credit and put them in a position to touch some of the best coke that had ever touched the Midwest. He sold the fact that they would be able to get the best quality at the cheapest price and become a member of an elite squad. This meant a lot of things, but at the top of the list was the built-in army that served as protection. No one declined to get down.

He spent the first two weeks just setting up shop before he re-leased one single drug. Under Kane's direction he was literally setting up a Wall Street for drugs. It was to be an open market, and if Basil controlled the whole projects and everyone worked for him, it would be harder for the feds to infiltrate.

Through all of the preparation, Basil still stayed in school and on top of his studies. It was the last day of class and as usual Basil sat in the back, but there was a difference to him. Instead of his usual urban casual attire, Basil wore a suit and looked more like a broker than a hustler. He focused on Kane, who was in the front of the lecture hall.

"Always remember: Keep your enemies far. Keep . . . your . . . enemies . . . far, not close. Life isn't a Scarface movie. This is real life. This is business. In the corporate world, if you let a snake into your circle . . . ," he dramatically paused as he carefully looked around the room, "you can watch your whole empire crumble in the blink of an eye. Build a strong team around you and one built solely on integrity, hard work, and loyalty. That, my friend, is how you succeed.

"With that I want to thank you all for spending these last few months with me. Business Philosophy 101 is officially over. Good luck, guys, and may each and every single one of you assist with or lead a change in the world," Kane said as he stood front and center, totally engaged with his students. It was at that moment the entire class stood up, giving Kane a standing ova-tion. The thunderous sounds of claps and whistles took over the spacious lecture hall. He was an enlightening, humble professor whom everyone seemed to love. Kane smiled and took in the love from his class. As the students filed out, he either hugged or shook hands with every student as they walked out. He took his time thanking each one for making his first teaching experience a good one. It was an epic experience for everyone involved.

Basil was the last one to leave as usual and Kane smiled, seeing his guy looking like a million bucks. Fat Rat, who stood by the door as he did every class, closed the door once the last student left.

"Congrats on completing the class," Kane said as he extended his hand. Basil smiled and shook Kane's hand. Kane pulled Basil in close and whispered in his ear, "Now the real class begins. It's time to get rich. That shipment came in this morning." Kane was smiling because he was beginning to get the hustler's rush that he had been missing for seven years. He knew what time it was. It was time to get money. Basil nodded his head with a grin, knowing his time had finally come.

"I want you to come over for dinner tonight. It's time to celebrate," Kane said as he grabbed his suit jacket off the back of the chair.

"No doubt."

"Fat Rat will come pick you up this evening. Around seven," Kane added.

Just as Basil was about to respond, the door opened and in walked a young lady. She wore neatly twisted dreadlocks and a sundress that flowed freely at its hem. Basil looked at the woman and never saw skin so beautiful and smooth. He then realized that she was Kane's daughter. She came in, hugged Fat Rat, and headed to her father. Basil couldn't help but stare. He had seen her once before, at the welcome-home barbecue for Kane. Her full lips and cat-like eyes were stunning. She was gorgeous. He slid his hand into his pocket.

"Hey, baby girl. What are you doing here?" Kane asked as he opened his arms. His daughter quickly fell into them.

"I wanted to surprise you and take you out to lunch. Wanted to celebrate with you on completing your first semester," the lady said in a soft, smooth voice.

"You got a date," Kane said as he smiled from ear from ear. Kane looked over at Basil, who was standing to the side, and realized that he never introduced them. He tried his best to shelter Moriah. He always kept his daughter and his street business completely separate.

"Basil, I want you to meet someone," Kane said as he unleashed his grasp on his daughter. He then held her hand and smiled at her. "This is Moriah. Moriah, this is Basil. He is one of my top students."

"Nice to meet you, Basil," Moriah said as she extended her hand.

"Likewise," Basil said as he shook her hand. He noticed how soft her hand was and her nails were perfectly manicured.

"Listen, sweetheart. Give me a few seconds to wrap up with him and I'll be out in a few minutes," Kane said just before he gave his daughter a kiss on the cheek.

"No problem, Dad," she said as she smiled. She looked at Basil and smiled too. "Nice to have met you, Basil."

Kane watched his daughter out and remained quiet until she completely exited. He then shot his attention back on Basil.

"Don't even think about it," he said calmly as the smile quickly turned upside down and became a scowl. Basil, at that instant, knew that Kane meant business when it came to his daughter. He took a mental note and just nodded his head, letting Kane know he understood.

"Understood," Basil said as he put both hands up in surrender.

Kane smiled and turned around to grab his jacket. He put it on and then checked his cuff links. "Fat Rat will send a car to come get you this evening. You know how to play chess?" Kane asked as he closed his briefcase.

"Nah, I never played."

"Learn to play. It'll help you in everyday life. Trust me," Kane said as he buckled the clamps and pulled his briefcase off the desk. He shrugged his shoulders to make sure his jacket fit right and headed to the exit. "See you this evening. Take a look behind the desk before you leave. Return my luggage I let you borrow," he said without even looking back. Fat Rat opened the door for him and they disappeared into the hallway. Basil frowned, as he didn't understand. He walked around the desk and saw two duffle bags sitting on the floor behind the desk, tucked away. He bent down and unzipped the first bag. When he looked into the bag his heart dropped. He saw so much white his eyes hurt. So many neatly plastic wrapped bricks were in front of him. Bricks that were going close to forty thousand apiece on the street. It was almost too overwhelming for Basil. Kane had graduated him into the big leagues and he had officially been plugged with the Cartel family. It was time to get rich. Basil felt a rush that no drug could ever provide. He got the rush that a hustler's ambition provided. It was his time.

He scooped up the two heavy bags, one in each hand, and headed out. He was about to flood the streets, particularly his own projects. He was finally plugged and he would not let the opportunity go to waste. Basil was out to get rich and he wasn't letting anything get in his way.

CHAPTER TEN

You're only as strong as your team.

—KANE GARRETT

Kane watched as his daughter cooked and slowly snaked her neck from side to side while she enjoyed the sounds of Sade. It made him smile, because he saw her mother in her so much. What a great woman Moriah had turned out to be. She was twelve when he went into prison, so he missed so much of her life, which pained him. The fact that her mother had died while he was incarcerated really saddened him. The doctors said she had a weak heart and died because of heart complications, but everyone knew the real reason of her death. She died from a broken heart. No science could explain that theory but deep inside Kane knew what the truth was. He abandoned them and his lifestyle got in the way of their happiness.

Kane was in the den playing chess all alone. He was taking turns making moves against himself. Kane paused briefly and looked up. He glanced over and watched Mo from afar, jamming to the tunes. He smiled as he crept up on her. He stepped into the kitchen and smoothly crossed his arms and cleared his throat, letting her know he was there.

"Hey, Daddy," she said without even turning from the stove.

"Hey, baby girl. You got it smelling good in here tonight. What's on the menu?" he said as he leaned against the counter.

"Just a Venezuelan dish Mama taught me. You are going to love it."

"I'm sure I am, baby girl," Kane said as he admired his daughter. "Your ma would be proud of you. The things you are doing at the Hurley Children's Clinic are amazing. Those kids really gravitate to you," Kane said proudly.

"Yeah, those are my babies up there. Seeing them be so strong, it makes me strong, ya know? I really appreciate life more after seeing how hard they have it at such an early age," Moriah said as she wiped her hands on the towel and turned to face her father.

"You never cease to amaze me," Kane said, in awe of the woman she was. Moriah volunteered at the medical center that cared for and housed terminally ill children, and it had become her life. It warmed his heart because her mother had volunteered at the same hospital and had a big heart as well. Kane knew exactly where Moriah got her kind heart from. She had it honest. Just as Kane was about to speak again, the doorbell rang.

"That must be our guests," Kane said. "Go get that while I go get freshened up for dinner, sweetheart." He kissed Moriah on her forehead.

"Sure thing, Daddy," she answered with a grin.

———————

Basil stood at the front door next to Fat Rat and waited. Basil was amazed by this brick mansion that sat on a hill. It was about an hour from the city and tucked away; the country setting had a welcoming feel. The ranch-style house was gorgeous, by far the most impressive residence he had ever been to, and he'd seen only the outside. The fifteen-thousand-square-foot palace instantly motivated Basil. *I want some shit like this,* he thought as he looked around in awe. The door slowly opened and Basil locked eyes with Moriah. Their eyes seemed to stick to each other. Basil admired her smooth skin and her long dreads, which flowed to the middle of her back.

"Hello. Welcome. Step in," she said as she smiled beautifully. She moved to the side, giving them a path to enter. "Hey, Uncle Rat," she said as Fat Rat walked by first. Basil walked by and Moriah smiled as she smelled his clean-smelling cologne. She closed the door and led them to the spacious den, where a chess board sat on the coffee table. Basil admired the cream and black marble floors and the tall ceilings. A masterpiece of a chandelier hung from the ceiling and lit up the entire space. Basil looked up in admiration at the crystal monument that hovered over his head. The long corridor leading to the back had stunning artwork lining the walls. Everything from original Jean-Michel Basquiats pieces to originals from the Dean's collection decorated the lavish spot. Cultured pieces, rich with soul and flavor. This home was one of the most immaculate things Basil had ever seen. It looked more like an art gallery than a house.

"Can I get you two anything to drink?" Moriah asked kindly.

"I'll take a scotch," Fat Rat said as he took his seat.

"I'm good," Basil replied in a low tone.

Basil also took a seat and sunk into the large leather sofa. Basil sat back and admired the cozy setting that Kane's home provided. He then watched as Moriah walked to the mini-bar that sat in the corner of the den and grabbed a bottle of scotch. As she poured a glass of the scotch for Fat Rat, Basil admired her from afar. Although she had on a sundress, Basil could still see her curves and plumpness. Her skin was so shiny and flawless. Just as he took his eyes off of Moriah, he saw Kane coming into the room, rolling up the sleeves on his dress shirt.

"Good evening, gentlemen," Kane said as he smiled. He walked over and put his hand on Fat Rat's shoulder.

"Yo, what's up, Kane?" Fat Rat said as he never took his eyes off the game. He took the glass from Moriah and took a sip, eyes still glued to the screen. Basil looked at Fat Rat and noticed that he seemed nervous and on edge as he watched the closing minutes of the intense game. Kane looked over at Basil and said, "He's locked in," as he smiled, knowing how his right-hand man could get on Sundays when the games were on.

"Basil. My man. Let me show you the ranch," Kane said as he motioned for him to follow him out the back patio door. Basil instantly stood up and followed Kane out the back, but quickly took a glance at Moriah, who was in the kitchen. To his surprise, she was looking at him as well. Just before he faded out the back entrance, she smiled and he returned the favor.

Kane led the way as they walked into the huge backyard. Gorgeous horses ran around inside of the wooden fence and the grass was green and vibrant.

"You have a beautiful place here, Kane," Basil said as he strolled alongside him.

"Yeah, this is one of the only things they didn't take from me," Kane said as he slid his hands into his slack's pockets.

"I plan on getting something like this," Basil said.

"Don't worry. You will . . . in due time. How's that last batch coming along?" Kane asked, cutting straight to business.

"Everything is running smoothly. They loving that shit. We don't step all over it, so we got people flocking from the north and east sides trying to cop from us. They taking it back to their area and turning ones into twos. Everybody eating," Basil stated.

"Good. Good," Kane said as he slowly nodded in approval. "You got you a solid team in place?" he asked, covering all bases with his young protégé.

"Yeah, I got that for sure," Basil said confidently.

"That's good. Always let your right-hand man eat. You have to let him be a boss in his own right. If you don't, he will always envy you and envy your position. He has to feel like a boss as well. That's how the love stays strong. You the plug; he needs you, but he has to also feel needed. Let him run a crew. That will keep your team solid and him loyal to you."

Basil nodded, soaking up the game Kane was giving. Basil was a thinker, so he instantly began to analyze Kane's words. He started to think about Kane's advice and how he wasn't practicing what he preached. Basil slightly frowned without even knowing he was doing it. The wrinkles in his forehead gave him away.

Kane put his hand on Basil's shoulder and spoke. "I know what you're thinking. You asking yourself, 'Why doesn't he put Fat Rat in place?' The answer to that is . . . he gambles. In order to be in a position of power, you can't have any vices. I'm not saying he's flawed because that man is the most loyal gangster nigga I know. He is as solid as they come. However, with any vice comes moments of weakness. He is too close to me for me to chance it. So I keep him fed to watch my back. He's probably the highest-paid security in history," Kane said as he added a smile and winked at Basil.

Basil smiled, amazed how Kane always seemed to read his mind. What Kane said made a lot of sense to him and he took a mental note to potentially use it later. They walked toward a gigantic brown barn that was about a quarter mile from the house. Basil was amazed by how much land Kane owned.

"This is my barn. My favorite part of the property. Let me show you why," Kane said as he slid the steel door lock. As soon as he pulled open the tall door, the smell of filth invaded their nostrils. The spacious barn was filled with haystacks and red mud. Basil quickly dipped his nose into his shirt, trying to mask the horrendous smell.

"Don't worry, you'll get used to it. Come on," Kane said as he led him to the steel skyway staircase that stretched from bottom to top. It overlooked the entire barn. Basil followed Kane and couldn't get over the pungent smell. *What the fuck?* he thought as he shook his head in disgust. They got to the top of the platform and Kane looked down onto the red mud and hay. They formed a big oval ring that you would see at a bull riding arena.

"This is where I solve all of my problems," Kane said just before he put both of his pinky fingers into his mouth. He blew, a loud whistling noise, and almost immediately, the sounds of rumbling and pitter-patter filled the air. "This is where I make things disappear," Kane said without displaying any particular emotion. A herd of warthogs began coming out of stables as they scrambled in a frenzy into the oval-shaped area. Basil was taken by surprise as he stared down at the hairy, gruesome-looking creatures. They were the biggest pigs he had ever seen. Their hairy, wet bodies and excessive snorting made Basil's soul uneasy.

"What the fuck are those?" Basil asked as he looked down at the massive group of wild animals.

"Those, my friend, are African warthogs. A gangster's best-kept secret. You see, I use them to take care of problems that I need to disappear, feel me? I feed them just enough to survive so they always stay ready. So they are always in survival mode, ready to eat anything that is put in front of them. Bones and all," Kane said as he stared into Basil's eyes, seeing if he would flinch at the thought. Basil didn't budge, though.

"Humans, so they eat humans?" Basil asked, trying to fully grasp what was being told to him.

"They eat anything. When beasts are pushed into a corner and have no other choice, they go into survival mode. They even eat their own if it comes down to it. Think about that."

"So how do you keep them from eating each other?" Basil asked.

"I can't. You see how many are down there now. Uhhh ... about twenty, right? Last month I had thirty-four. I constantly have to get more shipped in to keep them around for a rainy day. You never know when you have to feed a nigga to the wolves ... feel me?" Kane said, brutally honest with the kid. "If I put someone in here, a week later, everything is gone. No bones ... no anything. They disappear as if they never existed." Basil just nodded his head in approval and looked in amazement at the pigs. He made a mental note to never eat pork again.

Kane glanced at his watch and then put his hand on Basil's shoulder. "Let's head back for dinner. Moriah has been over the stove all day. I don't want to keep her waiting," Kane said as they headed down the stairs, out of the barn, and back to the house. Needless to say, Basil's mind was blown. He truly understood the coldhearted nature that came with being a boss. Kane had always showed him the strategic side of his job, but at that moment he had just showed him the colder side of the position.

Kane, Rat, Moriah, and Basil sat at the table eating. No business was discussed at the table, just as Kane instructed. He never wanted to let his daughter hear about the business that they were in. Although Moriah had heard stories and knew about her father's legend, he never directly put it in her face. Basil was slightly nervous, but not because of what he had just seen in the barn. Moriah was by far the most beautiful woman he had ever seen. Her skin was so smooth and her lips were full and puckered. He kept catching himself staring at her in amazement. Just by chance, Moriah caught Basil staring at her and they locked eyes. Moriah discreetly grinned and Basil couldn't help but return the gesture.

"Moriah, please clear the table and give us time to talk business," Kane said, interrupting their short-lived stare-down.

"No problem, Daddy," she said as she got up and began to clear the table.

"Let's go in the den, shall we?" Kane suggested as he stood up and grabbed the bottle of scotch and headed to the den. The men followed suit. Basil looked back at Moriah and noticed she was staring at him. They had an obvious connection and Basil was interested in learning more about the beauty queen. But he instantly felt that Moriah was out of his league. She seemed so sophisticated and reserved.

She probably dates a square-ass, corny dude, he thought to himself as he tried his best not to stare at her for an extended time. However, it was hard. Her skin was perfect, her eyes were perfect, and her aura was perfect. She was a good girl and he was a bad boy who was about to get badder. What he had in his possession were the tools to become the street's next king. She would never go for a guy like him; that's what Basil was thinking.

"Daddy, I'm going to the university library to study with my friend Maria. I'll be kind of late tonight," she said as she peeked into the den.

"Okay, don't stay out too late, honey. Love you, baby girl."

"Love you too," she replied.

The men sat down around a beautiful red oak coffee table, and in the center of it was a chess board. Fat Rat and Kane sat across from each other and Basil sat in the middle as he watched closely and listened.

Kane and Fat Rat began to set up the board, pulling the chess pieces from underneath the table. A subtle calm took over the room. Both men were ready to have a friendly war. Kane took off his diamond cuff links and set them to the side. The diamonds sparkled in the light, and Basil couldn't help but stare at them in awe. Kane began to roll up his sleeves, slowly displaying his jail tats, which were drawn up both arms.

"Pour us some scotch, Youngblood," Fat Rat said to Basil as he threw his head in the direction of the scotch bottle, now sitting on a china cabinet in the corner of the room. Under different circumstances, Basil wouldn't have fetched drinks for any man, but this was different. He was in the middle of something epic. The streets had talked about Kane and his reign for years and they would talk about it more for years to come. Basil couldn't believe that he was right there with the plug. Basil pulled out three glasses and then grabbed the crystal container that held the golden-brown aged scotch. Basil poured the drinks and took a seat as the game began.

It was an intense match with not much being said, just slow, strategic moves with random chuckles between the two men when a respected move had been made.

"The pawns are the soul of the game," Kane said as he pushed a piece on the board. "Francois Philidor said that many moons ago," he added as he looked over at Basil. Basil nodded his head in agreement as he soaked up the game Kane was trying to teach him.

"See, ya pawns are very, very important. They are there to protect you. They are there to protect the king. So as a king, you do everything to protect them. You are only as strong as your team," Kane said as he picked up his glass and downed the remaining scotch.

"Yup, got to treat your soldiers like kings or they'll resent you," Fat Rat added.

"You have a chance to make some real paper. You have the keys to the empire. Make sure you put a strong team together and make sure they feel appreciated. It'll take you a long way, trust me. Like I said before, pawns are the soul of the game," Kane said as he focused back on the board to make his move.

"Checkmate in three," he added and shot Fat Rat a menacing grin, knowing that it would be over soon. Kane watched Basil closely and noticed that he didn't take his eyes off of the chess board. Fat Rat reached toward the board, preparing to make a move, and Basil instantly sucked his teeth, knowing that Fat Rat was about to make a bad move. Both Kane's and Fat Rat's eyes shot to Basil, surprised by his impromptu interjection.

"What? You see something, Youngblood?" Kane asked, already knowing what Basil saw on the board. Fat Rat was setting himself up for destruction as he held the queen between his index finger and thumb. Basil calmly nodded his head.

"You should do this," Basil said as he reached over to the board and made a move for Fat Rat. Kane smiled, admiring his sharpness, and then he made his move.

Basil made another move.

Kane countered.

Basil grinned and made another move.

Kane frowned and made his move.

Basil made a swift move. "Checkmate," he said proudly as he rubbed his hands together.

"Ain't this about a bitch?" Kane said as he smiled from ear to ear. They all burst out into laughter as Fat Rat and Kane nodded their heads in approval. Kane, at that moment, knew that he had chosen the right kid to take over the streets.

CHAPTER ELEVEN

You're playing with fire.

—FAT RAT

The moist summer night was lit up by a full moon. Basil, Lil Noah, and a few members of their Regency crew all were in attendance. Basil had made the call and told everyone that he wanted to go out and relax before they put the bag in the streets. With the fish scale that Basil had in his possession, he knew that things were about to change. He was sitting on gold. Basil wanted to make sure his team was in order and moved as a unit, so he told Noah to gather the streets. The streets would feel their presence on that specific night. They were at the club Purple Moon, a popular spot right in the heart of the ghetto. This is where all the gangsters met to show off and toss their names in the hat for king of the streets. Basil had instructed Lil Noah to meet up with the owner earlier that day to prepay for their table and bottles of champagne.

Basil and his crew entered through the kitchen and avoided

the long line. All of them draped in black, they came through like a mob. The owner guided them through the back of the club and then to the main floor, where the party was. The music pumped out of the speakers and the bass seemed as if it shook the floor every time it hit. They made their way through the crowd and to their table, where buckets of ice and champagne bottles were waiting.

After they got settled in, Basil didn't say much. He just sat back and observed his crew having a good time. He rarely drank and the club scene wasn't his thing. His main goal that night was to establish comradery and a presence with his crew. While everyone was thinking about partying, Basil was thinking about the things to come. He had a plan and it was flawless, in his eyes. He thought about how much game that he had soaked up over the past semester. Kane had given him the blueprint to take over the projects and he had never seen things so clearly. He stood in the VIP section, which overlooked the main floor of the club. Basil stared at the people and thought about how everyone in that club would know his name soon. Lil Noah came from behind and threw his arm around Basil's shoulder.

"Yo, bro, we about to set the city on fire!" he said in an excited voice, holding a bottle of champagne in his free hand. He took a gulp and looked down at the crowd alongside of his partner.

"A yo . . . ain't that Kane's daughter?" Noah asked as he pointed to the corner of the dance floor. Basil's eyes shot in the direction that Noah was referring to and just like he said, there she was. Moriah danced with an attractive Latina girl as they laughed, talked, and grooved to the music.

"What is she doing in here?" he asked himself, totally not expecting a girl like Moriah to be in a party in the middle of the ghetto. *I know Kane doesn't know she's in here,* he thought to himself. Basil watched her slowly wind to the beat of the drums and grind her hips in the air. He admired the small black dress that hugged her curves and showed her wide hips and bubbled ass. Basil smiled, appreciative of her figure. She was a far cry from the good girl he had seen previously. That good girl and meek young lady was looking like something else. Basil couldn't take his eyes off of her. Her bright red lipstick matched the bottoms of her nude-colored heels, which seemed to light up the room. Basil watched closely as Moriah danced with another lady and laughed, displaying a beautiful smile. Basil smiled too, as his admiration for her grew.

"She bad," Noah whispered to him as he watched as well. He looked closer when a tall bearded guy approached her with lustful eyes. Noah laughed and nudged Basil, and nodded his head down toward Moriah.

"Look at Boone's thirsty ass trying to get some play," Noah said as he watched the man creep behind her and begin to dance on her while aggressively gripping her plump ass cheeks. Basil looked down and watched the scene unfold. Basil didn't care for Boone too much. He was the first cousin of Viv, and Basil always had a bad feeling about him. He never trusted him. As they looked closer they saw that Moriah was trying to push Boone off of her and he was becoming increasingly aggressive. Boone had grabbed both of her arms and Moriah was struggling, trying to get him to release her from his grasp. Basil quickly headed down the staircase to get a better look at the situation.

"Tired of stuck-up bitches like you," Boone said as he drunkenly barked at Moriah.

"Get your fuckin' hands off of me," Moriah said as she dug her nails into Boone's arms, trying to get him to release her.

"Let her go, asshole," Moriah's female friend said as she stood by and watched the drama unfold.

"Shut up, bitch!" Boone said as he glanced over at the young Latina woman. He then focused his attention back on Moriah. The thought of rejection angered him even more as he looked at her with eyes of hatred.

"Let me go!" Moriah yelled. Almost as a natural reaction, Boone reached back his hand to smack her. He was taken aback when he felt a strong hand grab his own. He turned and looked directly into the face of Basil.

"What the . . . ," Boone said, confused.

"Fall back, Boone," Basil stated calmly as he squeezed Boone's wrist with all his strength.

"Yo, Basil, mind ya business, bruh. This has nothing to do with you, potna," Boone said as he matched Basil's scowl.

"See, that's where you're wrong. This has everything to do with me," Basil said as he released Boone's hand. Noah and the rest of the crew began to crowd around Basil. It was their first time being able to flex their muscle for their new plug, so every one of them had something to prove. The tension built and Boone looked around and saw that he was outnumbered. He threw his hands up in defeat.

"Whoa . . . you got this one," Boone said as he put on a fake smile.

"Good. Go have a drink. It's on me," Basil said, still calm. He looked at Noah and then Noah shot to the bar and waved over a waitress.

"It's on you, huh? You grew up, didn't you? You got plugged and stopped fuckin with li'l ol' me," Boone said, jealousy oozing out of him. He couldn't hide it. He continued, "Didn't know this was your piece," Boone said as he looked over at Moriah, now standing next to her friend.

"Nah, it ain't like that. I know her people, though," Basil stated as he crossed his arms and stood there ready for whatever came his way. Boone stepped closer to Basil. He saw an opportunity to get in on Basil's operation. He had been hearing through the streets that Kane had plugged him with the Cartel and Boone wanted in.

"I been trying to bump into you anyway. Heard you plugged in. Put me on. Don't hog the plug. Remember what I did for you," Boone said smoothly as he tapped Basil's chest with the back of his hand. Boone was a few years older than Basil and had always looked at him as a kid. Basil looked down at Boone's hands like they were foreign objects, and realized that Boone didn't understand what he was doing.

" 'Remember what you did for me'? What? You mean charge me out the ass for them stepped-on bricks? You never blessed me. I paid for every joint I ever copped from you. Oh, you don't remember that, though, right?" Basil said as he smiled, trying to calm himself down. He felt his temperature rising but knew that this wasn't the place for him to step out of his usual square.

"I'm just trying to eat with you, my brother," Boone said as he threw both hands up, as if he wasn't a threat.

"We will talk later. Now isn't a good time," Basil said. He immediately knew that he would never do business with Boone. Boone was too sloppy and too reckless. Basil had learned this through hearing the stories through Viv. Basil stepped to the side and approached Moriah.

"Seem like you needed a little help. This doesn't look like the university library," Basil said as he released a small grin and looked around the club. Moriah couldn't help but return the smile, feeling impressed by Basil's authority. She watched how his crew had moved at his command and the sense of power was evident.

"Thanks, Basil. I don't know what was wrong with that mu'fucka," she spat, anger still in her voice.

"Oh shit, didn't know you cussed," Basil said, taken by surprise by her potty mouth.

"Like a sailor," she said, causing both of them to burst out into laughter.

"This doesn't look like a poetry jam," Basil said as he again sarcastically looked around the club.

"Yeah, I know, right? My father is so overprotective. I have to move around a tad differently than others, ya know," Moriah said.

"Your secret is safe with me," Basil responded as he put his index finger on her lips.

"Thanks. Listen, that nigga ruined my mood. Can you walk me to my car?" Moriah asked.

"Sure," Basil said as he looked into her cat-like eyes, once again admiring her beauty. Moriah whispered something to her Latina friend, Nia, and moved next to Basil as they prepared to make their exit. Basil's guys gathered around him, and Basil began to feel his power. He waved them off.

"Let me know when you make it home," Nia said as she kissed Moriah on the cheek and walked back to the bar area. Basil took a glimpse at Nia. She was a petite full-blooded Latina and had a mean walk with a model's posture. Basil then focused his attention back on Moriah.

"Listen, you can't tell my father I was in here. If he found out his daughter was in the middle of the hood, he would put security detail on me like I was the pope," she said, just before they both burst out laughing in unison.

"Scouts' honor," Basil assured her and walked her to the parking lot, to her luxury truck. As he opened her door for her, Moriah stepped in closer to Basil and stood on her tiptoes, delivering a kiss to his cheek.

"Thanks, I owe you one," she said, just before getting into her truck. Basil smiled as he shut the door for her. She then rolled down her window and just stared at Basil for a second. She took a good look, admiring his features: his strong jawline, caramel skin, and infectious smile. "Let me repay you. Lunch tomorrow?" she suggested.

"Come on, ma. You know I can't do that. Kane—"

"Oh, I see. You're scared of my father like everyone else in this city," Moriah said with a slight smirk.

"Nah, it ain't like that. I'm not afraid of anyone, actually. I'm just saying. Your father and I got some things going on together and I want to keep it respectful," Basil said as he looked around and slid his hands into his jeans.

"I thought you were a G. Guess I was wrong," Moriah said, intentionally trying to get under Basil's skin.

"Meet me here tomorrow around noon. We can do lunch," Basil said as he tried to show that he was a man of no fear.

"See you tomorrow, Basil," Moriah said, right before starting up her truck.

"See you tomorrow," Basil shot back, smiling. He watched as Moriah pulled off and stood there wondering how he had just made a date with his mentor's daughter. He smiled to himself and shook his head left to right. As she disappeared into the night's darkness, Basil didn't even notice the black Benz creep up on him. The car pulled up right alongside him and down rolled the window. Basil quickly turned around and stepped back, all while pulling a gun from his hip and pointing it at the driver.

"Put that mu'fuckin' gun down, Youngblood," Fat Rat said as he looked down the barrel of the gun. Fat Rat wasn't fazed at all as he gave Basil a stern look.

"Oh, my bad, Fat Rat," Basil said, surprised at his presence. Basil quickly put the gun back in his waistband. "What you doing out here?" Basil asked in confusion.

"Kane doesn't miss a beat. Trust that. I'm always watching Mo's back," Fat Rat said as he threw his car in park and stepped out. His expensive Italian shoes hit the pavement and he walked over to Basil and stood toe to toe with him.

"Listen to me and listen close. You're playing with fire. Leave that alone, Youngblood. Kane doesn't play about his daughter," Fat Rat said in a harsh whisper.

"It wasn't like that. I just walked her to her car," Basil responded. Fat Rat then placed his hand on Basil's shoulder and got even closer, as if he were telling him a secret.

"Listen, I don't care what you trying to do, I'm telling you what it looks like. It's not a good look. Just fall back off of Mo, understood?" Fat Rat exclaimed.

"Understood," Basil said, not wanting to spend more time explaining himself.

"Good. I'll keep this between us, kiddo. Don't want to rock the boat with Kane because he really has taken a liking to you. But do me a favor and keep it innocent with her."

"I got you, big homie," Basil said.

"Cool," Fat Rat said as he patted Basil's shoulder and gave him a smile. He spun on the spurs of his heel and headed back to the car. Just before he reached the car he looked back at Basil.

"Yo, how much money you got on you?" he asked as he squinted his eyes and began to walk back in Basil's direction.

"I got a couple racks on me," Basil said as he tapped his own pockets. Fat Rat then held out his hand and wiggled his fingers.

"Yo, lemme get that. I have to shoot a move real quick," Fat Rat said with an open hand. Basil didn't think twice about reaching into his pocket, pulling a wad of money out. Fat Rat was a legend, so passing money to him, there was no risk in it. He knew he would be good for it.

"Here you go." Basil handed the money to him without even counting it.

"I'll give it back to you next time we see each other," Fat Rat assured him. He then quickly retrieved the money, stuffed it in his pocket, and got back into his car. Basil watched as Fat Rat pulled off and out of the parking lot. Basil shook his head at what had just happened; he didn't want to crush his empire before it even started by offending Kane. However, there was something about Moriah that drew him to her . . . she was different.

CHAPTER TWELVE

The quietest person in the room is the most dangerous.
—KANE GARRETT

Basil anxiously tapped the steering wheel as he kept checking his mirrors. He looked down at his watch to check the time and noticed that it was a few minutes past noon. Moriah was late for their lunch date. He began to rethink his decision about meeting her. He knew that he was playing with fire, but there was something about Moriah that he was drawn to. He wanted to learn more about her, to say the least. Just as he was about to start up his car and pull off, he saw her truck enter the parking lot. He craftily smiled to himself, admitting self-consciously that he was excited to see her. He totally disregarded Fat Rat's orders about messing with Moriah. He had to learn about the most untouchable woman in the city. Moriah pulled up next to him and rolled down her window, exposing her beautiful smile.

"Hey there," Moriah said.

"Hey, ma," Basil replied.

"Sorry I'm late. I had to shake off Uncle Rat. He was on my tail," Moriah said, laughing but serious.

"He didn't follow you here, did he?" Basil asked as he looked around to double-check.

"Relax, we're good. I pinky promise!" Moriah said as she waved her pinky in the air.

"Cool. Follow me. If you can keep up," Basil instructed right before he pulled off. The screeching of his tires echoed through the air, and a small cloud of smoke emerged from under his back tires. Basil zoomed out of the parking lot, leading the way. Moriah let out a thunderous laugh and followed him onto the street. Basil looked in his rearview mirror and saw that Moriah was keeping up. He quickly turned into a back street and decided to have a little fun. He hit every corner he came across, trying to shake her with each turn. Moriah maneuvered around the corners skillfully as she laughed uncontrollably, having the time of her life. Basil was laughing also as he took her through the back streets, heading to his neighborhood, his projects: the Regency.

Basil finally pulled into the projects, to the back, where an unoccupied building resided; it had been vacant for years and boarded up because of the city's discovery of asbestos. He exited his car and leaned against his hood.

"What's this?" Moriah said as she stepped out of her truck and looked at the tall vacant building.

"This is where we are having lunch. You game?" Basil asked as he gave her a smirk. Moriah looked up at the building, not fully understanding what he was getting at, but agreed.

"Yeah, I'm game," she replied.

"Come on," he said as he extended his hand to her. Moriah placed her hand inside of his and Basil led her to the fire escape.

"You first," he said as he pulled down the ladder that led up to the roof. Moriah was kind of nervous but there was something about Basil that made her feel safe. So she began to climb . . .

Fat Rat pulled into a small parking lot that was just outside the city limits of Flint. It belonged to a small, well-known bar that sat in the middle of the Irish district. He frequented the place mainly to place bets and gamble without being noticed by anyone from his hometown. The brick building was owned by a notorious family who specialized in illegal gambling and loan sharking. He sat there and thought about not entering, but the monkey on his back had different plans. He was already hundreds of thousands down and knew that he had no room for error, but his demons haunted him daily and he always thought he was one lucky day away from hitting it big. He always told himself that if he ever struck big that he would walk away for good. Sadly, that day never came. He won at times, but mostly he came up with the bad end of the stick. He was currently on his worst streak of bad luck and couldn't catch a break. He gripped the steering wheel tightly and took a deep breath. He had knots in the pit of his stomach and suddenly the nervousness began to turn to excitement. The mere thought of walking out with a bankroll gave him an adrenaline rush that was similar to a high that an addict received from his preferred drug. Fat Rat parked toward the rear of the bar and approached the back door. A tall, overweight man in a suit stood at the back door smoking a

cigarette. His hair was slicked back and the four-leaf-clover tattoo on his neck was a dead giveaway of his Irish decent.

Fat Rat walked up to him and reached down into his pocket,
retrieving the wad of money that was wrapped in a rubber band.
Almost instantly the bouncer stepped to the side, giving Fat Rat
access to the spot. Fat Rat entered and walked down a dark hallway that led to a large steel door. He knocked on the door in a
rhythmic pattern. Seconds later, the sliding peephole opened
and a set of eyes focused on Fat Rat, followed by the sounds of
bolts unlocking and the large door being cracked open. The
smell of cigar smoke, and the noise of various conversations hit
him like a ton of bricks. He walked into the spacious room and
saw poker tables and crap tables scattered throughout the room.
This was the home of a secret society of gamblers and Fat Rat
was in heaven. He was a known player here. Today, he was
lighter than usual. The minimum bankroll was twenty thousand and the stash he had was just under five. He knew he was
playing with fire, but he needed to scratch that itch of his addiction. He took a seat at an open table and took off his blazer. He
rolled up his sleeve and let the games begin.

A spread of half-eaten sandwiches and fruits were placed on top
of a blanket. The sun beamed down on Basil and Moriah as they
laid on their backs staring up at the clouds.

"That one looks like a giraffe a little," Moriah said as she
puffed on the weed-filled joint and inhaled. She slowly blew out
the smoke and then tried to pass it to Basil.

"Nah, I'm good. I don't smoke," he said as he put his hands

behind his head and stared at the cloud. "You know what? That mu'fucka do look like a giraffe. Look, there go the neck." Basil smiled and pointed at the sky.

"Told you," Moriah said as she nudged him with her elbow. They both shared a chuckle as they were three hours into their lunch date and were enjoying each other to the max. In that three hours they had managed to talk about politics, religion, music, and knowledge of one's self; a well-rounded conversation. They were mutually feeling each other and it seemed so wrong, but it felt so right.

"Basil, you're not like the others I see working for my father. You're different," Moriah said as she sat up and pulled her knees close into her chest.

"I don't work for your father. We are doing business together," Basil corrected her as he sat up as well.

"Is that right?" Moriah said as she took another pull of the joint and then put it out.

"I'm about to take these entire projects over. Watch and see," Basil said calmly but confidently as he thought about what was to come. He then stood up and walked toward the edge of the rooftop. He overlooked the entire projects and knew that he was about to take over the reins. Kane had taught him a blueprint to the game and he planned on using it and becoming king. Moriah looked on in admiration as if she could read his mind. She had a notion that one day he would be king.

A short, stocky, red-haired man slowly paced the room as he looked at the situation that was in front of him. His skin was as pale as snow, which made his freckles stand out even more. His red-peppered face was distinctive and the tattooed clover on his neck matched that of the various members of his organization. He slid his hands into his Italian slacks, his collared shirt loosely unbuttoned, establishing his relaxed business-casual look. It was no other than Landon McVey, the Irish gangster who ruled the Irish district in the small town of Flushing. Landon looked down at the bloody man bound to a chair, his hands tied behind his back. Landon shook his head in disappointment as he walked over to his son, L.J., who was the spitting image of him. L.J. was breathing heavily, a bloody bat in his hand, as he looked at Fat Rat in disgust. L.J. was Landon's only son and a hothead and known enforcer for his father's organization. Sweat dripped from his forehead and his brows. He had beat Fat Rat relentlessly for his violation.

"How long did you beat him?" Landon whispered calmly as he tried to analyze the situation.

"About thirty minutes," L.J. responded, locked in on Fat Rat, ready to continue the beating. Landon took a deep breath and looked at his watch. He looked over at his henchmen and whispered, "Get Kane on the phone." Landon pulled up a chair and flipped it backward, right before he straddled it and faced Fat Rat, whose head was down. His chin was buried in his chest as he sat there, bloody and unconscious.

"Hey. Hey!" Landon said as he snapped his fingers, trying to awaken Fat Rat. "Come on, buddy, wake up," Landon said as he gently smacked Fat Rat's cheeks. Fat Rat slowly regained consciousness and breathed heavily as his mouth leaked blood. He spit out a good amount just before he looked up and focused on Landon.

"Listen, they didn't know who you were. We're going to get you out of here," Landon said as he signaled for his goons to untie Fat Rat. A man quickly came over to Fat Rat and unleashed him. Fat began to rub his raw wrists, attempting to soothe them.

"However, it seems that we have a problem. They say you didn't pay your bill. What's this? A man of your stature pisses on that type of money," Landon said as he reached into his pocket and pulled out a phone. "Just make a call and have someone bring the money here, so we can square this deal. Once again, I apologize for this. My son has a hot head, you know. He didn't know that you were made. We can make this problem go away," Landon said while giving a half smile. Fat Rat mumbled something incoherent. Landon squinted his eyes and looked closer at Fat Rat, attempting to figure out what he was trying to say.

"Come again?" Landon asked.

"I . . . don't . . . have it," Fat stammered in embarrassment.

"You don't have it?" Landon said as he stood up and moved the chair to the side. He slowly began to pace the room as he positioned both of his hands behind his back, obviously in deep thought. "So you came into my establishment, placed bets that you knew that you could not cover, and thought that was okay? See . . . you've dug yourself quite a hole. We don't operate like that in this district. You can go back to Flint with the 'nigga business.' Now you've left me no choice," Landon said as he walked toward his son and whispered something in his ear. L.J. nodded and smiled as he focused back on Fat Rat. Landon

walked out of the back room and left his goons inside with Fat
Rat once again. It was time for Fat Rat to pay his debt . . . in full.

As the sun set, the faint light peeked from over the clouds, causing a hint of orange and red to illuminate the skies. The irony
of witnessing something so gorgeous on the roof of one of the
deadliest and ugliest places in the world was surreal. Moriah
and Basil sat there staring at Mother Nature's personal sky show
for them. They had been there for hours just talking to one another about every possible aspect of life. They spoke about politics, love, music, and their future plans. They connected on a
higher level and both of them impressed each other but for different reasons. Basil was surprised by her game. She wasn't as
innocent as one would think. She was gamed up and her street
knowledge far exceeded Basil's expectations. On the other hand,
Moriah was impressed by Basil's intellect and knowledge of
things outside of the street realm. His intelligence intrigued her.

"It's crazy but this is my first time watching the sunset. It's
so beautiful," Moriah stated as she looked over at Basil. Basil
looked over to her and they locked eyes, and they were like deer
caught in headlights. They seemed stuck to one another as the
connection grew stronger with each second that passed.

"You're beautiful as well," Basil said as he leaned in to kiss
Moriah. Moriah closed her eyes and Basil did too. Just as their
lips touched, it was as if shots went through both of their bodies
simultaneously. Basil loved the way her thick, full lips felt
against his. He slowly placed his right hand behind her neck
and leaned in even closer as he continued to kiss her. Moriah

couldn't contain herself. A small moan came from the pit of her stomach as she melted into him. It all came to a halt when Basil's phone began to buzz. He instantly grabbed the phone from his waist when he realized it was the "Bat phone." The one that Kane had given him that was specifically for them to communicate.

"Damn, it's your pops. I have to take this," Basil said as he looked down at the phone as it lit up. Moriah nodded her head in agreement while beginning to get butterflies in her stomach. She instantly got the feeling that her father knew that she was with Basil. He was stern about keeping her separated from the streets and would blow a fuse if he knew that she was entertaining a street guy, especially a guy that he was working with. In Kane's eyes, Moriah was still his little girl and his being overprotective was an understatement, to say the least.

Basil stood up and walked to the edge of the building so he could take the call. Moriah watched as Basil discussed something over the phone, but he was out of earshot so she didn't hear what was going on. Moments later, Basil rushed back to her.

"I have to go. We have to go," he said as he hastily motioned to the ladder.

"What's wrong?" she said as she followed him to the fire escape that led down to the ground level. Moriah was confused but Basil didn't have a chance to explain to her what was going on. Just like that . . . their special moment ended abruptly.

Kane and Basil approached the back door of the Irish pub. Kane had on a gray tailored suit with a perfect fit and was noticeably irate. Basil had a duffle bag in his hand as he walked right along-side Kane. Kane had called him and told him he needed him to roll with him to handle something. Basil had no idea what was going on, but agreed to accompany him. They approached the bouncer, and Kane stood front and center as he crossed both of his arms just in front of his belt buckle and stood with a firm stance.

"My name is Kane Garrett. I'm here to see Landon," Kane said without a hint of anger or impatience in his voice. Although Kane was irate, he always held his composure and acted as a gentleman. Basil watched the legend at work. He too knew that Kane was angered, but not from his actions. It was the way that Kane clenched his jaws tightly, displaying the muscles there. Basil stood directly behind Kane, also with his hand just over his belt buckle, where his chrome .45 was tucked into his waist. Kane had instructed Basil in the car ride over not to say any-thing, but just to watch his back. "The quietest person in the room is the most dangerous," Kane had said just moments ear-lier to Basil. Basil replayed the quote in his mind over and over, taking notes. The bouncer stepped to the side, and Kane and Basil swiftly entered and made their way to the back. Landon was in the hallway waiting for Kane, standing with his arms crossed. Kane walked up to Landon and at the same time they extended their hands and shook. The two had known each other for years and had a mutual respect for each another. Both of them did time in the federal penitentiary together years back. Even though they had never done business together, they were col-leagues in the black-market corporation known as the streets.

"Where is he?" Kane asked.

"Downstairs," Landon answered as he threw his head in the direction just to the right of him, where a staircase led to the basement of the pub. Landon led the way as they all went down the damp, dark stairwell. When they reached the basement it was a wide-open space with beer and liquor boxes lining the walls. As they got deeper into the spacious room, they saw a single lightbulb swinging from the low ceiling and just beneath it was a man in a chair, bound and bloody. Kane instantly became infuriated.

"Release my man, now!" Kane screamed as he stood before Fat Rat. Face and veins began to protrude from his neck. Basil instantly placed his hand on his gun strap and waited for the scene to unfold.

Landon nodded to L.J., signaling him to release Fat Rat. L.J. frowned and reluctantly began to untie Fat Rat's hands.

"How much?" Kane said as he regained his composure, but his eyes couldn't hide the fury.

"A bean," Landon said, using a slang term meaning one hundred thousand dollars.

"It's seventy-five grand in the bag. We can call it even. You guys took twenty-five of it in my brother's blood. Fair enough?" Kane said as he turned, staring Landon directly in the eyes. Even though Kane's voice was calm, there was an obvious tension in the room. Kane knew that he had no space to act in any other manner than respectful. Fat Rat was dead wrong and Kane understood that.

"Fair enough," Landon said. As he gave his son another

signal, L.J. walked over to Basil and grabbed the bag. However, Basil didn't let go of the bag. He didn't like the fact that they had beaten Fat Rat so brutally. His pride wouldn't let him act in the same manner that his mentor Kane was. His willpower and discipline over his emotions weren't as developed yet. Those were vital traits that only experience could groom. L.J. yanked the bag again and Basil still didn't release it. Basil and L.J. had an intense stare-down, neither conceding to the other.

"Let it go, Youngblood. It's not the time for that," Kane said, understanding the game. They were on enemy turf and the wrong side of the potential argument. Basil reluctantly let the bag go.

"Nigger," L.J. whispered as he snatched the bag from Basil.

"What the fuck you say?" Basil hissed as he stepped directly into the face of L.J. They were so close, Basil's nose touched L.J.'s. He reeked of whisky and tobacco. L.J. said nothing. He just smiled while staring down Basil. He wasn't backing down in any form or fashion. He stood toe to toe with Basil as the tense engagement drew on.

"Let's go," Kane yelled, breaking up the showdown. He then walked over to Fat Rat as he sat there, disoriented. Kane helped Fat Rat up and acted as a crutch for his best friend. Fat Rat held his aching side with one hand and threw his free arm around Kane's shoulder, and they made their way up the stairs. Just before Kane exited the room, he yelled out.

"Landon!"

"Yeah," Landon answered as he thumbed through the bag as his son held it for him.

"Next time ... when it comes to my family, I might not be so diplomatic. Have a great evening," Kane said, a fair warning. He then focused back on Fat Rat and whispered, "I got ya, bruh," as Fat Rat almost lost his balance. Basil quickly grabbed Fat's other side. They exited the building and climbed into the car outside. Basil remained silent as they rode back to their neck of the woods, wondering how Kane could stay so calm during the heated ordeal. Kane was teaching him a vital lesson. Power wasn't what you did in the time of adversity ... sometimes it's what you didn't do during that time.

CHAPTER THIRTEEN

This girl is a savage.

—BASIL

Kane lit his cigar as he watched Basil stare at the chess board, his index fingers slowly massaging his temples. Kane had finally found a worthy opponent and it was nothing like an easy Sunday morning slow game with cigars and family. Although Fat Rat had had a rough week, he was still there. They hadn't missed a Sunday together since Kane had been out of prison. Fat Rat sat in the corner sipping cognac as he watched along. He still was sore from a few days before, but there was no way he was going to miss the Sunday dinner. Basil made his move and then sat back and relaxed. He took a sip of the scotch that was in front of him and then glanced at Kane. Stevie D was there as well, and Kane felt comfortable because it felt like old times, when he was knee deep in the game with his crew. Curtis Mayfield played faintly in the background as the fellas congregated.

"Your move," Basil said as he looked over at Kane.

"Indeed," Kane responded as he sat up and examined the board. "Are we all set on that other thing?"

"Yeah, everything is set up and all the product is in the streets. They loving that shit. Never seen anything like it. The way things are looking, we might need to re-up," Basil said nonchalantly.

"Re-up?" Kane said as he frowned in disbelief. Basil calmly nodded his head in agreement, knowing that he was pulling off the unbelievable.

"That's amazing. We are three weeks ahead of schedule," Kane added.

"That's right. The Detroit niggas are in love with that new pack. They can step on it a few times and it's so strong, they customers don't even feel the effect. This new shit that the Cartel got is like no other. You really plugged me with a gold mine," Basil said.

"Very impressive," Kane said, proud of the young man sitting before him. He knew that he was making the newest version of himself through his protégé. Kane looked at the Italian slacks and loafers that Basil wore and couldn't help but smile. Basil had taken his advice and begun to look the part of a boss. Basil's aura was changing and Kane was loving every bit of it. Fat Rat could see the change as well and the green-eyed monster began to slowly creep into the room. Fat Rat took a mental note to begin changing his ways or he might lose his position as Kane's right hand. Fat Rat didn't look at Basil in malice; he was more like a reminder to tighten up.

Kane never said a word to Fat Rat about what happened in

the Irish district, not wanting to cause any more embarrassment than he already was going through.

"Dinner is done," Moriah yelled from the kitchen.

"Okay, baby girl. Here we come," Kane yelled back as he stood up and began to rub his hands together. He absolutely loved his daughter's cooking and it always reminded him of her late mother. Everyone followed the smells into the dining room and there was a magnificent spread of food waiting on the long marble table.

"Dig in, guys," Moriah said as the assortment of lamb chops, fresh mixed vegetables, chicken marsala, and salad awaited them. The chairs were already pulled out. Moriah had the perfect setup for them.

"This is amazing," Basil said as he took his seat, directly across from Moriah.

"Why, thank you . . . ," Moriah said as she squinted her eyes. "Uh, what was your name again?" she added, not wanting to tip her father off.

"Basil," he answered, playing along with her and giving her a smile. He couldn't help but smile. Mo was so witty in his eyes and this only heightened the intrigue he had for her.

"Yeah, that's right. Thanks, Basil," Moriah responded.

Fat Rat looked on in disgust, as he knew that she was putting on her father. They all began to place the food on their plates and small talk began.

Kane, Fat Rat, and Stevie D were immersed in conversation; however, Basil and Moriah seemed zoned into each other, exchanging extended stares. Basil couldn't help but stare at the gorgeous woman in front of him. Midway through the dinner, Basil felt a foot creep into his crotch area. He jumped at the touch but quickly realized what was going on. He looked at Moriah and she was focused on him with a slight smirk. She winked at him, letting him know that the games had begun.

This girl is a savage, he thought to himself as she tried to look normal and engaged in the talk with Kane and his crew. They were in discussion about connecting with some of the hustlers outside the city limits to expand their distribution network. However, Basil's mind was totally somewhere else. It seemed like all the blood had left his brain and headed down to the area in between his legs. Basil enjoyed the massage as she used her foot to fondle his tool. She switched from his sack to his rod as if she were using her hands. Basil was growing with each touch and it was driving him wild as her toes began to curl. He repositioned himself in the seat as he spread his legs apart a tad bit more so that she had better access to his crotch. This silent game that they were playing was giving both of them a rush that they had never experienced before. Basil tried his best to pretend that he was engaged in the conversation with the men, but it was hard to do with his growing member under the table. He was at his capacity and rock solid.

"Excuse me. I have to take a leak," Basil said. The way Moriah was working her foot, he felt as if he would be exploding at any moment. Basil hastily made his way to the restroom and took a deep breath.

"What the fuck is she doing here?" he whispered to himself as he rested both of his hands on the sink while he looked at himself in the mirror. He turned on the faucet and then splashed water onto his face. He had to gain his composure and re-enter the dining room. He knew that he was playing with fire by playing games with Moriah in Kane's presence. He exited the bathroom and went into the kitchen to grab something to drink. He needed to cool down and make sure that his rod wasn't sticking out of the slacks that he wore. He walked into the kitchen and was startled to see Moriah there, putting her plate in the sink. He was frozen and didn't know what to say to her. She looked at him and smiled. She walked over to him and they instantly began to kiss. Moriah had never felt a thrill like that in her entire life. She was so used to being this daughter of a kingpin and not being able to let loose, but Basil provided a new feeling for her. She reached down and began to rub him through his pants once again. She absolutely was impressed by his thickness and wondered what the real thing looked and felt like.

Basil pulled away from her after he realized how close they were to someone walking in and catching them. "What are you doing?" he whispered as he grabbed her by her shoulder blades and held her away from him.

"Stop being a wuss. You supposed to be a G, right? Stop acting like a pus—" Moriah smirked and said just before Basil interrupted.

"I'm not scared of anything, ma. Trust that," Basil said with confidence. He looked back and made sure that no one was coming. "You're crazy, you know that?" he said playfully as he looked into her eyes. They both were having the time of their lives.

"I'm out of here," Basil said lightheartedly.

"Scaredy cat," Moriah said as Basil started to walk out of the kitchen. He looked back and stuck his tongue out at her, which made her burst out into laughter. She covered her mouth to suppress the sound. Basil shook his head and faded into the hallway.

Basil entered the dining room and the men were still talking. He felt uncomfortable and decided to leave early. Moriah was putting him in a tight spot and he wanted to get the hell out of there because it was getting too heated.

"I have a headache, OG," Basil said as he extended his hand to Kane. "I'm going to call it a night." He slapped five with Kane.

"Young nigga can't hang," Stevie D said just before he downed a shot of scotch. They all burst into laughter.

"Cool. Have a good night, Youngblood," Kane said as he began to pour himself another drink. Basil slapped hands with his other two old heads. He kept thinking about what Moriah had called him and shook his head in disbelief at her boldness. Basil walked out of the house with Moriah heavy on his mind.

Moriah had just finished with the dishes and made her way up to her room to prepare for bed. She still heard the music playing downstairs and the laughter of the fellas on the main floor. She couldn't get Basil off of her mind and was feeling his whole vibe. She reached her room and began to take off her clothes. She walked into her bathroom and started the shower. Just as she was about to step in, she felt a strong hand grab her from behind. She tried to scream but the man placed his hand over her mouth, muffling any sound that she could attempt. Moriah's heart began to beat so rapidly, it felt as if her heart was trying to jump out of her chest. Fear overcame her body as she tried to get away, but the man was too strong.

"Don't move," the man whispered in her ear, as he gripped her tightly against his own body. "Who's the scaredy cat now?" the voice said as he released her. Moriah swiftly turned around and saw Basil, smiling at her. She couldn't believe it. He had snuck up to her room and waited for her.

"Basil. Oh my God," she said as she playfully hit him in the chest. "You have to get out of here." She crossed her arms, covering her exposed breasts.

"Do you really want me to leave?" Basil asked in an undertone. They stared into each other's eyes and the sexual tension dominated the room. Basil impressed himself with his level of slyness and brazenness. He knew that Moriah was worth the risk. All his bases were covered and he was ready to see if she was as good as advertised. He parked around the corner and walked back to the house to avoid any suspicion from Kane. He was all in. Moriah was speechless as she gazed into Basil's eyes. "Do you want me to leave?" he asked again.

"No, Basil . . . I don't want you to go," she admitted just before she let her arms fall, displaying her now erect nipples. Basil was lost in Moriah's eyes as he let his hand gently cup her face. He leaned in and tenderly kissed her lips. Her full, juicy lips felt so soft to him. It felt so right . . . it felt so real. Basil's tongue slipped into Moriah mouth, which sent a signal directly to her clitoris, making it begin to pulsate. Moriah squirmed as the euphoric feeling began to take over her body. The feeling was so strong and intense and overpowered any logic or willpower that she had. Almost on key, their tongues began to circle one another as Basil wrapped his arms around her and pulled her closer to his body. Moriah pulled away and whispered, "Hold on," as she grabbed his hand and led him to her bed. She pushed him down, causing him to fall onto the king-size, cozy bed. She then walked to her door and Basil's gaze was glued to her backside. Her slim waist and petite frame were candy for Basil's eyes. He watched as her bubble-shaped ass slightly jiggled with each step. She reached up and pulled off her hair scarf, and her long dreadlocks fell onto her back. Basil looked at the gap in between her thighs and noticed her cleanly shaved lovebox hanging perfectly. Moriah locked the door and turned around and saw that Basil's eyes were locked in on her. She slowly walked toward him and placed her finger on her lip, gesturing for him to keep quiet. Basil bit his bottom lip and nodded his head in agreement. He swiftly pulled his hoodie off and positioned himself in the middle of the bed, crawling backward. Moriah approached him and got onto the bed. She straddled him and admired him. She was on fire. Her body was craving him desperately and she felt the wetness underneath her. She was soaked and had never wanted a man so badly. Maybe it was his mind or maybe it was the fact that he had crept into her room without fear of her father. She couldn't put her finger on it exactly. The only thing she knew was that she wanted him. She leaned down and they began to kiss passionately. Basil gripped her succulent butt cheeks and she began to grind against him and lightly moan, wanting so desperately to feel him inside of her. Basil began enthusiastically kissing Moriah's neck while massaging her back. At that point, he was rock hard and ready to show her what he had, but Moriah had other plans. She aggressively pushed him back down onto his back. She then crawled up, lining her lovebox directly over Basil's mouth, and all of a sudden she dropped down, putting all her weight on his face. She smashed her soaked, hot lovebox onto his mouth, which caused a loud slurping noise throughout the room. Basil hands automatically went to her cheeks and Moriah began to slowly ride his face as she rested her hands on the bed, directly in front of her. She moved her hips in slow, circular motions. She was moving like a snake as Basil showed off his mouth skills. He gently sucked her erect clitoris and flicked his tongue from the bottom to the top of it. He smacked her ass, encouraging her to keep going as he noticed her getting more and more into it with each second that passed. Moriah felt an orgasm approaching and her pace began to pick up. She began to grind against his mouth vigorously as she approached her peak. Basil couldn't take it anymore and began to pull down his pants as Moriah did her thing on his face. He unleashed his curved beast and was standing at full attention. He then grabbed Moriah by the waist and sat her square on his tool, causing her to shriek in pleasure and pain. Moriah panted heavily as Basil's width filled her up. That's when she felt the difference that only his curved penis could provide. She was pleasantly surprised; she had never been with a curved man. She moaned and quickly put her hand on her mouth as she closed her eyes, feeling them beginning to roll to the back of her head.

She slowly slid all the way down on his shaft and began to gently rock back and forth. Basil dug deeply inside of her as he snaked against her from the bottom. Her plump cheeks slammed down on his testicles as they grooved in unison. They were playing the "quiet game," neither of them able to let out the moans and nasty talk that they both desired to release so desperately. There were having the best sex in history and they were equally blowing each other's mind. Basil picked her up with authority, wanting to switch positions. Moriah bit her bottom lip as she got on all fours. She buried her face in the bed and then tilted her backside up for easier access and busted it wide open for a package only Basil could deliver. Basil slowly entered her from the back and rested his hands on the small of her back as he began to move in and out. Moriah gripped the sheets as she experienced pleasure and hurt simultaneously. As Basil made love to her, Moriah's eyes again rolled to the back of her head out of pure bliss. She almost moaned out loud, but quickly buried her face in the pillow to muffle the sound. Basil looked down as he stroked and watched as the ripple effect went through her plump cheeks. He was totally engrossed in the woman in front of him. She looked back at him while he stroked her, and her look made him even firmer as he admired her effortless beauty. Sweat dripped from his face and dropped down onto her back as their flesh slapped against each other. Moriah reached underneath herself and placed her two fingers directly on her clitoris. She began to rub in circular motions as Basil continued to please her. The action heightened her senses, which brought her closer to a climax. Basil noticed that she was becoming even more soaked as she played with herself. His sack swung back and forth with each stroke, causing a smacking noise to fill the air. He slowed down, not wanting to make too much noise, knowing that Kane and his company were in the house. Basil pulled out of Moriah and laid flat on his back. Like clockwork, Moriah turned around and straddled him. She then grabbed his pole and guided him inside her leaking lovebox. She slowly began to gyrate her hips while sliding up and down on him. They were now looking into each other's eyes and almost instantly they both smiled, knowing that they had found something special. They had a mental, spiritual, and physical connection that was simply explosive.

They made love until the morning light and whispered under the covers, laughing and enjoying themselves. Basil snuck out just before the sun rose. It was the beginning of a love that would shake both of their lives. They were connected souls and their secret love affair would be one for the history books.

CHAPTER FOURTEEN

Once the streets grab ahold of a person, it's hard to shake loose.

—UNKNOWN

Basil watched as Vivian walked across from the television with nothing on but a small T-shirt. Her brown, heavy ass cheeks hung out of the bottom of the shirt as she strutted across the room like a championship stallion. He admired her well-oiled legs, hips, and cheeks. He instantly was ready for their sexual appointment. While walking, she began wrapping up her hair.

"So, I heard you was playing Superman to some chick at the club the other night." Vivian said as she walked into the bathroom, stood in front of the mirror, and placed bobby pins in her dark silky hair. She tried to pretend that she was unconcerned, but her jealousy was blatant.

"That's what you heard, huh?" Basil answered, knowing exactly where she'd got her information. *Boone talk like a damn female,* Basil thought as he shook his head.

"Yeah. So, who is she?" Viv quizzed.

"Yo, you bugging. Bring yo' ass over here, ma," Basil said smoothly. He knew what she needed to get straightened out. Viv crossed her arms and made a pouting face. But she followed his orders and walked over to him and climbed into the bed. She was on all fours and slowly crawled over to Basil with her pouting lips.

"I know what you need. You asking me about things that are irrelevant. Your focus is on the wrong thing, ma. Your focus should be on this," Basil said, exposing his thick tool under the covers. Almost instantly Viv attacked it as if she were a predator. She grabbed it with her right hand and covered the top with her salivating mouth. She began to circle her tongue around the top of his shaft while slowly stroking him. Basil threw his head back in complete pleasure and he placed his hand on the back of her head. She began to stuff him in her mouth and she swallowed him whole and moaned as she felt his tool touch her tonsils. She used her free hand to begin to massage his balls as the moans grew louder with each slurp. She worked her mouth like a professional as she performed her magic on Basil. After getting him rock solid, she stopped sucking and popped his tool out of her mouth as if it were a lollipop. Her lips were glazed with her own saliva and it dripped from her mouth. She wiped her face and laid on her back and began to rub her clitoris with two fingers. Her body was on fire and she desperately wanted to feel Basil deep inside of her. Nobody could touch the back of her cave like Basil did and she needed to feel that unique massage that only his dick could provide. Basil knelt and looked down at Viv's fat lips, which were now glazed. He saw her erect clitoris peeking out as she rubbed it with authority. She begged for him to enter her and began to move her hips seductively, slowly lifting her cheeks off of the bed with each motion. She then smacked her own vagina, creating a wet, slapping sound. She slapped it repeatedly, trying to entice Basil to dive in. His self-control was legendary and was driving Viv crazy. He just sat there and watched as she pleaded to him repeatedly while masturbating.

"Put it in, daddy. Please. I'm want to feel you," Viv crooned, her eyes locked onto his. "Please." Viv slid her fingers into herself and curved them upward so that she could stimulate her G-spot. She was in need of Basil badly. She needed to feel him and she did. Basil leaned into her warmth and commenced to giving her long, deep, and rock-solid strokes while gently kissing her neck. Basil was masterful and it drove Viv crazy.

Basil made her orgasm over and over. After a half hour, he ended it by releasing himself from her. Sweat dripped off of their bodies as the moonlight gave them a blueish hue, and they laid on the bed panting and their hearts racing. Their relationship was a different kind. Basil looked at Viv as something short-term, and a dependable piece on his chess board. She kept his money and provided great sex. At this point in his life, that was all he needed from a female. He didn't understand the affect that great sex could have on a woman's mental state. He was blowing her mind and making her fall deeply in love with him. The more they made love, the more she fell for him. Basil's lack of life experience didn't allow him to understand that most women's hearts are attached directly to their clitoris and he was playing a deadly game. He was in the middle of that mind game but he was unaware of it. Little did he know he was feeding her addiction with every sexual rendezvous they had. Her drug of choice was him.

Although Basil enjoyed being with Viv, lately his mind always seemed to drift to Moriah. As the sun came up and Basil laid there in deep thought, he made a note to himself that he would no longer continue his sexual relationship with Viv. *Straight business,* he thought as he looked over and saw half of her oiled body hanging out of the white satin sheets. One of her plump, big, brown ass cheeks peeked out and it was attached to a thick thigh. He shook his head, knowing that he would miss the experience. However, he wanted to get focused and remove anything from his life that wouldn't feed his mind, body, and soul equally. He was ready to become king and knew that this was the first step. He was searching for a queen, not a temporary stand-in. He decided not to tell Viv his plans, but to slowly wean her off of him so there wouldn't be any conflict. He still wanted to keep a professional relationship with her as far as her being the caretaker of his money and the mule for his monthly shipments. He had been stashing his money and drugs over at her house for years so he hoped his new stance wouldn't change their standing agreement. Only time would tell.

Fat Rat sat at the race track and watched the horses closely. He wore a casual jogging suit and a Dobbs hat with a red feather in it. He considered it his lucky hat and was hoping to the heavens that it did its job today. He had borrowed ten grand from Stevie

D earlier that morning and took it straight to the track. He'd had a dream while unconscious from the beating by Landon's goons and the number seven kept recurring in the dream. So when he saw that a horse named Seven Heaven was racing that day, he took it as a sign from the gambling gods. Fat Rat watched the horses that waited in the stables, on edge as he anticipated the gunshot to start the race. The smell of horse manure and popcorn filled his nostrils as he sat in the stands rubbing his hands together. It seemed like his mind was bombarded with thoughts before the race started. He began to think about every-thing that he'd lost due to gambling over the years. It was like he kept digging a hole that just got deeper and deeper. He always had this burning desire to get back even, so he could quit and not feel defeated by the game. However, that day never came. Little did he know, that day would never come . . . it was only an illusion. He reflected back on the times that gambling had forced him to do things that he thought he never would. The guilt weighed heavy on his shoulders as he reflected on the times in his life when his morals were compromised because of his strong addiction. He dropped his head and shook it, yearning to drop his gambling problem.

"Are you winning at least?" a voice said. Fat Rat looked up and there he was. Sharply dressed as always, in a designer suit and standing tall and firm. It was his best friend, Kane. Fat Rat instantly grew embarrassed as he clenched his teeth and the bet-ting paper in his hands. Kane took a seat next to him and watched the race alongside his partner in crime.

Fat Rat began to hear the random hoots and hollers of the

other gamblers in the audience as the race neared its end. The horses were on the home stretch and everyone rooted for their particular pick. Fat Rat locked in on his horse, which was in second place.

"Come on, you bastard," Fat Rat yelled at the horse as he perked up and stared. "Come on, come on, come on," he said in a low tone as he stood up. Although Fat Rat was in the stands and the horse was on the track, in his mind he was right there running with him. Fat Rat was in tune with the horse, praying to the gambling gods that the horse would pull through. As the horses neared the finish line, Fat Rat's horse tapered off and finished third. Fat Rat instantly threw his betting slip down in anger and sat down in frustration.

"Listen, you got to let this shit go," Kane said in a concerned voice. "It's slowly making you a different person, man. I need my old partner back. We got some good shit going on. We have the streets again, just like old times." Kane placed his hand on Fat Rat's shoulder.

"I'm cool, man. I'm just having a bad streak, that's all. You know how that shit goes," Fat Rat said nonchalantly.

"Bro, you been having a bad streak for twenty years," Kane said as he cracked a smile. It was almost as if the humor were contagious: his joke made Fat Rat smile and temporarily broke the tension. "Check this out. You are bigger than this. You are all I ever had. We are each other's keeper," Kane said as his eyes watered. Although a tear never fell, it was evident that his words were evoking a strong emotion from a deep place. He continued, "I need you to be strong and standing firm with me.

You can beat this, man. Basil has to go away for a minute and I need you to step up."

Fat Rat sensed the sincerity in Kane's words and in his eyes. He knew that his friend truly cared about him and needed him to quit. Fat Rat had never seen Kane that vulnerable.

"I'm going to quit this shit, man. I'm done for real. I'm ready to take over like we did before you got locked up. I just kind of lost my way while you were away," Fat Rat admitted.

"That's what I want to hear. I'm going to be with you every step of the way," Kane said.

"Thank, Kane. I love you, man."

"I love you too." Kane stood and buttoned his blazer. "Now, let's get out of here. These seats gon' fuck up my five-thousand-dollar suit," he said. They shared a chuckle and Fat Rat stood. Kane put his arm around his best friend and they walked out and back to business. Fat Rat vowed to himself that he would never gamble again.

CHAPTER FIFTEEN

Power wasn't what you did in the time of adversity . . .
sometimes it's what you didn't do during that time.

—UNKNOWN

"That movie was amazing," Moriah said as she looped her arm inside of Basil's. Her heart felt warm as she walked next to the man who had been keeping her happy for the past six months. They were inseparable and they managed to spend every free second they had with each another. They were in the Irish district after enjoying a Saturday night movie, outside the city limits of Flint to avoid anyone who might see them and report back to Kane. It was just after one and the streets were almost empty. They stuck out like sore thumbs in the mainly Irish community, but they didn't care. They were in love and in their own world. They strolled out of the theater and onto the street while holding hands, discussing the powerful film that they had just witnessed.

"Yeah, I agree. Systematic oppression stemmed from those times," Basil said, referring to the film *Birth of a Nation*.

"Absolutely. Just to think that our people had to endure that for four hundred years. Just to think, in the grand scheme of things, we haven't been free that long," Moriah said as they strolled along. The street was well lit and the warm summer night was just right.

"True. True . . . the narrative has to change with this country as a whole to—" Basil said before stopping, feeling his phone buzzing on his hip. He reached down and pulled his phone out and saw that it was Lil Noah calling. He whispered to Moriah, "Excuse me," and picked up the call.

"Yo," he said as he placed the phone to his ear. He listened attentively as he got an update from his head soldier. A few seconds passed and Basil released a slight grin. "Good, good. I'll put in an order for a re-up. Great work, youngster. I'll be by the spot later tonight," he said with authority as he ended the call and focused back on Moriah. She was staring at him, smiling.

"What?" he asked as he noticed her childlike smile.

"I love the way you can talk about social issues and thought-provoking subjects and then talk street talk effortlessly. A real gangster and a gentlemen," she said, impressed.

"Oh yeah?" Basil asked while returning the smile. Moriah stopped and turned toward Basil. She then wrapped her arms around him and looked up into his face.

"Yeah, look at you. You are changing. You remind me of a great man I know," Moriah said as she looked at Basil's attire. His entire look had transformed. Italian-cut slacks and loafers replaced sweatpants and sneakers. Basil was becoming king and the entire city knew it. Over the past six months, he had made close to a million dollars' profit and on top of that, he'd made his connects, Kane and Carter, even more. Basil had taken like a duck to water and expanded his business tenfold. He was seeing more money than he ever had, just as Kane promised. Basil leaned down and kissed his woman. Just as he was about to tell her he loved her, a group of men walked past them and one of them bumped Basil. Basil was instantly offended as the group of well-built Irish guys kept walking as if they hadn't bumped against him.

"Watch where you going, potna," Basil said loudly as he watched the men walk down the sidewalk. Once they heard Basil's comment they all turned around and began walking toward him and Moriah.

"Or what, nigger?" the man in the middle said, a beer in his hand. Basil realized who the man was as he approached. It was L.J., Landon's overzealous son. L.J.'s face was red and he was obviously drunk, as were his three friends. L.J. walked directly into Basil's face and they revisited the tension that they shared during their previous meeting. "Or what?" L.J. repeated as he stood toe to toe with Basil.

"Just forget it, Basil. Let's go, baby," Moriah said as she tried to pull Basil away.

"Better listen to your bitch and get the fuck out of here. You're in the wrong part of town, motherfucker. Go back to Flint wit' the rest of your kind," L.J. stated aggressively. Basil's jaws were clenched so tightly that veins began to form in his forehead. The fact that L.J. had called Moriah a bitch and blatantly disrespected her enraged him. Basil was on fire! He heard

Kane's lesson in his head, *Power wasn't what you did in the time of adversity . . . sometimes it's what you didn't do during that time.* Basil shook his head and looked down at Moriah. She placed her hand on his jaw and whispered, "Let's just go, okay?" She knew that Basil was outnumbered and didn't want anything violent to go down.

"Yeah, you're right. Let's go," Basil said as he nodded in agreement. He grabbed Moriah's hand and led her away from the men. Basil had already begun to plan how he would handle L.J. at another time. They didn't get five feet away before L.J. poured beer over Moriah's head, causing it to trickle down her entire body. L.J. and his crew erupted with laughter.

Moriah stopped in her tracks and gasping as she held her hands in front of her while beer dripped down her body. Infuriated, Basil reached for the gun that was in the small of his back, but Moriah grabbed his wrist, stopping him from pulling it out. So Basil decided to handle his business the old-school way: with his hands. He charged L.J., tackling him to the ground. Basil began to pound him and L.J. was no match for Basil's wrath and strength. L.J.'s crew attacked Basil, knocking him off of their friend. They all began to jump on Basil, and Moriah screamed, trying to get them to get off of him, but it was to no avail. They tried to stamp him out, but Basil managed to get to his feet and began to fistfight with all of them at the same time. He caught some blows, but he landed his share as well. The fight ended up in an alley as they rumbled like savages. Basil stumbled and his back was against a brick wall but he kept his footing.

Moriah tried to run over and help him but L.J. delivered a

haymaker to her chest that landed her flat on her backside, clutching her chest in pain. Basil snapped. He reached into the small of his back and pulled out his handgun. L.J. was about to deliver a hard kick to Moriah, when a single shot rang out. The bullet ripped through L.J.'s chest. L.J. gripped his chest in agony, letting out a roar, and dropped to his knees. L.J. stared at Basil as if he couldn't believe that he had been shot, his eyes as big as golf balls. His eyes rolled up in his head and then he fell flat on his face and into a pool of his own blood.

Moriah stared in horror while L.J.'s crew ran out of the alley. Basil watched as L.J.'s body jerked for the last time, then snapped out of his daze. He grabbed the bottom of his shirt and wiped off the gun before he tossing it aside. He swiftly helped Moriah up off the ground.

Basil had called Kane and told him everything about the murder that occurred the night before, except the fact that Moriah had been with him.

"This isn't good, Youngblood. This isn't good at all," Kane said calmly as he faced Basil and slid his hands inside of his pockets. His custom-tailored suit fit him flawlessly and signature diamond cuff links shone as the sunlight bounced off of them.

"I know," Basil admitted as he dropped his head and shook it in disappointment.

"I sent someone over there and they have it all taped up. They shut down the entire block. The good thing is that it was in the Irish district. That's all old buildings over there. There were no surveillance cameras. But that's not our problem. Landon is a very powerful man with a long arm," Kane explained.

"What do you want to do?" Fat Rat asked.

"That man just lost a child. He is going to want blood. However, we are prepared for whatever should come our way. We are a family and we stick together. One of our battles is all of our battles. I already got word that Landon wants a meeting with me. I'm going to check his temperature and see what it is," Kane answered.

"I'm a man. I will stand on my own. I'm prepared to deal with anything comes my way. I have an army of young niggas that's ready to go to war," Basil said fearlessly.

"See, that's where your downfall will be," Kane said as he walked close to Basil. He placed his hand on Basil's shoulder. "This is chess, not checkers. You have to think about your moves. You're making more money than you have ever made. Do you know the number-one killer of street business?" Kane asked. He then continued, answering his own question. "War. War is horrible for business. Murder brings cops. Cops bring the feds. Feds bring life sentences. A true hustler flies under the radar and gets money . . . as he should. You can't do that while in the middle of a war."

"I see. What should I do?" Basil asked.

"Nothing. That's what you have me for. This is an OG call that I have to make. We might have to drop off a bag to show our remorse for his loss. I'm anticipating that Landon will respect the game. He has to know how much of a hothead his son was. He knows how the game goes. He's been in the streets for a very long time. Let's just hope he sticks to the code and nothing comes of this," Kane stated.

"I didn't get a good look at him. They got into a slight altercation and the next thing we knew, shots rang out. It all happened so fast," the young man said as he sat on the couch inside of his uncle's office. It was L.J.'s cousin Tony, who was there the night of the shooting. Two detectives were standing in front of him with notepads in hand. Tony looked over at his uncle, who sat quietly at his desk as he supervised the interview.

"So, what race was the guy?" one of the detectives asked.

"I'm not too sure. He had tan skin. Maybe he was black . . . maybe Mexican. Could have been Middle Eastern. I don't remember," Tony said nonchalantly, blatantly giving them misleading answers. The detective shifted his stance and placed his hands on his belt line. He was noticeably growing impatient with the lack of cooperation.

"Look, you have to give us something, kid. We can't find out who did this if you don't give us some sort of information. There were no cameras in the area, no witnesses, and no trace. If you don't help us this will be an unsolved mystery. You might want to think deep and hard before you give your next answer. Who murdered your cousin L.J.?" the detective asked sternly.

"I'm sorry. I don't remember," Tony lied. Landon had heard enough and walked over to the detective and placed his hand on his shoulder.

"I think that we're done here, fellas," Landon said as he extended his hand for a shake. The detective gritted his teeth, exasperated. He knew what was going on. Landon and his family had a different type of justice in mind. They sought street justice and it was apparent. The detective reluctantly took Landon's hand while shaking his head in disappointment. He knew what was to come and the only thing he could do was watch the plot unfold.

"We will be keeping a close eye on this situation. Move wisely," the detective said before he exited the office and out of the pub. Landon turned on his heel and walked toward his nephew. He leaned down and kissed him on the forehead.

"Thatta boy," he said encouragingly. He closed his eyes and took a deep breath. His nephew had told him the truth and gone through what happened on that night for what seemed like a hundred times.

"Are you sure it was Kane's boy?" Landon asked, not wanting it to be true. Landon respected Kane and knew that it would be the start of something catastrophic if he pushed the button for a street war. Nevertheless, Landon was furious and vengeance for his son was a must.

"Yeah, I'm sure. His fucking nigger face is sketched into my brain," Tony said as his own face grew red with hatred. Landon nodded as he crossed his arms and began to pace the hardwood floor.

"He was alone?" Landon asked, getting all of the facts straight.

"Yeah. Well, he had some bitch with him. But he was the only guy," Tony answered.

Landon placed two fingers in his mouth and whistled,

signaling for his bodyguard, who also acted as a bartender for his pub. Moments later, a man stepped into the office while drying his hands with a towel.

"Get Kane on the phone. Set up a meeting tomorrow morning," he demanded as he walked over to his desk and slipped on the blazer that rested on his chair.

"Yes, sir," the man answered before he disappeared back into the pub. Landon reached into his inner coat pocket and pulled out a pair of shades just before sliding them onto his face. He felt the tears coming and he had to hide them from the world. He had to quickly shake it off and go visit the coroner to identify his only child.

Basil stood on the roof of the projects along with Lil Noah, who sat on one of the air-conditioning units. Basil looked over the projects and realized that in under a year, he had taken over the whole premises. Everyone in the projects either worked for him or was on his payroll in some manner. He had even gotten the senior citizens on his side by offering all-expenses-paid weekly buses to the casino and free Sunday dinners at the rental hall. He was beloved and a man of the people. Although Flint had a mayor, within those project gates, Basil was the dictator and the beloved son of the ghetto. He grew up in these projects and everyone felt they were a part of his success because they had witnessed his rise to power. Lil Noah looked at his mentor and saw that he was in deep contemplation.

"I say that we just go push it to them niggas. Why should we be on defense when we could be an offense? You got an army out here, bruh. The only thing you have to do is give me the green light. Push that button and the whole projects will light that Irish district up," Noah suggested with passion. He was ready to go full force.

"Nah, we have to be smart. It's more at stake than just what lies on the surface. Money has never been this good for us, bruh. Just look at you. You not a little knucklehead anymore . . . you bossed up, eating more than you ever have. Why would we throw that all away with a street war?" Basil said as he paced back and forth with his hands slid into his pockets. Lil Noah watched and listened closely just before he unleashed a small grin.

"What's funny?" Basil said as he caught a glimpse of Lil Noah smiling.

"Look at you. You are starting to sound and act like the god Kane," he said half jokingly. Basil looked down at his hands tucked in his pockets and quickly snatched them out. He returned the smile and shook his head, knowing that his comrade was correct.

"All bullshit aside, though. I think I may have to go away for a second until shit die down. Kane said it's too hot for me to stay in town right now," Basil said, not happy with the circumstances but he understood it was the smartest thing to do. Basil was more worried about trouble with the law than the street aspect.

"Damn, B, you know the streets need you. We got a well-oiled machine going on here. We have to keep it going," Lil Noah said as he stood up and pointed toward the projects.

"That's right. We do have a well-oiled machine. That's why

I can leave and we won't miss a beat. Everything will still be the same. I will still have Viv bring the joints up and nothing will change. I will just be running it from out of town, that's all. I'll be back. I just need to step away until shit dies down. You feel me? By winter all of this shit will be forgotten about and I can return and it will be business as usual," Basil explained confidently.

"No doubt. I'm with you, bruh," Lil Noah said as he walked up to Basil and dapped him and hugged him directly after. Basil and Kane had a long talk earlier that morning and they both decided Basil leaving would be the best thing to do. So it was confirmed. Basil would have to be away for a while. He had to explain that to his mother and also his love Moriah. The thought of leaving them made the burden a few tons heavier.

"Where you going, by the way?" Lil Noah asked as they released their embrace.

"Miami," Basil answered as he nodded.

"You bring me a suitcase full of money in return for peace? I was expecting to see Basil's head on a stick. That's his name, right? Basil?" Landon asked.

"Yeah, that's his name," Kane answered as he slowly nodded.

Landon took his time before he spoke. He picked up a cigar that rested in his ashtray and one of his goons immediately walked over to light it for him. Landon took a couple of puffs to make sure his favorite stick was lit and then blew out a few smoke rings. He watched as they danced in the air and followed it by blowing out the remainder of smoke rapidly. He then looked at the big faces on the hundred-dollar bills. They were neatly lined up inside of the briefcase as it was popped open on top of his desk facing him. Kane had put it there just before he took his seat. Landon then looked at Kane and Kane met his stare and neither of them blinked as they played a silent game of mental chess. Neither of them wanting to look away first.

Kane sat in the chair in front of Landon's desk just as cool as a cucumber. His leg was propped up on his knee, displaying his silky designer socks and expensive loafers. His hands were collapsed into one another and his shoulders were broad and straight as he sat there without an ounce of fear in his body. Although Landon had five goons in the room with him, Kane did not bust a sweat. He'd walked in alone and came to handle business as usual. It was high noon, but the office was dim. The sunlight was blocked from shining in because all of the blinds were closed. Only the lamp that sat in the corner illuminated the room, giving it a grim orange hue. Landon had Frank Sinatra playing in the background as he took his time puffing his cigar. Kane decided to break the tension by addressing the issue.

"I came here out of respect. My respect for you is the sole reason why I came with a briefcase instead of something else. I understand that you lost a son and I could never imagine that pain. I feel for you. You have my deepest condolences. However, your son wasn't the most diplomatic young man. You know that and I know that. That's why I'm asking you to take that into consideration before you push any buttons." Kane slowly stood up and buttoned up his blazer. He walked closer to the desk and crossed his hands while putting them down by his belt line, signaling that he wasn't a threat. "Because I have buttons I could push as well," Kane warned.

"My problem isn't with you, Kane. I want your boy and I want him now," Landon said as he sat forward and put the cigar out in the ashtray. "Bring him to me!" Landon yelled, not able to hold his composure.

"I am sorry, my friend. I can't do that. Not him. Not Basil," Kane said calmly but sternly.

"So, you are going to flush our friendship down the drain for a mere soldier? We played chess every morning for two years straight upstate. We have the same morals, the same ideologies, and you are flushing that down the drain for this piece of shit. I just want him, nothing else. No war, no cops," Landon said as his face turned plum red in anger.

"Oh, now we are friends? We weren't friends when you nearly beat my friend half to death," Kane reminded him.

"You know and I know that was purely business. No one forced his hand and made his ass-bet," Landon said, referring to a gambling term describing a bet that can't be honored.

"That's neither here or there. The bottom line is, I'm not going to give you Basil and if so much as a hair is harmed on him . . . I'm going to make it rain forty days and forty nights. But it won't be water. It will be bullets," Kane said, still calm.

"Motherfucker. You come in my fucking establishment, the day after I bury my son, and make threats? You must be out of your cotton-picking mind. I could have my guys fill your body with holes with a snap of my fingers," Landon threatened. Kane chuckled lightly and put his hand over his mouth and then rubbed his goatee in a downward motion.

"Please pardon my laughter. It's getting too tense in here. It's kind of dark as well. Do you mind?" Kane asked politely as he slowly walked over to the blinds. He pulled the string that opened the blinds of the huge window that displayed the main street the pub sat on. As the sun crept in, something else did too. Fear crept into Landon's and his goons' hearts. At least fifty black gunmen were standing outside of the window, on full display, ready for war. Kane smiled and continued, "See, you might could fill me with bullets . . . but everyone in here would die a horrible death. I would hate to see that happen, Landon."

"Get the fuck out," Landon said, burning in rage.

"I had planned to. So this is how this is going to go. I'm going to leave you with two things. One, a suitcase full of money. Two, a fair warning. Good day, sir," Kane said as he smiled and headed toward the door. Just as he reached the door Landon spoke calmly.

"Kane, losing a child is the most painful thing a man could ever go through. I want you to remember that," Landon said.

"I'm sorry for your loss. I wish this never happened," Kane said without turning around.

"Thank you. I will not retaliate. I don't want to put my family through any more bloodshed. I wave my white flag humbly. Take care," Landon said in a low, conceding tone.

Kane chose not to respond and exited the building and then the Irish district along with his street army. Checkmate.

CHAPTER SIXTEEN

Never count favors with your family!

—KANE GARRETT

"Hello. My name is Frenchie and I am a recovering addict," the lady said proudly.

"Hello, Frenchie!" the group of people responded as they sat in a circle. Frenchie looked over at her son, who leaned on the wall near the door and smiled proudly at his mother. She had been clean for over six years and had never missed a meeting since her sobriety. Basil couldn't have been prouder of his mother because he'd seen her battle her addiction and conquer it. He waited patiently as his mother met with her group of recovering addicts. He knew that he would be leaving for Miami for a while and wanted to break the news to his favorite woman in the world. He watched as his mother hugged and spoke with her group, and the smile on her face was constant and she glowed. Her happiness was oozing out of her.

"Hey, baby boy," Frenchie said as she smiled widely and approached him with her arms extended. She looked him up and down and laughed while shaking her head.

"My handsome son. You sure know how to wear a suit," she complimented him as she admired his new look. His well-tailored grayish suit was complemented by a black-collared shirt, black diamond cuff links, and a black pocket square that just barely peeked out of his top left pocket. Basil was neat and put together, just as Kane had taught him to be.

"Thanks, Ma," Basil said as he cracked a rare smile.

"Kane sure has you looking like a distinguished gentleman," she said as he brushed a piece of lint off his shoulders. "I saw you come in a while back. I was surprised to see you here. You haven't sat in one of my meetings since you were a little boy," she said as she hugged him, rubbed his back, and rocked back and forth. Her warm embrace made Basil feel so good on the inside and he closed his eyes, enjoying the moment.

"Just thought I would come take you to lunch," Basil said as he smiled.

"You sure know how to make an old lady feel good," Frenchie said. "Just make sure you get me home by six. I have Bible study tonight, she added as she put her arm inside his and they began to exit the community center.

"I think I can do that," Basil said as they strutted out of the building and toward the parking lot. Basil looked at his mother and the love he had for her could move mountains. That's why what he was about to tell her would be a difficult thing to do.

"Ma, I need to talk—" Basil started as he opened the door for her. He stopped mid-sentence when he saw the black-tinted Land Rover creeping by.

"Ma, get in the car!" he said in a harsh whisper. He moved his hand to his belt buckle, where his chrome .45 rested.

"What's wrong, baby?" Frenchie said, not fully understanding the sudden change of mood and tone of her son.

"Don't worry about it. Just get in," he said quickly as he stared at the Land Rover's windows, trying to see inside. He watched his mother get in the car and closed her door just after she got both feet in. His eyes never left the Rover as he slowly made his way to the driver's side. There was something eerie about the slow, creeping truck and Basil didn't feel right about the situation. The fact that his mother was with him raised the stakes and he was willing to protect her at all costs. Even if it meant making fireworks in broad daylight at a community center. He watched as the car cruised by and passed him, slowly exited the parking lot, and then drove out of sight. Deep down inside, he knew that an Irishman was in that vehicle and it only affirmed his hiatus to Miami. He quickly got into the car and went the opposite way.

Basil began to think as if he were playing chess with the Irish. He knew that by murdering Landon's son, the gloves were off. He didn't want his mother to fall victim for something he had done. He immediately decided not to take her back home. He headed toward Kane's house because he knew that he would know how to handle the situation. His mother talked to him on the ride there and he nodded and agreed, but his head was elsewhere. She didn't understand how close she was to a potential shootout but Basil did, and now his nerves were on edge as he checked his rearview mirror at every turn just to make sure that they were not being followed.

"We're going to make a stop real quick before lunch, okay, Ma?" Basil stated as he looked over and gave her a fake smile, trying to hide what was going on from her.

"That's fine, baby. I'm riding with my favorite guy in the world. I don't have any complaints," she said as a huge smile spread across her face. Basil smiled and patted his mother's knee as he guided his car through traffic.

After a brief ride, they arrived at Kane's estate. Kane had hired some of his henchmen to secure his home during these heated times. Basil noticed the two men standing by his gate and knew that Kane had already took the precautions of dealing with a street war. This was the exact reason Basil had brought his mother to Kane's spot. He had to do everything in his power to protect the woman that gave him life. With him having to go to Miami for a while, he knew his mother would be an easy target. Basil knew too that Frenchie wouldn't up and leave for Miami so he had to protect her while she was home.

Basil rolled down his window so the gunmen could see his face and they promptly let him through the gate leading to Kane's home. Basil crept through the entrance and up the long, snakelike driveway.

"Oh my God," Frenchie said as she set her sights on the

big luxurious home that they were approaching. "This is amazing, Basil. Where are we at?" she asked as she admired the immaculate landscaping and sculptures that sat in the yard.

"This is Kane's house, Ma. I have to come and talk to him for a second," Basil said as he entered the circular driveway and pulled in front of the main door. Frenchie smiled as she looked around in amazement. It warmed her heart that Kane had taken Basil under his wing. For some reason, she didn't worry about Basil as much when she knew that he was with Kane. She was very appreciative even though she never mentioned it. She had not fully accepted that her son was a gangster, but it made it more bearable to know that Basil was under the tutelage of one of the best. Basil stopped his vehicle right by the big red welcome mat in front of the entrance. A well-built man in all-black suit stood guard at the front door. Obviously he was guarding the place. This was something that Basil had never seen when visiting Kane. Kane had bulked up his security to the max and wasn't taking any chances with his family's protection.

Within seconds of their parking, Kane emerged from the house. He stepped out of the front door wearing a casual walking suit with house slippers on. He approached the car and opened the door for Frenchie.

"Hey, Frenchie. Long time no see," Kane said with a welcoming smile on his face.

"Hey, Kane." She took his hand as he helped her step out of the car. They hugged each other and rocked back and forth as they remembered the good times. "I haven't seen you since

Keema's funeral," Frenchie said, referring to his deceased wife.

"Yeah, it has been a while. But you looking good now," Kane said as he looked her up and down.

"Yeah, I've been clean for almost seven years," Frenchie said proudly. Basil exited the car and walked around, meeting them.

"What's up, Kane? Sorry for popping up unannounced, but I had to talk to you about something important," Basil said as he stood before his mentor.

"Never apologize for coming to see me. My doors are always open for you," Kane assured as he placed his hand on Basil's shoulder.

"Thanks. Can we talk alone?" Basil asked as he looked over at his mother.

"Yes indeed," Kane answered. He then waved for the henchman who stood at his front door to come over. The big burly man came quickly and Kane wrapped one of his arms around Frenchie.

"Show her around the house. Also have Maria give her a manicure and pedicure," Kane said. "You came on the right day. My manicurist is here," he explained as he looked down at Frenchie.

"Well, I'm not going to turn a good mani/pedi down," Frenchie said jokingly as she smiled from ear to ear.

"It would be my pleasure," the henchman said with a smile as he reached out his elbow, inviting Frenchie to latch on. With no hesitation, Frenchie hooked on to the man and they headed toward the door. Just before they reached the door Frenchie stopped in her tracks and turned around, looking at her son and old friend. "I'm glad that you two found each other," she said happily. There was so much joy in her eyes and sincerity in her tone. Kane and Basil both smiled, knowing that she was unware of the turmoil that surrounded them. They were in the midst of a potential war.

They both watched as Frenchie disappeared into the house and focused their attention on each other.

"Let's take a walk," Kane suggested. He slid his hand into his pocket and pulled out a Cuban cigar and lit it. They walked through the compound with nothing but green grass around them. The sun shone down on them, but the aura was cold. Basil knew that he had potentially started a war. Something that Kane adamantly was against. There was no money in war and Basil felt culpable for what he had done.

"I know what you are thinking and don't worry. I'm not upset. I know you and how you move. You are a hustler, not a troublemaker. I know that Landon's son must have left you no choice. The little fucker was a bonehead and everyone knew that. He got what was coming to him. Just so happen that you had to be the one who give it to him," Kane said.

"That shit happened so fast," Basil replied as he shook his head.

"It comes with the territory, young G. You had to catch a body. Luckily, it wasn't a civilian. Because if it was, it would have been a whole different set of problems. You killed a street cat, so that's where we have to hold court. I'd rather deal with this than dealing with a judge and twelve jurors that was put there just to put you in jail for the rest of your life. So now, we have to lace up our boots and move accordingly. As I said before, I want you to go to Miami for a while. Ya know, to lay low? I have already put the word in and they are waiting for you to arrive. Just go down there until this thing blows over and I can get a firm grip on the situation," Kane instructed.

"I understand. But it's something that I need you to do for me," Basil stated.

"Sure. What's that?"

"It's my mom. I need her to be looked after while I'm gone."

"Absolutely. I'll make arrangements for her to be moved out of city limits and also will put a detail on her twenty-four hours until further notice," Kane said assuringly. A great burden had been lifted from Basil's shoulders. To hear that his mother would be protected made his departure easier.

"Thanks, big homie. I will pay whatever to—" Basil began but got cut off mid-sentence by Kane. Kane stopped walking and blew out a cloud of cigar smoke. He then faced Basil and put his hand on his shoulder, looking Basil directly in the eyes.

"Listen, we are family. We don't keep count with favors. Never count favors with your family! We move as a unit. Your problem is my problem and I don't need any money to take care of family. This is not just your problem. It's our problem," Kane said sincerely. Basil and Kane slapped hands and hugged. At that moment, their bond was even further cemented. Kane wanted to keep Frenchie safe just as much as Basil did. He and Frenchie

had a history as well. Kane took a mental stroll down Memory
Lane as he embraced his understudy.

Circa 1989

Kane and Carter Diamond sat at the card table while the sounds
of Stephanie Mills filled the air. They were on the south side of
Flint, ducked off in a small apartment in the Howard Estates. The
apartment belonged to Keema, a young lady that Kane had taken
a liking to. She was half black, half Venezuelan. She was the product of a hooker for a mother and a foreign father who was a trick.
This mix gave her a distinct look and growing up in the middle of
the ghetto, where nearly everyone was black, she was a hot com-
modity. Kane took her off the market quickly and they become an
item. Seven people were in the apartment; Carter, Kane, Polo, Fat
Rat, T, Frenchie, and Keema. All around twenty years old, they
were a small social clique. It was the night of the NBA championship and the Detroit Pistons were on the verge of becoming the
world champions. The television was on mute but they could see
the crowd going wild and the seconds ticking off the shot clock.

Keema's best friend, T, was the girlfriend of Carter so they
double-dated frequently. She also had a friend named Frenchie
who refused to talk to Fat Rat or Polo so they were always just
the spare wheels. But it worked; they were a crew. Just like any
other weekend, they were all together smoking, counting, and
partying in Keema's tiny spot. They had just sold out of their
product and were counting up the profits so that they could re-
up and do it all again.

"Life is good," Kane said as he put another stack of money through the money counter.

"Life is good," Carter repeated as he wrapped a rubber band around the stack of money that he pulled from the money counter. Fat Rat sat by the door with a pistol in his lap as he always did, and Polo stood at the window and slightly pulled down the blinds as he kept an eye on the parking lot. They were all from the same neighborhood and grew up together. They were a solid crew and the brotherhood ran deep.

"Your plug is on a million watts," Kane said to his business partner, referring to Carter's newfound Miami cocaine plug, the legendary Emilio Estes.

"Yeah, we got a good thing going on for sure," Carter answered as he focused on the money while talking. He was back home in Flint visiting and picking up his money from Kane. Kane ran the Midwest while Carter was just getting his footing in Miami. Carter Diamond had met Estes down in Miami and set his childhood friend up nice. He gave Kane bricks of cocaine for the cheapest price and on consignment. They were setting the drug market on fire and were on their way to being millionaires before the age of twenty-one.

T was dancing to the feel-good music as they were counting. She looked over at Carter, who was focused on the money, and she instantly got turned on. She looked at his smooth baby face and the Kangol hat that slyly tilted to the side and smiled. His thick pork-chop sideburns and small Afro that perfectly peeked out the sides of the hat were so sexy to her. He was a smooth player, as she liked to say. The record changed and Teena Marie and Rick James's "Fire and Desire" began to play. T threw her hands in the air and swayed back and forth.

"This my song!" she yelled as she began to snap to the beat. She made her way over to Carter and straddled him as he focused on the money.

"Put that down for a minute, baby," she said as she threw her arms around him, continuing to snap to the rhythm.

"Whoa, whoa," Carter said as he lost count. He focused on T and chuckled, admiring her beauty.

Keema yelled from across the room and she began to groove in her seat. "Yeah, come over here to mama," she said playfully as she patted the empty space between her and Frenchie.

"Don't have to tell me twice," Kane said as he stopped what he was doing and made his way over to the couch.

"Yeah, it's time for a break, baby," Keema added just before she laid a big wet kiss on her man as soon as he sat down.

"Kane, will you take me home? I have to get up for class tomorrow," Frenchie said as she stood up and stretched her arms. Kane was snuggled up closely with Keema, making out.

"Can't you see I'm busy?" Kane said as he briefly stopped what he was doing and looked over at her.

"Take her home! It's only around the corner. You might get lucky when you get back," Keema said as she playfully grabbed her breasts and wiggled them.

"Uh oh! You better get to moving," Carter said playfully as T sat on his lap, drinking a beer. Everyone burst into laughter and Kane smiled. He leaned over and gave Keema a kiss, right before he stood and grabbed his keys out of his pocket.

"I guess the queen has spoken," Kane said as he smiled and walked toward the door. Frenchie went over and hugged T and then Keema.

"Love y'all. See ya this weekend," Frenchie said as she put on her peacoat.

"Love ya too, girl," Keema said as she smiled and watched her friend exit the small apartment. Just before Kane closed the door, she flicked her tongue and mouthed "Hurry back" as she playfully grabbed her breasts and squeezed them together.

"Yes, ma'am," Kane said as he tilted his hat and gave her that famous smile. Kane and Frenchie headed out and Fat Rat watched the door.

"Why don't your girl give me any play? She cold-blooded," Polo said as he watched Frenchie and Kane walk to the car from the window.

"Frenchie ain't worried about no nigga. That girl is going to be a lawyer someday. She focused," Keema said proudly about her childhood friend.

"Yeah, Frenchie's going be something one day. She is almost done with school. She goes to Mott and don't need a thug like you to knock her off her square," T added as she shot a look at Polo, sticking out her tongue, teasing him. Polo laughed and shook his head, knowing that she was right. Frenchie was a good girl and honestly, too good for him. He knew she was out of his league. In time, her position in life would drastically change. But as for his: once the streets grab ahold of a person, it's hard to shake loose.

CHAPTER SEVENTEEN

We are family.

—KANE GARRETT

Basil sat in the presidential suite at the Atheneum Suite Hotel in downtown Detroit. The old building had a lot of character and had been a staple within the city for years. Only "old money" stayed at the hotel and Basil had figured it would be a great low-key spot for a meeting with Mo. He looked at the duffle bag that was by the door and the thought saddened him. The next morning, he would be on a flight to Miami until further notice. Kane instructed him not to come back until he gave the go-ahead. Basil had to break the news to Mo that he would be leaving for a while. He walked to the window and looked at Detroit's skyline, thinking about how he had come up in the drug game in such a short time. Nevertheless, his drug reign would be short-lived because of his current dilemma with Landon. Just as he finished his thought, a knock at the door sounded. He walked over to the door, looked in the peephole, and unlocked the top locks as his heart began to pound in anticipation. He opened the door and looked at the beauty that stood before him. It was Moriah, standing there with glowing skin and nude-colored lipstick on. She wore a black head wrap and huge vintage sunglasses that covered almost the entire top half of her face. She quickly stepped in and was noticeably shaken. She snatched off her sunglasses and exposed her beautiful face, which warmed Basil's heart. She immediately hugged Basil and squeezed him tightly.

"I missed you so much," she said as they hugged each other, followed by a heartfelt kiss. They both were mutually happy to be in each other's arms. The past week without each other seemed like a lifetime, considering that they had been together every day for the past six months.

"This past week has been torture for me. I missed your touch." Moriah laid her head on Basil's chest, searching for his heartbeat. Basil clutched her tightly and realized that their souls were connected. A wave of sadness overcame him as he thought about the bad news that he was about to break to her.

"I missed you too, ma," Basil said as he leaned down and kissed the top of her head. "This week has been crazy for me too. It's caused me to change the way I move. The guy I hit was made. Meaning, there is consequences . . . heavy consequences that came with the bullet I gave him," Basil explained.

"I have been watching how my father has been acting and I knew something was going on. Who exactly was that guy?" Moriah asked, trying to get a better understanding of the situation.

"The guy I hit, name was L.J. He was the son of the Irish gangster Landon McVey. Their entire family comes from a long line of gangsters from Chicago. Landon's father used to work under Ronald Dermody out of Boston, an infamous hitman with heavy ties. They moved to Michigan in the eighties and started an underground gambling ring. So their connections run deep. And wide; they have connections across the country. Which makes it bad for me and my crew. I didn't murk just any-body. This mu'fucka was a somebody," Basil explained as he shook his head in disbelief at the chain of events. He gave Mo-riah details, repeating the info that Kane had given him earlier that week. He wanted her to understand the magnitude of their situation.

"Damn," Moriah whispered, being streetwise enough to know what type of problem that Basil had on his hands.

"Yeah, it's nothing I can't handle, though. But I have to move strategic. I have to take off for a while until things calm down and we get a full clear view of the board, feel me?" Basil said as he released her and walked toward the window. He was deeply pained that he was leaving Moriah. He had never met a woman like her and their connection was something that he had never experienced in his life.

"I understand," Moriah said as she dropped her head, know-ing that she couldn't do anything to change his decision. She knew it was the right thing to do. She felt slightly guilty, know-ing that the only reason they were in the Irish district was the fact that they had to hide their love for each another.

"Kane is like . . . he's like a father to me. If he finds out about us, he would never forgive me. He told me on countless nights how you were his precious gem. He doesn't want you anywhere near the streets or anybody involved in it. And what did I do? I fell in love with you," Basil said as he gazed at the lit-up skyline. "We can't do this anymore," he added, as he dropped his head in sadness. What he was saying was difficult, but he knew that it was necessary. He was playing with fire and being disloyal to the one man whom he had the most loyalty to. He kept replaying the conversation that he'd had with Kane during their walk. Kane had emphasized, *We are family*. Basil kept hearing his voice and remembering the deep sincerity in his eyes. He knew that Kane truly looked at him as family. Basil had fallen weak to a woman who was off-limits and she had a strong grip on him. It pained him, but he understood deep inside that he had to let her go. He felt a pain in his heart that he had never felt before.

"Mo, we can't do this anymore. It isn't right. I'm so sorry but it has to be over. It has to be . . ." Basil shook his head. "I love you," he whispered for the first time to her. He placed his hand on the window and leaned slightly, using it to balance him; somehow hoping that the window could help him with the weight of the world, which seemed to be on his shoulders. The words he had spoken were crushing to Moriah and Basil both. But they knew that this moment was inevitable. They were not meant to be together. It was wrong on so many levels.

Something was telling Moriah that this would be the last time she'd see Basil for a while. As she slowly approached him, she began to silently cry. Tears fell down her face as she stood behind him. She rested her head on his back and wrapped her hands snugly around his body. She hugged tightly as the smell of his cologne heightened her senses. She closed her watery eyes and cherished the moment. Moriah couldn't see it, but Basil had dropped a single tear, knowing what was to come. The pain was too much to bear. He hadn't cried since he was a little boy. He had to say goodbye to his soul mate. He slowly turned around and they now faced each other, both of them seeing the other one's pain.

"I love you too, Basil," Moriah said as she reached up and gently cupped his cheeks. She kissed him and Basil wrapped his hands around her lower back. The more they got into the kiss, the lower Basil's hands got, and they eventually landed on Moriah's backside. Each one of Basil's hands gripped a cheek and he began to caress them while pulling her closer, causing Moriah to moan. She felt her clitoris pulsate, thinking about Basil's masterful stroke. She felt his member beginning to grow against her. Still kissing, Basil slowly walked her to the bed.

Basil gently pushed her onto the bed. Moriah hurriedly pulled off her coat and pulled up her dress, exposing that she wore no panties. Basil looked down and saw that she was freshly shaven and her glazed lips were shining and noticeably soaked. Her small, erect clitoris peeked out of her lips. Moriah reached down with her fingers and slowly spread her lips, exposing her pinkness to Basil. Basil just stared and admired, wanting to remember every moment because it would be his last.

He pulled off his shirt and slowly dropped to his knees. He reached onto the bed and pulled Moriah closer to him so that her pelvis barely hung off its edge. He then put his hands behind her knees, firmly holding her legs in the air. Her ebony-colored, plump peach sat perfectly in front of his face and he could see her womb contracting in and out. She threw her head back and moaned in anticipation. She couldn't wait to feel his tongue on her. Basil took his time and made her wait. He studied her love-box carefully as if he were a surgeon about to perform a precise operation. He slowly kissed around her clitoris, knowing exactly what he was doing. He kissed everywhere but where she desired him to. Moriah began to squirm, moving her hips in a circular motion, as she began to rub her nipples in ecstasy.

"Please, please, Basil. Suck it," she begged.

"Nah . . . ," Basil said in between the strategic kisses to her inner thighs.

"Please, baby. Please," she pleaded again, but in a whiny voice. She was feigning for his tongue. At that point, her clitoris was almost twice its normal size and it felt like it had a heartbeat in it. She had never wanted to be touched or licked so badly. Basil was driving her to the edge of insanity. She felt her wetness drip down and fall into her asshole. She propped her pelvis up even more by sliding down slightly. Her entire ass was hanging off the bed as Basil's strong hands held her up in the air. Basil watched her squirm as she bit her bottom lip and pulled her nipples. He knew that she was ready. He attacked her box with his mouth and slowly began to suck on her clitoris. He wrapped his lips around it while moving his head in and out. He then began to flick his tongue across her clitoris and then down into her open-ing and repeated this for five minutes straight. Moriah was to-tally turned on and felt an orgasm approaching. Her entire body began to shake and she aggressively put her hand on the back of Basil's head and sat up and looked down so she could see him in action. Moriah pushed Basil's face into her lovebox so hard that he couldn't breathe and she began to grind against his face rapidly. She moaned loudly while staring down at him. She felt herself beginning to explode as she panted heavily and her mouth was wide open. Grunts and sounds that she never heard before came from the pit of her stomach and out of her mouth as she began to orgasm and jerk sporadically.

Basil slowly let her shaking legs down and stood. Moriah's body quivered as she scooted onto the middle of the bed. She spread her legs open as she began to rub herself, ready to orgasm again. Basil began to remove his clothes. He pulled down his boxer briefs and his rock-hard pole popped out, pointing directly at Moriah as she waited in anticipation. A heavy vein ran down the center of his thickness and the sight alone made Moriah whimper. Basil climbed onto the bed and onto his knees as he hovered over the love of his life. They locked eyes and gazed into one another's soul as they both smiled at the same time. Moriah dropped a tear while smiling widely. Basil wiped her tear away with one hand and with the other slowly slid into her wetness, causing her back to arch and her mouth to open. Basil began to rock back and forth while never breaking eye contact with her. He took his time as he inched his way deep inside of her, filling her up. He slowly drove in and out of her. Every time he plunged, he wiggled his hips as if he were dancing inside of her. It was driving her completely insane as she placed her hands on his tight buttocks, digging her nails deep into him with each stroke.

"I love you from the bottom of my heart, Mo. You're always my girl," Basil said as he stroked her with authority and precision.

In.

Circles.

Out.

In.

Circles.

Out.

Basil was erect to his fullest potential as he tried his best to satisfy Mo. His ball sack hit her other hole with every stroke and the wet smacking noise sounded each time he dove in. The sound itself drove Basil wild as he licked his lips in excitement. They traded "I love you's" for twenty minutes as Basil stayed consistent and strong the whole time. He ran his fingers through her dreadlocks and kissed her softly as he put his game down. He felt himself begin to climax and sped up his thrusting and spread his legs wider, attempting to get even deeper inside of her.

"I about to come," he announced as he closed his eyes and dug deep.

"Me too, baby. Don't stop. Please don't stop!" Moriah yelled as she smacked his ass and helped him plunge harder into her.

"Ahhhhhh!" she yelled as she exploded on him, her inner walls contracting so rapidly that it sent him over the edge. He then released a walnut-size load deep inside of her. He grunted loudly as his entire body tensed up and veins began to bulge out of his neck and temple. He fell on top of her and their sweaty bodies seemed to melt into one another. They both just laid there for an entire minute, saying nothing. Just deep breathing and body rubs. After he caught his breath, Basil moved to pull his semi-erect tool out of her, but she hugged him and pulled him closer.

"Just stay in," she whispered, not wanting it to be over. Basil paused and he followed her command. He stayed inside of her and they slowly began to grind on each other until he was fully erect again. They took their time and made love the entire night, while enjoying each other's company, savoring every precious second. This was their final goodbye . . . so they thought.

CHAPTER EIGHTEEN

You got all of these hitters and scared to use them.

—LIL NOAH

Basil slowly opened his eyes and looked over at Moriah's naked body as she slept peacefully. Her face was partially buried in the white fluffy pillow. Basil smiled as he admired her beauty, while slyly sliding out of the bed. He tried his best not to wake her as he stood up and stared down at the love of his life. The sun's rays peeked through the blinds; it was the crack of dawn on the day of his departure from the only place he ever called home. He showered and slipped on his clothes and headed out without a sound, but not before he gave Moriah a kiss on the forehead and whispered that he loved her. With that, he was out of the door and on the highway heading to Flint to take care of a few loose ends. He was set to leave for Miami later that evening, so he had to make sure his affairs were in order.

His first stop was in the Regency projects to check on his soldiers, Lil Noah in particular. Basil pulled into the gates and drove to the rear of the projects, where Lil Noah usually set up shop and monitored the operation. He parked in the lot of the vacant apartment building and just as expected, Lil Noah was on the stoop with about five other guys. Basil stepped out of his Range Rover, neatly dressed in his Italian-cut slacks and crisp white button-down shirt that tightly hugged his body, showing off his athletic physique. His snakeskin, black leather Hermès belt wrapped around his waist tightly. He looked like a Wall Street broker on a lunch break. The only thing that gave him away was the chrome pistol handle that was tucked snugly in the small of his back. Basil's expensive red-bottom loafers hit the pavement and all eyes were on him. His new stylish look was a far cry from what he had once been. His legend only grew with his upgraded appearance and everybody respected the young king. Basil hopped out and walked up to the stoop, joining his team. Everyone immediately showed respect and slapped hands with him, including Lil Noah. The man who gave them a pipeline to the riches was present, so their gratitude was unmistakable.

"Yo, what's up, family? Let's go talk in my office," Basil said as he locked hands with his head street general.

"Absolutely," Lil Noah said as he stood up and stepped off the stoop. Lil Noah held both of his pinky fingers to his mouth and blew as hard as he could, causing a loud whistle to echo through the air. He looked up at the top of the building, where two men stood with sniper rifles, acting as lookout boys and the first line of defense as they looked through the scopes, patrolling the projects. They quickly put their guns down and began to walk to the stairs. The roof was Basil's office and the boss was home. Basil looked up and watched as the two men disappeared from the rooftop.

"Let's go up, fam," Lil Noah said as he headed to the fire escape so that they could climb up. Basil and Lil Noah made their way up to the rooftop and they both stood at the edge, looking out over the projects.

"I still don't see why you have to go down south, bruh. We can bring it to them Irish mu'fuckas. You see that?" Lil Noah said as he waved his hands over the projects. "We all riding for you at the drop of a dime. You the king of this. You! Why won't you push that button and show the muscle that you have? You got all of these hitters and scared to use them," Lil Noah said as he patted his waist where his gun was tucked.

"Nah, kid, I aint scared of nothing. Trust that. However, what's the good in starting a street war? Blood is going to spill and that's going to bring nothing but the feds and indictments. Which will lead to niggas like you getting football numbers in prison. And when the heat is on . . . I'm going to do what I should have done in the beginning. Go down south and lay low. I can't put my soldiers in harm's way like that. I have to be smarter than that. So I'll just skip the drama and lay low until things calm down. Plus, on top of that, no money can be made if y'all worried about shooting at niggas and getting shot at," Basil said, explaining the logic in his moves. The way he broke it down, it made total sense to his young general. He was ready to go to war, but understood how it could be harmful.

"I see," Lil Noah admitted as he nodded his head in agreement.

"Just because I'm gone away doesn't mean the show stops. This is still a well-oiled machine. I will still set up the work to be brought in on the twenty-eighth of every month. The only difference is that I will be making the plays from afar. Nothing changes, got it?" Basil ordered as he slid both of his hands into his pockets and looked Lil Noah in the eyes, establishing his weightiness. "You don't have to worry about anything. I'm going to hold it down and make sure shit run smoothly. You already laid the blueprint for this thing to run as designed."

"True. True," Basil said; he trusted the work that he'd put in to get them this far.

"What about them north side niggas? They been coming through here trying to cop," Lil Noah said, updating him on the latest.

"Nah, that's Boone's crew. Let them niggas stay at that side. I ain't fucking with Boone like that," Basil said, sticking to his guns on his decision not to do business with Boone. He thought about all of the intel he had got from Viv about her grimy cousin. He had a funny feeling about Boone and didn't want to mix his new connections with him.

"You sure? He was talking about copping ten. Plus, he wasn't asking for a discount. He was willing to pay the full yard," Lil Noah pleaded, as he thought about the money and the money only.

"What the fuck did I say?" Basil said sternly as he looked at Lil Noah with piercing eyes. He never went against his gut feeling and he wanted to make that clear. "Do you work for me . . . or is it the other way around?" Basil asked through clenched teeth, noticeably agitated by Lil Noah's persistence.

"I got you, boss man," Lil Noah said as he put both of his hands up.

"Good. Good," Basil said as he lightened his demeanor. He adjusted his cuff links and continued to debrief Lil Noah. "Viv is still going to do the pickups and drop-offs of the bricks. Every week drop her off my cut as usual and I'll take the rest up with her."

"I got you. Everything is going to run smooth, bro," Lil Noah said as he rubbed his hands together and nodded his head with confidence.

"Bet. I have a flight to catch. I'm about to get out of here," Basil said as he walked to Lil Noah and slapped his hand. Basil locked their handshake firmly and pulled his little man into him to embrace. "I love you, bro. Remember that."

"Love you too, big bro. Be safe out there and I'll hold it down," Lil Noah assured him. With that, Basil climbed down the fire escape and took off. He didn't let anyone other than his immediate circle know that he was leaving for a while and that was just the way he wanted it.

Basil had reached Vivian's doorstep to pick up his money for the week and break the news to her. He had sent her a text earlier that day, so she could have his money together for him when he arrived. He didn't intend on staying long.

Basil knocked on the door and waited for an answer. Moments later, he opened the door and his jaw almost hit the ground. Vivian came to the door in a full-length see-through robe. The sheer robe had white trim and left nothing to the imagination. Vivian had her hair pulled back, and her baby hairs rested perfectly along the edges of her hairline. Her dark ebony face was glowing and she had bright red lipstick on that made her smooth skin seem even more perfect. She stood in a nude-colored pair of stilettos that were five inches tall. The smell of cocoa butter and flowery perfume came off of her body as she stood in the doorway while her hand rested on her waist. Basil looked her up and down and she was simply stunning. Her thick thighs were on full display and just above them were her slightly pudgy hips. Her stomach wasn't flat but it was imperfectly perfect as a belly button sparkled in the light. Her neatly cut triangle of hair hid her vagina; however, her plump, meaty lovebox was on display. The faint sounds of Drake pumped out of her home speakers and the flickering of candles were her source of light. Basil wanted to pounce on her but he was too calculated to do that. He hated that she chose they day he was quitting her to put on the current spectacle.

"Hey, daddy," she whispered as she batted her eyes.

"Damn," Basil whispered as he looked at her big brown nipples. He could see that they were erect and it seemed as if they stuck out two inches from her areolas. Vivian looked like a goddess. Basil stepped in and walked right past her and shook his head in disbelief. Not disbelief in her, but the disbelief that he was about to turn all of that down. Vivian closed the door and met him in the living room as he stood by the light switch. She then walked into the kitchen, where a bucket of ice was sitting on the counter. A black bottle of champagne stuck out of the bucket along with two flute glasses.

"I've been waiting for you all day," Vivian said in a seductive voice. Basil watched as she walked across the room. Her sheer robe showed her plump ass. It seemed to have a mind of its own as it wiggled every which way as she strutted.

"Listen, we have to talk," Basil said as he continued to shake his head.

"Yeah, we can do all that. But I need you to hit this pussy first. I'm trying to feel that curve ASAP. Been thinking about him all day. Trying to squirt all over it," she confessed as she opened the bottle, making a big popping noise erupt throughout the place.

"No, listen. You're not hearing me. We have to talk," Basil said again as he switched on the lights, killing the mood.

"Damn, what you tripping for?" Vivian said as she frowned and quickly grew agitated at Basil's rudeness.

"We can't do this anymore."

"Do what? What the fuck are you talking about, Basil?" Vivian said as she put the champagne back in the bucket and placed both of her hands on her hips with a heavy attitude.

"This! This shit. I ain't fucking with you like that anymore. My mind is somewhere else right now," he said as he tried to stay on task.

"Oh, I see. That bitch got yo' ass wide open, huh? She gave you a li'l bit of pussy and you don't know how to act," Vivian said as she jerked her neck from left to right as she talked.

"You're funny," Basil said calmly as he shook his head and gave her a fake chuckle.

"I ain't said shit funny. That natural, Erykah Badu–looking bitch got you whipped," Vivian said as she slowly approached

Basil. She folded her arms as she walked over and stopped right in front of him. She began to talk again as she dropped her hands and untied the belt, allowing her robe to fall open.

"Look, I know you like that girl. I can see it all in your eyes. You ain't dropped no dick off in months. I'm not stupid. I'm gamed up and you know that. A blind man can see that you're in love. But dig this. I just want that dick from time to time," she said as she cupped her breasts and began to caress them. She then lifted her right breast and leaned down to suck her own nipple.

"Nah, we can't do that," Basil said, knowing that he had to stay disciplined. He was too seasoned to fall for that trick. He knew that if he laid pipe to her, it would lead to her wanting what they used to have. He wanted to have a business-only relationship with Vivian from that point forward. Strictly business.

"Are you sure?" Viv said as she circled her nipple with her long pink tongue. Basil looked on and began to enjoy the show. He felt his dick begin to harden and quickly brushed past her and stood by the couch.

"Yo, I'm good, ma. I'm going to pass on that. We can still get money together and all that but the sex is dead. Go to the back and get my bread out of the safe," he demanded.

"Yo, this is crazy. It's many niggas that want all of this. Don't flatter yourself!" Viv said, almost yelling. She was irate and couldn't believe that Basil was cutting her off. Basil couldn't believe it either, but he knew that he had to stay focused and keep things in perspective. He was in the middle of a potential war with the Irish and understood that most wars were lost because of a woman. He wanted no part of it. He also loved Moriah and she was the only one that he was attracted to. After experiencing a woman like Mo, it was hard to accept anything less. Mo's intellectual conversations trumped any sexual escapade that he ever had with Viv. On top of that, sex with Moriah was amazing because of the deep connection their minds shared. He couldn't go backward if he tried. Moriah showed him what real was, and once you tasted real, everything else left a bitter taste.

Needless to say, Viv didn't like the new scenario but she went to fetch his money. She cursed him out during his brief visit, but she didn't go overboard, not wanting to disrupt her honeypot. She made good money with Basil and she understood that. But she silently vowed that she would get him back for embarrassing her.

Basil instructed her on the business structure and how she would get paid double for not only doing her monthly trafficking, but for holding his money for him until he returned. Basil took just over eighty thousand in cold cash from Vivian's house. He was headed south with a duffle bag and all his ducks in a row. He hated that he had to leave but he knew that it was a smart move. He was playing chess . . . not checkers.

"Miami, here I come," he whispered to himself as he got on Interstate 75 South. Next stop, Miami, Florida: Cartel land.

CHAPTER NINETEEN

*Always give a man just enough room to jump out of the
window and escape.*

—UNKNOWN

Five months had passed since Basil had left Flint and to his surprise, he was enjoying his extended vacation. He was comfortable in Miami with his Cartel counterparts. Carter Diamond
had set him up a spot in South Beach that he was in charge of.
Basil ran it just as he did back home; like a business. He was
more hands-on in the smaller operation and was making good
money while doing it. With what he was getting sent from back
home and his current hustle, he had stacked up north of a million dollars in the short stint. He liked this new spot in particular because the majority of the clientele were college kids and
tourists searching for a party drug, cocaine in particular. He
moved powder cocaine instead of crack rock and loved the
climate of his new hustle. He even tapped into the local professional athletes and was their exclusive provider. Word got

around that there was a new guy in town that the pro athletes could trust and cop blow from. Basil fit right in and was embraced as if he were born there. To be frank, Basil loved Miami. Less stress, warm weather, and more upscale clientele. He ran his operation out of a small storefront and loved the smoothness of it. From the outside, the storefront looked like a convenience store but much more was getting moved out of the back door. Although Basil had reservations when he found out what spot they had offered him, he quickly had a change of heart when he began to see the traffic and residuals. Carter Diamond had made sure he was set up to win and within the first week of his arrival he had a crew, built-in clientele, and an unlimited credit on his coke supply. Not to mention the fact that the Cartel had the local police in their back pocket, and the possibility of raids or interference from the law was nonexistent. Basil immediately began to see the muscle and power of the Cartel umbrella.

Basil sat in front of the storefront and watched as the skaters, dog walkers, and bicyclists went past him. He wore an unbuttoned white linen shirt that displayed his physique and a khaki bucket hat blocked the sun rays from hitting his face. He looked over at the older black man who sat at the small table before him. Basil had befriended the older gentleman after they discovered their common love for chess. The man owned a newsstand that was next to Basil's spot and they played every time Basil was at the spot. The slow-moving older man had a head full of gray hair and his skin was black as tar. His big purple lips and smooth-shaven face gave him a unique look. Winston was his name and he didn't say much. He just had a passion for the mental game of chess and although he was in his seventies, he was still sharp as a tack. Winston always wore old-school Cartier glasses and most of the time he was shirtless. He once told Basil jokingly, "When you're my age, you don't care about the small things in life . . . like shirts." Winston had a toothpick sticking from his mouth as he slowly twisted it with his thumb and index finger. He stared at the board and made his move.

Basil took his focus off of the strip and back to the board and quickly made his countermove. He had gotten the habit of daily chess from Kane and was relieved when he found someone to play with. Basil stayed to himself while in Miami, other than Mecca. He didn't want other friends . . . Winston did just fine for him. Basil was down there strictly for business and he anticipated the day that Kane gave him the okay to return back up top.

A cherry-red Lamborghini pulled onto the curve just in front of the store and a few feet away from where Basil was sitting. Basil looked closer and saw that it was Mecca. Mecca hopped out and threw his hands in the air with a big smile. Mecca's hair was all over his head and his long mane was past his shoulder blades. "What's good, B?" Mecca said as he approached Basil.

"Mecca. My guy. What's good?" Basil said as he stood up and slapped hands with his friend. They had grown pretty tight over the past few months and had a mutual respect for each another. Basil usually dealt directly with Mecca with the Cartel's bricks and through that, they bonded. Mecca showed Basil around town and got him acclimated to Miami's street culture.

"Just came to check you out. See how you holding up," Mecca said as they released their embrace.

"Everything is good, fam. Business as usual," Basil said as he looked up the strip.

"Good. Good," Mecca said as he rubbed his hands together. He then leaned in and whispered, "Yo, how that bag moving?" He was referring to the bricks that he dropped off to Basil about a week earlier.

"All gone," Basil said calmly and confidently.

"All gone?" Mecca asked as one of his eyebrows raised.

"All gone," Basil confirmed, cracking a small smile.

"You are God. Never seen anything like it," Mecca admitted as he smiled from ear to ear. Let's go inside and talk."

"Absolutely," Basil answered as he stepped to the side, clearing a pathway for Mecca to enter the store. Basil watched as Mecca entered the store and then walked to Winston and reached down and moved a piece on the chessboard.

"Checkmate in three, old man," Basil said as he pointed and smiled at Winston. "Don't go too far and dodge this ass whooping. I'll be right back," Basil added as he faded into the store, but not before flipping the sign to "Closed."

Basil entered the store and saw four of his appointed goons scattered throughout the store sitting in folding chairs. Loud hip-hop music pumped out of the small radio that sat on the floor in the corner of the room. The store was mainly empty. The only thing they had for sale to the public were drinks: three large standing coolers, filled with water and different-colored

Gatorades. Mecca slapped hands with the goons, greeting them, and then he and Basil made their way to the back.

Basil walked into the back and opened the large safe. He then reached in and pulled out a brown paper bag that was filled with rubber-band-wrapped stacks of cash. He handed it to Mecca, and Mecca looked at the bag in disbelief.

"You running through them joints like water," he admitted, as he was thoroughly impressed.

"You know how I do," Basil said calmly.

"Cool, I'll have the new joints sent through tonight. You want the same order, right?" Mecca asked.

"Yeah, that's cool. Matter of fact, I need an extra one on top of the usual order. I got some shit going on this weekend that I need to be prepared for."

"I got you. What you got going on?" Mecca asked, interested in what Basil was referring to.

"You know, the all-star game coming this weekend," Basil commented.

"Oh yeah, you right. I'mma need you to get us some floor seats. You still got that plug, right?" Mecca asked.

"No doubt. I got you covered. We can fall in that mu'fucka together if you want," Basil offered.

"Hell yeah. I'm with it," Mecca agreed as he smiled, thinking about how he was going to floss on the floor seat of the national televised event.

"But check this out. Like I was saying before, the all-star weekend is here this weekend. You know I got my guy that play on the Heat. Big. He's throwing a private after-party at his mansion and want me to supply the blow for all of his NBA niggas that flying in for the festivities. Listen to this, the nigga buying a whole brick for them to blow that night. A whole fucking brick, bro. I charged that nigga fifty just to see what he would say. He prepaid for that shit like it was nothing. Sent his little cousin over here and dropped off a bag that same day," Basil explained as he began to think about the easiest fifty grand he had ever made in his life. He had charged Big double what bricks were going on the street for. Basil put his tax on it and the naive athlete paid for it without a care in the world. Basil understood that Big was paying for the secrecy just as much as the product. Big was a veteran that rode the bench, but was a popular player in his heyday. He was on his way out of the league, but had received multiple max deals in his career, so he had money to blow. Everybody loved Big of the Miami Heat. Especially Basil.

Kane swung at the ball with his tennis racket while releasing a small grunt. His all-white Polo outfit was soaked in sweat and he watched closely as the small lime-green ball flew across the net. On the opposite side was Moriah. She swung at the ball, sending it crashing back to the other side. Kane ran to beat the ball to the spot, but it was too fast.

"Game, old man!" Moriah said as she threw both hands in the air and gloated in her victory.

"What can I say. You got me. I'm getting old," Kane said as he breathed deeply and rested his hands on his knees. Beads of sweat dripped off of his brow and onto the court. He caught his breath and walked over to the net where Moriah was waiting.

They shook hands and Kane kissed her on the cheek. "Good game, baby," he said as they headed to the side, where their gym bags were waiting. They both scooped up their bags and began walking side by side.

"Thanks for coming to play a few games with me. You made my morning," Kane admitted.

"I enjoyed myself. It's always good to spend time with you. Also, I know you let me win that game," Moriah said as she poked her father.

"You got me," Kane admitted and they both burst into laughter. Kane looked at his daughter and admired her beauty. She was the spitting image of her late mother and it gave him joy that he still had a piece of Keema through her. "It's good to hear you laugh," Kane said as he threw his arm around his daughter's shoulder as they walked off the court. He continued, "You haven't been the same for the past few months. You seem down. Is everything okay?" Kane asked in concern. He had noticed the change in her and couldn't seem to put his hand on the problem. Little did he know she was suffering from a broken heart. She missed Basil so much that it hurt. She hadn't spoken with him since he left and it was taking longer than she expected to get over him.

"I'm good, Daddy. Just, this new semester has me buried in work. Kinda stressful, ya know?" she lied, trying to cover up the real reason she was down.

"I hear ya. You will push through. I have faith in you," he said just before he kissed the top of her head.

They reached the parking lot of the country club but Kane

wasn't yet ready to leave. He wanted to play a couple of rounds of golf, so he instructed Mo to go ahead and he would see her later that night. He watched as she got into the car and put on her seat belt.

"Maybe you need to take a weekend getaway of some sort," he recommended as he tried to figure out a way to get her out of her funk.

"You know what? That may not be a bad idea. My friends asked me if I wanted to go to the all-star weekend with them. I might take 'em up on that offer," Moriah said, hoping that that would get her mind off Basil.

"You should. You're young! Get away and see different places," Kane said. "Wait." He reached into his bag and grabbed his wallet. He pulled out his black credit card and handed it to his daughter. "It's on me. You and your friends go and enjoy yourself. First-class," he added as he smiled.

"Aw, thanks, Daddy. You're the best," she said as she grabbed the card. Kane leaned into the car and got a peck on the cheek and then stepped back as he watched her pull away in the white Mercedes Benz 6 series. Kane waved to her as he headed to the locker room of the country club to get dressed for a few rounds of golf.

"Nice doing business with you, my nigga," Boone said as he slapped hands with Lil Noah. Boone had just copped a quarter brick and was elated because he knew that he was getting the best product in town. Boone was deep in the projects and it was his first time copping from the Regency. He had run into

Lil Noah at the club and convinced him to let him get work from him.

"No doubt," Lil Noah said as he side-eyed Boone. He didn't care too much for Boone, but unlike Basil he didn't let that get in the way of making money. He watched as Boone stepped off the stoop and got in his custom painted purple '84 Cutlass. He had gold rims on it and tinted windows that were black as midnight. Lil Noah shook his head in disbelief, as he didn't care for the flashiness of his new buyer, and began to see why Basil didn't like him.

"Thought y'all didn't fuck with homie," one of the henchmen said as he stood on the stoop and watched Boone pull off.

"We don't. But he spending money so I'm not discriminating. That's Basil that ain't fucking with him. Me, on the other hand, I don't give a fuck," Lil Noah said as he thumbed through the bills that Boone had just placed in his hands. He then added, "Yo, while we on the subject. Get Basil's money together so we can send it down with the mule. Get that bitch Viv on the phone and tell her come pick up this bag." Lil Noah grabbed his phone from his pocket and texted Basil, letting him know that the bag was on the way. They did the same routine every month, sending Viv down with the re-up money and Basil's cut. She then would come back with the bricks of cocaine for distribution.

Kane eyed the golf ball, the beautiful silence allowing him to keep his focus. A cigar hung from the corner of his mouth as he closed one eye to get a precise look at the target. He took a powerful swing, knocking the ball off its tee, causing a loud pop to fill the air. "Fore!" he yelled as he watched the ball soar in the air. Kane placed his hand over his eyebrows to block the sun as he kept an eye on the ball while it traveled rapidly through the blue skies. It eventually fell onto the green about 280 yards away. A few of his Caucasian golf buddies clapped as they joined him in a friendly game between gentlemen.

"Good one, Garrett!" one of the men said as they slapped five with him. Kane smiled and then took a deep pull of the Nicaraguan robust cigar that was half smoked. Kane walked over to his golf cart to head over to the green, and saw another cart approaching him. Just as he put his club into his bag, he looked closer and saw that it was Landon. Kane made eye contact without looking away and Landon did the same. As they got within three feet of each other, Landon tapped his caddy and told him to stop. He apparently had some words for Kane.

"Top of the morning," Landon said as he stepped off the cart and began to pull off his right leather glove.

"Top of the morning," Kane replied, trying to feel out how Landon wanted the situation to play. Kane looked in Landon's eyes and to his surprise, he didn't sense any tension. Landon walked toward him and stopped just in front of him. Landon extended his hand and Kane paused. He looked down at Landon's hand, surprised, and thought twice about returning the gesture. He saw that Landon was conceding and he knew the laws of the street. If someone doesn't want a war, never press it. Always give a man just enough room to jump out of the window and escape. That's exactly what Landon was doing. The kitchen that was called the streets was too hot for him, so he'd decided to jump out of the window, avoiding war. Kane smiled and felt dominant, seeing a powerful man of Landon's stature bowing down. Kane reached out his hand and grabbed Landon's as they shared a firm shake.

"Can we take a walk?" Landon asked as he looked around and then focused back on Kane.

"Sure," Kane responded. He looked back at the guys he was currently in a game with and told them to go ahead so that he could discuss business. Landon instructed his caddy to take a break as well. Kane and Landon began to stroll the walkway around the huge golf course. Landon was the first to speak.

"I know our last meeting was a tad bit intense," Landon said as he pulled out his own cigar and lit it while strolling. "However, I have mourned my son and that period is over. One can never get over a death of a child, but I'm learning to deal with it. I understand my son's horrible temperament and after numerous discussions with my nephews, the truth came out. He was absolutely the aggressor." Kane remained silent and listened closely, trying to see where Landon was getting to.

"So, if you are willing to bury the hatchet . . . I am as well."

"I appreciate you approaching me to talk. Once again, my condolences for L.J. Everyone wishes that night never would have happened. To be clear, I never had a hatchet to bury. I respect you and your organization. I just had to protect my family, as I know you can relate," Kane said smoothly.

"Yes, I can," Landon said as he blew out a cloud of smoke. "I have been wanting to talk to you about something."

"Sure, what's on your mind?" Kane asked.

"I am looking to expand. My family back home in Boston are looking for a supplier. The days of street gambling and extortion are over. We need to get in the winning game. That's where you can help me out," Landon said as he stopped and looked around. He leaned in close to Kane and whispered, "I need a cocaine connection, my friend."

"Oh yeah?" Kane said calmly as he stopped as well. He tossed his cigar, but not before taking a huge puff.

"Yes. I know we have had a shaky past but I believe the best way to mend things is to get into business and make money for each other."

"Agreed," Kane said, understanding the rules of the streets and engagement.

"We need fifty kilograms," Landon said.

"That's a lot for your first order."

"Well, I'm not your typical buyer. This is only the beginning. If you partner with me, we can make a lot of money together. So what do you say?"

"I say you have yourself a supplier. Twenty a piece," Kane said as he smiled and reached out his hand. Landon nodded his head in agreement and the beef was over right at that moment. The rush of selling a brick overcame him and it felt like the old days. This was selling coke at its highest level, and he understood the connections and thoroughness of Landon. He decided to let bygones be bygones and get to the money. They shook hands and established a connection that had the potential to be monumental.

"I will be in contact very soon. Thank you, Kane," Landon said humbly as he looked over to his caddy and waved. Within seconds, the golf cart arrived and Landon hopped in and took off.

Kane's mind began to turn; he would keep a close eye on Landon, but he refused to miss an opportunity to prevent a war and also gain a buyer, a potentially major buyer at that. He was ready for whatever Landon wanted to do. In his mind, it was clear that the Irish didn't want any smoke and he was content with that. He smiled, knowing that it was time to bring his boy back home where he belonged. He pulled out his phone and called Basil.

"It's time," Kane said simply.

"It's time?" Basil asked as a smile spread across his face.

"That's right. I'll catch you up when you get here. Welcome home, Youngblood," Kane said as he smiled as well.

"I'm on the first thing smoking back home. I just have to wrap up some business here this weekend. Some major players coming into town for the all-star weekend."

"Oh, okay. I guess that's the place to be. Moriah is supposed to be down there as well. Keep an eye on her for me, okay?"

"You know I got you, big homie," Basil said as his heart dropped at the sound of Moriah's name.

"I'll let you know where she's staying once she books. Make sure my baby girl stays safe. She's my precious gem. Just watch out for her."

"I got you," Basil reconfirmed.

"After that, get yo' ass up here so I can give you an old-fashion schooling on that chess board."

"We'll see soon enough," Basil said with his smile shining through his voice. Kane knew that his protégé was smiling and he was too. He was glad to have his best guy back up top with him.

CHAPTER TWENTY

He felt a tear drop from his eye as well. His soul rained for her; a beautiful rain.

—UNKNOWN

"What you mean, somebody ran in here? Who was it?" Lil Noah said as he looked down at Viv, who had tears in her eyes as she sat on her couch explaining.

"I told you before, I don't know. He had a mask on," Viv explained for the fifth time.

"How they get in the safe?"

"They put the gun to my head and said if I don't open it, they would blow my head off," she yelled as tears continued to flow down her face. Lil Noah was skeptical and was sure that it was an inside job. Or more likely, a made-up story altogether. He had been stashing Basil's cut at Viv's all month, and the day that she was supposed to go down to take it to Basil, she got robbed? Something was fishy and Lil Noah knew it. He instantly grew furious but tried his best to hide it.

"Okay, okay. Let's slow down and go through this one more time. Someone came in, put a gun to your head, and forced you to open up the safe. Right?"

"Yes, that's exactly what happened. I was so scared, Noah. I could have been killed," Viv said as she began to wipe her tears away.

"Okay, so let me ask you this. Who knows about Basil keeping his money here or you making runs for him?"

"Nobody, I swear!" Viv said, sensing that he was growing suspicious. "I keep my business, *my* business. I never told anyone," she pleaded as she instantly stopped crying. Still, Lil Noah knew something was fishy. He looked into her eyes and stared at her, searching for any hint of guilt in her mannerisms.

"Cool. Let me get to the bottom of this," Lil Noah said as he put his hand on her shoulder, assuring her that he believed her. "I'll give you a call later." He began to walk out and saw that the small window that was next to the door was shattered.

"This is where they must of broke in at, huh? They busted out the window and unlocked the door to let themselves in," Lil Noah said as he examined the door.

"Yeah, that's exactly how they got in. I was so scared," Viv said as she hugged Lil Noah from the back. "Thank you so much for coming by so quickly. I feel safe now." Lil Noah turned around to face her.

"Don't worry. Everything will be all right." Viv hugged him and then kissed him on the cheek.

"Thank you so much," she said as she reached back and slid Lil Noah's hands under her two heavy cheeks so he could feel the weight of her load. Lil Noah looked down at Viv and smiled. His natural instinct was to squeeze them so he did. Viv instantly felt him beginning to rise through his pants.

"No worries," he said as he removed his hands and pulled back. He looked her up and down and licked his lips. Her hourglass shape and thick stature was just his type; he'd always admired Viv's beauty but never acted on it out of respect for Basil. He shook his head and headed out the door. Vivian watched as he walked out and closed the door behind him. She placed her back against the door and smiled, knowing that he was putty in her hands. She had made off with Basil's money without any fingers being pointed at her. *Fuck that nigga. He shouldn't have quit me. I just made that nigga pay the tax owed when you cross me,* she thought as she continued to smile and think about what she was going to do with her cut. She reached into her blouse to text Boone.

We are in clear, she texted and then pushed the SEND button. Just then, a knock at the door erupted, startling her. She quickly turned around, looked through the peephole, and saw that it was Lil Noah. She smiled and already knew what time it was. He was coming back to get the kitty that she was blatantly throwing at him. She opened the door then turned on the spurs of her heels and began to walk back into her living room, knowing that Noah was looking at her backside. She had on shorts pulled up as much as possible so that her cheeks hung out the bottom of them. Her two big teardrop-shaped butt cheeks were on full display and her shorts were wedged in her crevice. Lil Noah stepped in and locked the door.

"I knew you were going to come back. You want some of mama's pie?" she said seductively as she turned around slowly, ready to wrap Lil Noah into her web. She instantly began to think how she would turn him out with her seasoned sex and make him become her new sponsor.

When she turned again, ready to pounce on her newfound prey, she shrieked in terror. She was staring down the barrel of a nine-millimeter. Lil Noah bit his bottom lip in passion as he dug the barrel into her forehead and placed his free hand over her mouth. He backed her into her couch and pushed her down.

"Bitch, if you make a sound I'mma blow your head off. Try me," Lil Noah said as he gave her a menacing scowl, praying that she made a wrong move so he could blow her brains out.

"Wait . . . Wait. Please tell me what did I do?" Viv pleaded as she put both hands in front of herself, as if she could block the bullets.

"First of all, your dumb ass don't know how to rob right. You said that someone broke in, but when I went outside the glass was on the outside of the door. Meaning, yo' dumb ass broke it from the inside. Second of all, you supposedly almost just got your life taken by a masked goon but somehow you willing to give me some pussy within the same hour. You didn't think your plan out, did you?" Lil Noah asked as he shook his head at her botched idiotic plan.

"Wait, I can—"

"Shut up!" he said as he pulled out his phone and dialed Basil's number.

"Hello," said Basil as he sat on the bed, counting the money that he had just gotten from Big for the party that coming weekend.

"You not going to believe this shit," Lil Noah said as he stared at Viv.

"What's up?" Basil said as he continued to put the money in stacks. Colorful bands for the small ones and beige ones for the big stacks, as usual.

"I got a call saying that somebody ran into Viv's spot, roughed her up, and made her open the safe."

Basil instantly stopped counting the money and frowned.

"Wait, what happened?" he asked.

"But dig this, this bitch set it up. She tried to throw me some pussy, thinking I was a tender dick. Plus the bitch didn't even think the shit out. She says they broke the glass to get in, but the glass was scattered on the outside of the door."

"Oh, I see. She bust them out, huh?" Basil said calmly as he smiled. "How much was taken?"

"It was about fifty here."

"Fifty? Check her phone," Basil said, still calm. Lil Noah reached into her cleavage and pulled out the cell phone that was slightly sticking out from it. She screamed, thinking he was about to harm her.

"Shut up, bitch." He went through the phone. "Bingo," he said as he saw the text she'd sent to Boone. "She just texted Boone that they were in the clear. I knew it."

"You know what? Tell her that'll be the last real piece of money she will see her entire life. She can keep that," Basil said as he continued to count the money that was scattered in front of him. "I just made that amount today. That's nothing to me. Don't touch her . . . let her go. Let her breathe. We will catch up to Boone later. Tell her if she tells Boone that we know, you'll come back for her. Keep it a secret in exchange for her life."

"You sure?" Lil Noah said, sounding disappointed in Basil's decision.

"I'm positive. Just cancel her. She can't eat with us anymore. We'll find another mule. Oh yeah, and I'll be home soon." Basil hung up the phone and continued to count his money. He smiled to himself and thought about returning home. He had bigger fish to fry than worry about the theft. The way he saw it, he just paid Viv fifty thousand to get out of his life permanently. So it was a fair exchange from his viewpoint.

"Today is your lucky day. Basil saved yo' life. He told you to keep that money. But you dead in these streets. You are no longer needed. Oh yeah, and don't tell Boone nothing or I'll be back around to see you," Lil Noah said as he tucked his gun and tossed her phone to her. Vivian sat there frozen in fear as her heart beat at what seemed like two hundred miles per hour. Lil Noah shook his head as he exited the place, wishing he would have hit it before he exposed her. Damn, he thought as a grin appeared on his face.

Every variation of beauty in a woman was in attendance. High heels and snug dresses were the dominant attire. It was the night before the annual NBA all-star weekend and the city was filled with A-list celebrities and the top professional athletes in the country. Miami was literally the hottest city in the nation that weekend. Meanwhile, Basil and Mecca sat in the cut at the multimillion-dollar mansion that was the home of Big of the Miami Heat. They were tucked a nook that was similar to a club's VIP section, and a few members of the Cartel stood around them wearing all black from head to toe, and draped in platinum jewelry that was encrusted with diamonds. They were shining more than the NBA players that were in attendance. Basil stuck out like a sore thumb, as he wore tailored slacks and a white-collared shirt that was neatly tucked in his pants. He didn't wear any shining diamonds or jewelry but his presence was still felt. Swagger oozed off of him and his confident stride and smoothness were of the likes of Kane Garrett, the man who'd given him the game that made him a street king. His Italian designer loafers were suede and the only thing that shined on them was the emblem on the toes that matched the buckle on his belt. Music blared from the DJ's speakers and the clock had just struck midnight. The private event was small and intimate. The men-to-women ratio was lopsided, with the women outnumbering the guys four to one. Phones weren't allowed and had to be checked at the front door. Also there were no pictures allowed, maybe because of the mounds of blow that were on tables scattered around the room. Basil watched everyone closely and only drank water while they drank champagne and cocktails. He looked over at a Cartel member who had a leather book bag on his back, knowing there were a few more ounces stashed in there. Basil was waiting for Big to tell him he needed more blow, so that he could run up his tab. By the way people were using their noses as vacuums, they would be needing more by the end of the night. Basil sat back patiently and watched his work, work for him.

Big approached Basil with another guy who was tall and lean. He was a clean-shaven, dark man with strong facial features. Big was all smiles as he slapped hands with Basil and they embraced.

"Yo, this the guy I was telling you about. T.D., this is Basil. Basil . . . T.D.," Big said as he pointed his thumb toward Basil. Big's friend extended his hand and Basil instantly recognized him. He was the star wide receiver for the Miami Dolphins.

"Nice to meet you. My guy Big said you're the man that made it snow in here," T.D. said while shaking Basil's hand.

"Is that right?" Basil asked modestly as he shot a look at Big and then focused back on T.D.

"Absolutely. I see you got this party stocked up. I might need you to do the same for mine," T.D. said.

"Indeed. I will get your number from Big and I will be in touch," Basil said smoothly, knowing that he'd made another strong connection.

"No doubt. I tried some of your product. That shit pure. Looking forward to becoming friends," T.D. said.

"Same here," Basil responded. A waitress walked by with a bucket full of champagne bottles. Big stopped her and grabbed one out. He then popped the cork and released a small fountain of bubbly volcanoes.

"Well, now that we got that out of the way, let's enjoy this party. I got my man to go to Club Liv and grab the baddest bitches in the club. The stretch limo just pulled up. So fellas, if you would . . . focus your attention on the door and look at God. Ain't he good?" Big asked in a joking manner. Almost on cue, the door opened and in came a member of his crew. The crew member held the door open and a line of the most beautiful women they had ever seen came in. A line of all dimes, nothing less.

"Gentlemen, welcome to heaven," Big said as the stampede of beautiful women entered. All eyes were on them, the top-twenty pick of the litter. Basil admired the view then his heart dropped when he saw a few familiar faces: Moriah with two of her friends from back home. Basil felt himself get short of breath and butterflies began to form in the pit of his stomach.

"Excuse me. I have to take a leak," Basil said just before he went to the opposite side of the room where the bathroom was located. He hurried into the bathroom and closed the door. He rested his arms on the sink and looked in the mirror. He dipped his head low and turned on the faucet. He splashed water on his face, trying to regain his composure. He took a few deep breaths and decided that he was ready to reenter the party. He knew that Moriah was coming into town but he didn't expect her at Big's private party. As Kane had requested, he had put some Cartel goons at her hotel without her knowing, but never had he thought that she would end up in the same spot as him. He hadn't seen or spoken to her since the night he left her back home. The love of his life had just walked into the room and it threw him completely.

Moriah, along with her friend Nia and Nia's cousin, walked into the private mansion party. They'd been picked out of the line at the club and asked to come party with the stars. Moriah wasn't impressed with the offer, but Nia was excited and wanted to go so Moriah went with the flow. Besides, Nia had gotten all three of them free first-class flights to Miami, paid for by a guy she'd met back home. Moriah didn't want to rock the boat.

"Girl, this is nice," Nia said as she looked around the lavish mansion with the highest ceilings that she had ever seen.

"Yeah, it is," Moriah said as she too looked around. All three girls had small black dresses on, all of them wore different designer heels. Moriah had her locks neatly pulled into a bun on top of her head and wore big diamond earrings. She was simply stunning. They went to the bar that was set up and ordered themselves a drink. As they ordered, a big tall man approached them and introduced himself.

"Hello, ladies," he said, making sure he looked at all three women, giving them an equal amount of attention. "My name is Big and I want to personally welcome you to my house."

"Thanks, Big," Nia's cousin said, her kitty getting wet just thinking about how much money he had. Nia was friendly as well, while Moriah was unimpressed. Mo had been used to money her whole life. Power was what intrigued her and she hadn't met anyone other than Basil that met her standards. Moriah put on a fake smile to be polite and let her friends do the talking.

Moriah got her drink and leaned against the bar, scanning the room while her girls engaged in small talk with Big. She noticed that there were mounds of cocaine on every single table and she instantly grew uncomfortable, never seeing anything like that before: people doing blow with not a care in the world.

She looked over the room and couldn't believe her eyes. Basil was walking out of the bathroom, looking as good as she remembered. He'd grown a small beard and was stylish as usual. Moriah instantly got butterflies and felt the urge to vomit. She grew nervous as she watched the love of her life walk across the room, and turned around facing the bar. She was embarrassed too. She didn't want Basil to know that she was picked up at the club and brought to a private party as if she were a gold digger.

"Moriah! Mo! Moriah!" Nia called, trying to get her girl's attention. Moriah snapped out of it.

"What's up?" she asked as she looked over at Nia.

"Big invited us to the VIP section upstairs, girl!" Nia said excitedly. Moriah, wanting to avoid seeing Basil, quickly agreed to go along with her.

"All right, let's go," Moriah said hastily. Nia whispered something to Big and moments later, he led the way upstairs.

Basil sat back with Mecca on the couch and skimmed the room. Moriah was nowhere to be found. *Where did she go?* All of the loud music, drinking, and blow-sniffing going on around him, and the only thing he could think about was Moriah. Mecca nudged him with his elbow and leaned over to talk.

"Yo, check it out. Big taking them bitches upstairs to get slayed," Mecca said as he laughed and clapped his hands.

"What? How you know?" Basil said just before he swallowed what seemed to be a bowling ball. He couldn't believe his eyes as he saw Moriah walk upstairs with the two other girls and Big.

"When you went to the bathroom he talked about the VIP section, where he got all the hoes getting down. T.D. already up there. Shit, that's where I need to be," Mecca said just before he turned a bottle of champagne up and took a few chugs.

"Looks like upstairs is where the party is at, family," Basil stated as he put on a fake smile, not believing Moriah was devaluing herself by being a groupie.

Moriah instantly wanted to go back to her hotel room and not run into Basil. She had already made up her mind that she would play it cool for a short while then leave. She wasn't prepared to see Basil, and even though she wanted to approach him, she couldn't do it. Not in this setting, at least. Moriah looked ahead as Big guided them through the long dark hallway. The house was the biggest she had ever been in. The farther they went down the hall, the quieter it got. Eventually there was no music at all, and the only sound was their heels clicking on the floor.

"We're almost there," Big said as he continued to lead the way. Big got to the door at the end of the hallway and looked back at them.

"Here it is. This is my special VIP room. Once y'all go in here, your life will never be the same. It's nothing but millionaires and good times through this door. Welcome," he said as he slowly opened the door. A red light illuminated the hallway and slow, sensual music by Sade came from the room. The girls walked in and what they saw blew their minds. There were numerous naked bodies throughout the room, grown men and women walking around naked. Moriah couldn't believe her eyes as some of the most well hung men she'd ever seen appeared before her. "Oh my God," Moriah whispered as the horse-hung men walked, talked, and sexed all around the room. There was a threesome going on in the corner as two black men slowly grinded a slim tall Caucasian woman, one in her mouth, the other was entering her from the back. Moriah was completely shocked as she put her hand on her chest. She looked in the opposite corner, where a man was being ridden by a voluptuous Latina woman as she swung her hair back and forth while crashing down on his pelvis. There were no screams . . . just moans and the sounds of bodies slapping together. It was like nothing Moriah had ever seen before. A full-fledged orgy was going on with no holds barred. Moriah looked at her girl Nia and she seemed to be into it. Her cousin wasn't fazed by it either, and Moriah was shocked even further.

"Girl, this shit is crazy. Let's get the fuck out of here," Moriah said as she grabbed Nia's arm. A bare-naked six-foot-something chocolate man walked over to Nia as Moriah was tugging her arm. He had absolutely minimum body fat and his body shone from head to toe. His abs were flawless, and his penis was slightly erect and hung just above his knees. Moriah quickly avoided eye contact, but Nia did the exact opposite.

"I know who you are. You're T.D. I watch you every Sunday," Nia said as she smiled, tremendously impressed with what she saw.

"That's right, baby. The one and only." He gently grabbed her hand and placed it on his ripped abdominal muscles. Nia squirmed in pleasure and giggled like a schoolgirl.

"Oh my," she said as her hand slipped down to his strong, semi-erect penis and gave it a stroke.

"Yo, let's go," Moriah said, not believing her eyes.

"Let's just stay up here for a while," Nia suggested without even taking her eyes off of T.D. Another man walked up and approached Nia's cousin and began whispering in her ear.

"Yeah . . . so . . . I'm about to go," Moriah said as she took a step back. She was overwhelmed; this was definitely not her type of party.

"Yeah. Yeah. I'll catch up," Nia said, as she was getting her ear whispered in by T.D. Moriah swiftly brushed past Big and exited the room. She hurried down the hallway, only to feel a hand grab her.

"Get the fuck off me!" she yelled, not knowing who had touched her without permission. She looked more closely at the man and saw that it was none other than the man of her dreams.

"Basil," she said, surprised.

"Hey, Mo," he said calmly.

"Hey," she said in a soft tone as she dropped her head.

"Where you going so fast. You don't wanna stay in the jump-off room?" he said, just before he cracked a smile.

"Forget you," Mo said as she laughed with him and playfully hit him in the chest.

"Come here, baby. I missed you so much," he said in a joyful voice. He embraced her closely, bringing her right next to his heart. They were where they belonged, in each other's arms.

"Basil, I missed you too. You don't know what I've been going through without you. It's been so hard letting you go."

Basil knew exactly what she was referring to because he had been going through the same thing. "You just don't know," she said as she shook her head, buried in his chest.

"I know . . . I know," Basil whispered comfortingly.

"I need you, Basil. You complete me," Moriah admitted, feeling herself about to cry.

"You complete me, ma. I love you." He felt tears welling up in his eyes as well. The love that they felt was eternal. The magnetic force that they shared was second to none and their souls were intertwined. The laws of attraction had brought them back together and both of them knew it without saying a word. The world had a crazy way of making what was supposed to happen . . . happen. It was something perpetually strong that pulled them together and neither of them could explain it. Basil placed his hands on her cheeks, making her look at him in the dimness. Moriah couldn't understand it but, even with no light, she saw him clearly. Her tears began to flow. Tears of complete happiness. She'd never cried before from happiness. It felt so good to her. That cry was better than sex or any other intimate encounter she could imagine. He slowly leaned in and kissed his soul mate with fire and desire. Basil couldn't believe it, but he felt a tear drop from his eye as well. His soul rained for her; a beautiful rain.

Basil and Moriah had slid off and talked in Basil's car for hours. They laughed, reminisced, and shared what they had being doing for the past few months. Three hours had passed and they didn't even realize it. Basil was parked right outside of Big's mansion and they saw the crowd begin to slowly leave, one by one.

"You came here with your girl, huh?" Basil asked as he knew the night was about to come to an end.

"Yeah, but I'm not sure if I'm rocking with her like that. She is not who I thought she was. She saw that big-ass horse ding-a-ling and went crazy," Moriah said, sending both of them into laughter. Then Basil grew quiet as he thought about their time together coming to an end.

"Changing the subject. I have something to tell you," Basil said as he positioned his body so he was facing her.

"What's that?" Moriah asked.

"I'm coming back home."

"Are you serious?" Moriah asked, excited, but then saddened when she thought about their situation.

"Don't worry. I don't care anymore. I can not let you go. Not again. Nothing is taking me away from you. We just have to keep it low until I figure something out. Cool?"

"Cool," Moriah said as she unleashed a big smile. Just as she finished speaking she saw her friend Nia and her cousin walk past Basil's car.

"I guess you got to leave with your friends, huh?" Basil asked, understanding the etiquette of girlfriends.

"Hold on, lemme see," she said as she kissed him and got out of the car. She called Nia's name and Nia quickly turned around.

"Hey, where were you?" Nia asked.

"Nowhere, just was talking to an old friend in the car. You good?"

"Girl, am I? Hell yea. I had the best—"

"Spare me the details," Moriah said as she raised her hand

with a smile. "But, I think I'mma call it a night. What you want to do?"

"Well, you know the nigga that flew us out, Boone? He wants to chill so I guess I have to go see him. I don't want to do him like that after he cashed out for the flights. I might as well squeeze a couple bands out of him before we leave," Nia explained.

"Oh, okay. If you don't mind I'mma just head to the room. I have a little headache."

"Okay, that's cool. He staying at the same hotel as us so if you change your mind, just come up. He's in the presidential suite. Room fifteen hundred. Just come up. He has a few friends too," Nia said.

"They got money too, girl," her cousin added as she snapped her hands in the air proudly.

"Nah, I'm good. I'll have my friend take me back to the room and y'all have fun," Moriah said as she hugged and kissed her friends on the cheek. She then returned back to the car to rejoin Basil.

"So what's up?" Basil said.

"They are going to go ahead. I'd rather be with you."

"I like that," Basil said with a smile.

"Cool, we can go back to my room. I'm at the—"

"The Waldorf in Boca Raton," he said.

"How did you know?" Moriah said as she frowned.

"You know Kane all over it. He called ahead and told me you were coming down. I got a few goons there right now."

"My daddy is a trip," Moriah said as she smiled and shook her head.

"You sure I'm not stopping you from having a good time with your friends?" Basil asked, just to double-check.

"No, not at all. They about to chill with some guys from back home. I think she said his name was Boo or Boone. Something like that," Moriah said as she frowned again, trying to remember the guy's name.

"Wait. Are you serious? Boone?" Basil asked.

"Yeah, that's what is was."

"He from the north side?" Basil asked.

"Yeah, she did say he was from that side earlier this week."

Basil already began to put a play in his mind.

"You know where he staying?" Basil asked.

"Yeah, he's staying at the Waldorf. She gave me his room number too. Why?" she asked.

Boone and his two friends bobbed their heads to the music as the sounds blared from the portable speaker. They were inside the presidential suite on the top floor of the Waldorf Astoria, right on the beach. Boone was living like a king, in his eyes. He had on one of the hotel-provided terry-cloth robes with all of his gold jewelry on. He had just come up on some cash a few days before from the robbery he did with his cousin Vivian. Two girls danced on the bed as the men watched and threw money at them as if they were at a strip club.

A knock at the door caused Boone to pause. He took another gulp of the champagne and then took the shot of tequila that was waiting for him on the bar top. He made his way over to the door to get the room service that he'd ordered. Five lobsters and a shrimp cocktail platter, to be exact. When he opened the door, he was greeted by two guns to his face. Two masked men backed him into the room as he held his hands up in fear. One of the men focused his guns on the other men and instantly ordered them to lay on the floor. The two girls began to scream in terror as they fell back on the bed, completely naked. One of the gunmen went over and delivered two blows, one for each girl, knocking them out cold. The other gunman was pistol-whipping Boone so badly that he lost a tooth and his mouth was leaking blood as his upper lip instantly began to swell. The once cocaine-colored white robe was now crimson red, completely soaked in Boone's blood. The gunman that stood over Boone pointed his gun directly at Boone's chest.

"I should burn you right now," he said as he looked in Boone's disoriented eyes. The gunman looked over to the corner and saw a duffle bag. He then looked over to his partner, who pulled out some hog ties and tied the other men's hands behind their backs as they laid flat on their stomach, pleading not to be murdered.

"Shut up!" the gunman yelled as he struck one of the men with the butt of his gun.

Basil had enough of the guessing games and wanted Boone to see who he was. H looked down at Boone, who writhed in agony.

"Look at me!" Basil said as he pulled off the mask. He gave Boone a swift kick to the gut. "Didn't think I would catch up with you, huh? You stole from me? Huh!" he yelled. He gave him another swift kick to the head, sending him flying onto his back.

Basil went over to the corner and quickly picked up the duffle bag. He looked inside and saw a few guns and rubber-band-wrapped money.

"I didn't steal from you, man. I wouldn't do that!" Boone said as he struggled to lift himself up.

"Yo, still left my rubber bands on her. Colored for the small money, regular ones for the big stacks." Basil smiled, then pointed his gun at Boone and walked toward him.

"Smoke 'em," Mecca said as he pulled up his mask and a smile spread across his face, enjoying every single second. He lived for moments like the one at hand.

"Nah, I ain't gon' smoke 'em. He ain't worth it," Basil said as he smirked. "Strip!" he ordered and he held the gun to Boone's chest.

"What? Come on, man," Boone pleaded, not knowing what was going on. Basil struck him again across the face, causing another bloody tooth to fly across the room.

"Strip!" Basil repeated.

"Man, I don't know what you into, but I like it. You a crazy mu'fucka like me!" Mecca said excitedly, hoping that Basil was about to do some torturing. However, Basil had other ideas. Boone frantically took off his clothes.

"Tie them bitches up too," Basil said, not wanting them to mess up his newfound idea. Mecca grabbed the girls aggressively and tied them up as well.

"Walk to the balcony," Basil instructed as he waved his gun toward the big balcony at the back of the suite.

"Please, man. Please," Boone pleaded as his naked body was

splattered with his own blood, which was leaking profusely. Basil struck him again, this time causing him to fall to the ground.

"Aggggh!" Boone yelled in misery.

"Balcony! Now!" Basil instructed again. "If I have to ask you again, I'm putting a bullet right in the middle of your head." Boone struggled to get to his feet, but he eventually did and stood up, wobbly. He faced the balcony and Basil put the gun to his back, guiding him to it.

"Now open it!" Basil said. Boone, with shaking hands, opened the door. Basil smiled and nudged him just barely so he was on the balcony. It overlooked the front of the hotel. Basil started laughing and then closed the door behind him and locked it. Mecca was confused but he soon understood what Basil had done. After a brief moment of silence, the sound of chatter and people flicking their cameras erupted. It came from the hundreds of paparazzi in front of the high-profile hotel to cover the all-star weekend. They were hoping to catch an athlete or celebrity walking out, but now they were getting so much more. Boone would surely be on every blog and major Internet social media platform. They had a field day as the tall butt-naked black man stood on the balcony for all of them to see.

"Man, you crazy," Mecca said as he joined in with Basil's laughter.

"Let's go, man," Basil said with a smile.

"What about them?" Mecca asked as he looked over at Boone's crew and the two girls.

"Leave 'em," Basil said. "We need someone to tell the story."

Basil and Mecca headed out, but not before Basil grabbed the duffle bag of his money. Just before they went into the hallway, they pulled their masks down for the camera and headed out the back.

Basil returned home that night with his girl and a bag full of money. He was headed back home to Flint, Michigan.

CHAPTER TWENTY-ONE

The streets will never love you back.

—KANE GARRETT

The Present

Boom! The loud blast momentarily caused Basil to go completely deaf in his left ear. It felt as if a loud bell were ringing in his ear. A small droplet of blood leaked from his eardrum as he covered his ear with his hand. The bullet ricocheted off the floor and into a hospital wall. People scattered in panic, while Kane and his crew stayed calm. Kane stood over Basil with a smoking gun and had just barely missed his skull by a half inch. Fat Rat had quickly pushed Kane's hand away at the last minute, saving Basil's life.

"Not here, Kane!" Fat Rat yelled, something that he rarely did. He held on to Kane's arm, trying to prevent him from doing something that would land him in jail for the remainder of his life.

"Cameras are everywhere. We can handle this, but not here, bro. Not here," Fat Rat whispered to Kane, trying to bring him back to reality. Fat Rat then looked down at Basil, who was holding his ear in pain.

"Basil, get out of here!" Fat Rat demanded as he breathed heavily, while trying to hold Kane back from firing another round. Basil scurried to his feet and ran out in a hurry. He knew that nothing would ever be the same.

Kane broke down in Fat Rat's arms as he thought about losing his own flesh and blood. "Moriah! No, no, no. Not my baby girl," he wept as he completely cracked. He cried a pool of tears on Fat Rat's shoulders and all eyes were on him. He quickly raised his head and tried to brush past Fat Rat and his other henchman. "I have to see her!" he said as snot ran down his nose and his eyes were bloodshot in agony. He tried to get to the back of the emergency unit, but Fat Rat and the other man held him back, knowing that a father should never have to see his child in that way. "Nooooo!" Kane yelled as he fell onto the floor, pulling both of his men down with him in the process. Kane was heartbroken. He was confused and hated that he had no control over the situation. His only child was gone and he never saw it coming. Kane Garrett was officially broken.

Basil drove along the highway with blood-drenched clothing and all of the windows rolled down. It was as if he was in a daze. His whole life had been turned upside down in a blink of an eye. He picked up his phone to call Lil Noah. He knew in his heart that Boone was the one who had tried to murder him. He was furious and confused. There was no doubt that at this point, he wanted blood. He heard a voice on the other end of the phone.

"Yo, Lil Noah! Someone killed Mo. They killed her. I know it was that nigga Boone," Basil yelled into the phone, getting straight to the point.

"Hold on, wait . . . what? Killed Mo?" Lil Noah responded, trying to figure out what was going on.

"Meet me at the diner on Corunna Road. I can't trust anybody in the projects. I have to figure out what is going on."

Kane and his entourage were walking out of the hospital. Kane was focused on one thing and one thing only, and that was getting to Basil. He didn't want to talk or reason with anyone. In his eyes, Basil was responsible for the murder. He told Basil that his daughter was off-limits and Basil knowingly broke the rules. He would have to pay.

"Put out the word. I want Basil's head. I have two hundred and fifty stacks for whoever brings him to me. A quarter million dollars," Kane said as he spoke calmly and stared at nothing in particular. It was as if he had snapped and inhabited a completely different mental zone. Kane was about to devote his life to finding out what happened to his daughter. Every single chess piece attached to his daughter's murder would be wiped off the board. Kane wasn't playing any games with anyone. He was about to go on a cold-blooded murdering spree, starting with Basil. But first, he had to do the hardest thing he ever had to do and that was to bury his daughter. After that was done, he would find out what led to this event. Kane was on the verge of going mad.

Meanwhile, on the other side of town, Basil sat in the corner of a diner with two pistols on his lap. His fingers lightly traced the triggers as he prepared for anything and everything. His eyes frantically rocked from left to right, right to left, while watching all movement inside of the diner. He couldn't trust anyone. He didn't know exactly who attempted to kill him and until he found out for sure he would be on high alert. Thoughts of Mo lying dead, mixed with paranoia, had Basil on edge. He didn't know who was coming for him at this. The only person he trusted was Lil Noah.

Lil Noah walked in and immediately focused on Basil, who was sitting in the corner tucked away. He hurried over to join his comrade and took a seat across from him.

"What the fuck is going on, bruh? The streets is going crazy right now. The whole projects is talking, saying you got shot up," Lil Noah said as he looked at his best friend. He saw the blood-stained shirt and the lost look in his eyes.

"They killed my girl, man. They fuckin' killed her," Basil said as a tear dripped down his face. He quickly wiped it away. He clenched his jaws tightly and gripped the pistols even tighter.

"Damn, bruh. Sorry to hear that. We going to get those niggas. Whoever is responsible." Lil Noah began to rub his hands together. "You didn't see who did it?" he asked.

"Nah, nigga had a mask on. I never saw it coming. Emptied the whole clip into the truck," Basil said as he shook his head in disgust. He knew that he had got caught slipping and the guilt began to weigh on his shoulders heavily. "Something in my gut is telling me it was that nigga Boone. He was mad salty that I didn't put him on. Nigga always been a jealous-type nigga. I never trusted homie."

"So let me get this right. Homie was masked up and hit you?"

"Yeah. I should've been on my A game." Basil continued to shake his head at his own irresponsibility.

"Just give me the word. I will off homeboy right now," Lil Noah said as he made a menacing gesture.

"I got to put some plays together. I'm about to go to Viv's pick her brain about this shit. Try to squeeze some info about Boone out of her. Then I'm going to get low for a while," Basil said as he looked into Noah eyes. "Yo, let's switch whips. Mine is too hot right now." Basil slid his car keys across the table.

"No doubt," Lil Noah said as he did the same. They shook hands and Lil Noah left Basil alone in the diner with his mind racing.

Kane was in the middle of the Regency projects and he called all of his OGs, longtime friends, and bosses throughout the entire Midwest. It was the G-code that if a respected boss lost a child you didn't send flowers, you brought them your condolences. That was a golden rule and all of Kane's friends came to the city of Flint to support him. Bosses from Chicago, Detroit, Milwaukee, and St. Louis flooded into the city once the news was out that Kane's daughter was murdered. It was a gangster party; a sad one. A row of luxury cars filled the spacious parking lot and two men stood dead in the center. All of the cars were parked in a circular pattern and their lights were pointed to the center. That is where Kane Garrett stood with a duffle bag at his feet. It was just before midnight and the moon and the streetlights helped illuminate the dark parking lot. Kane raised his hand and immediately every OG began honking their horn and flicking their headlights on and off, causing a scene. The horns echoed throughout the projects, a demonic orchestra. An eerie feeling filled the air and everyone in the projects felt it. A local police officer rode by in a squad car and Kane gave him the meanest look he could muster, with piercing eyes. The cop looked the other way and pretended as if he hadn't noticed the chaotic scene. He just rode his cruiser car through and then out of the projects. Word around town was that Kane's daughter had been murdered and it was as if the police respected what was about to happen.

As the horns were honked and the lights were flickering, people began to come out of their units to see what the uproar was about. Slowly but surely, as people began to trickle out. A crowd formed, and all eyes were now on Kane in the middle of the parking lot. Kane slowly turned, looking at the entire crowd. He took his time, as if he were examining everybody one by one. He made sure he locked eyes with as many people as he could. He was trying to catch any envious eye, any dropped head, or any sign of guilt in the audience's eyes. He wanted whoever was possibly connected to Mo's death to be punished . . . slowly. He then reached down and picked up the duffle bag that was at his feet. The horns still were blowing and people were confused, not knowing what was going on. Kane slowly raised the bag up high over his head and spun around so everyone could see. The car horns stopped and in silence, Kane continued to hold the bag up as if it was a trophy.

"My daughter was murdered earlier tonight. Right here in these very projects. The same projects that I have fed for years. The same projects that I have showed love to and loved me back. What's love? Huh? Streets don't show love. Not even the king gets love! The streets have no motherfucking king. The streets will never love you back. So, I want you to listen and listen loud and clear. In this duffle bag is a quarter million dollars. Cold cash. If anyone brings me Basil and the niggas responsible for it, it's yours," Kane said as he paused and took in the moment. He wanted to cry so badly, but he couldn't show weakness. His bottom lip quivered uncontrollably and his eyes began to water. One blink and the floodgates would have opened and tears would have fallen like a waterfall. He didn't blink, though. He had to be strong. He had to be strong for Moriah. He lowered the bag and walked to the SUV, where Fat Rat was standing by the door with it open for him. Kane slid in and Fat Rat closed the door.

There was a bounty on Basil's head and also on that of the mystery man who pulled the trigger. Nothing could prepare Basil for what was to come. In less than twenty-four hours he would have the entire projects gunning for him. Although he ran the projects and had respect, when that much money came into play, all of the respect went directly out the window. He was about to be prey in his own city. The drug empire that he had helped build had just turned on him.

Kane rode in the back of the car, staring out of the window. He was hell-bent on revenge and sleep wasn't an option. He looked up at Fat Rat, who was driving for him, and shook his head.

"They took my baby, Rat," Kane said, still not believing the reality of his world at that moment. "I'm going to punish Basil. Believe that."

"What happened if he skipped town? Basil is a sharp young dude. He's not going to wait around for someone to take him out," Fat Rat said, providing perspective.

"I'mma make him look for me," Kane said as he pointed to the left, "turn here."

Basil knew he had to get out of town for a few days, just to think things out. But first he had to go find Boone. He'd already made up his mind that he was going to kill him regardless of what he found out. Basil had never been in a position where he didn't know who his enemy was. It was as if he were fighting a ghost. A known enemy was fair, but one that stayed in the dark was dangerous and Basil understood this.

Who tried to kill me? he asked himself as he pulled up to Vivian's apartment. He parked away from her building and sat back and watched. He knew that he couldn't go to his spot because it was too hot. He knew that he could lay low at her spot until he put his plans together. He called her but it was going straight to voicemail, so he decided to go up and knock on the door. Basil parked Lil Noah's car and just when he was about to get out of it, he saw a car ride right past him and circle the parking lot. He instantly recognized the car. He looked closer and saw that it was Boone. The gold rims were a giveaway. He was the only one in the city with gold rims on an '84 Cutlass.

I can't believe this. This fool fell right in my lap, Basil thought as he sunk low in his seat, trying not to be seen. He gripped the two pistols that were in his lap. Basil knew that Boone probably didn't know he was parked across the lot because he had switched cars with Lil Noah. His trigger finger began to itch and he wasn't 100 percent sure that Boone was the shooter, but he didn't care. He had a gut feeling and at that point, that was good enough. There was no reasoning with Basil.

He watched as Boone got out of the car and looked around. Boone looked in the direction of the car and Basil instantly gripped his guns tighter. He watched as Boone threw his hands up and smiled. Basil instantly remembered that he was he was in Noah's car and not his own. Noah's car was tinted so Boone couldn't see who was inside. He must have thought it was Noah.

Boone began to walk toward the car with a smile on his face.

"I been blowing you up, fam. Why haven't you been answering your phone?" Boone said as he stood at the driver's door. Basil couldn't believe his ears. *Did Lil Noah set me up? What the fuck?* he asked himself as his heart dropped. Boone had threatened Basil's life before, so it began to make sense. Also the fact that he had a motive because of what Basil had done to him at the all-star weekend. So many thoughts were running through Basil's head as he tried to make sense of it all. *They tried to get me out of the way, so they could take my spot?* Basil thought to himself and instantly grew furious. He was at his tipping point and at that point, he only saw red. He thought about his love taking her last breath and he completely lost it. He slowly rolled down the window as Boone watched. Boone's facial expression changed when he saw Basil's face, rather than Lil Noah's. Basil was like a madman as he began to fire shots out of his .45 into the torso of Boone. Boone never saw it coming. He folded like a lawn chair as the bullets ripped through his flesh and then organs, killing him almost instantly. After letting off numerous rounds, Basil stepped out of the car and stood over him to finish him off. Basil was foaming at the mouth with anger as he released another two bullets into Boone's forehead. The sight was a gruesome one, Boone's insides splattered all over the concrete. Usually Basil wouldn't have been so careless, killing a man in public, but he was a man possessed. He was on a mission to avenge Moriah's death.

"Thank you so much for always looking out for Basil," Frenchie said as she sat at her kitchen table and placed her hands on top of Kane's, who sat directly in front of her.

"I just don't want him to get hurt. So if you hear from him, I want you to call me immediately so I can protect him. The streets are very dangerous right now," Kane said while playing possum with Frenchie. She hadn't heard about the shooting, so when Kane came knocking at her door at one that morning, it was news to her. He had told her that someone had tried to kill him and he left out the fact that his daughter had been murdered. He was hoping she could tell him where Basil was, but she had no answers.

"Oh my God. I pray for him every night and I hoped that something like this would never happen. I'm so glad he has someone like you that looks out for him. He really looks up to you and rightfully so," Frenchie said as tears began to well up in her eyes. "Listen, Kane, I want to tell you something that I vowed to keep a secret until the day I left this earth."

"What's that?" Kane said as he held her hands.

"Well, remember that night that we were all at the apartment back in the day? The night that the Pistons won the championship?" she asked as she tried to jog Kane's memory. It didn't take much, because Kane knew that night like the back of his hand. He could remember it as if it happened just the night before. He already knew deep inside that she would be telling him the story that she was about to tell.

"Well, I never said anything because of the friendship that I shared with Keema. I knew it would break her heart but . . ." Frenchie choked up as a tear fell. Kane rubbed her hand to comfort her. He shot a look to Fat Rat, signaling him to do what he did best.

"We should have never done that. We were dead wrong. That's the night that—" Fat Rat wrapped a chicken wire around her neck and pulled tight. Frenchie clawed at her neck, but there was no escape. Kane sat back and watched emotionlessly. Fat Rat pulled the chicken wire so tightly that his fingers began to bleed.

Frenchie tried to claw for Kane's hand as if she was begging for his help, but Kane slowly pulled his hand away and stood up. Unbothered, he slid his chair underneath the table, then stood and watched as her movements began to slow and her eyes began to roll back in her head. Only the whites showed in her eyes and her body began to jerk erratically. He watched as she took her last breath and her body went limp. Fat Rat continued to pull aggressively to make sure he finished the job. Kane calmly fixed his cuff link that Frenchie had disheveled. He then calmly said, "That's enough, Rat."

Fat Rat slid the wire from around her neck, letting her head fall to her chin. Just as her head was about to hit the table, Kane cradled her face and gently sat her on the table. He then brushed her wild hair from her face with his fingers. He stared at her and said nothing, regretting that she had to be a casualty of war. He left her lying on her kitchen table . . . lifeless.

Kane knew at that moment the hunt for Basil could be called off. There was no need for a bounty anymore. Basil would come looking for him and when he came . . . Kane would be ready. Kane snapped off his cuff links from his well-tailored suit and shook his head in disappointment. He gently placed them on the table, almost as a signature to this brutal death.

"Yo, I don't know how they had the drop on me. It was a setup. I know it," Basil said in between his clenched teeth as he balled up his fist and hit the table. The sound echoed through the restaurant, and Basil looked around and composed himself.

"Everything gonna be smooth, bro. Point me to whatever direction and I'm coming through blazing," Lil Noah said as he patted his waist while scanning around the top of the rooftop.

Basil looked at his protégé with skepticism and wondered if he was friend or foe. Basil was always cautious about how he moved and especially with Mo. He didn't know who to trust at that point. The fact that Boone thought it was cool to walk up on Lil Noah's car had Basil's mind spinning.

"Why are you so fucking calm? Did you have something to do with—" Basil stopped mid-sentence, catching himself.

"Look, I'm with you, bruh. I'm the last person you have to worry about. You're paranoid, bro. I never saw you like this," Noah replied in disbelief.

"You're right. I just don't know who to trust. I lost everything, man . . . everything. Mo didn't deserve this. She was everything I had. They didn't have to do her like that," Basil said as he dropped his head, feeling himself beginning to tear up.

"It's cool. I understand. We will get to the bottom of this," Lil Noah said as he reached over to put his hand on Basil's shoulder. He didn't even notice that Basil had reached for his weapon and now was pressing the tip of his gun to Lil Noah's stomach. "Yo, Basil, what are you doing?"

"Yo, you and Boone tried to kill me?" Basil asked as he stared down at Noah.

"Whoa . . . whoa. Fuck no. I just served him a few bricks. That's it. Strictly business, big homie. It was just business. You buggin'!" Noah pleaded as he put out both of his hands, showing that he posed no threat.

Basil didn't care about anything anymore. He didn't know who to trust and at that point everyone was an enemy.

"How you rocking with an enemy of mine? I showed you nothing but loyalty and this is how you repay me?" Basil asked in anger.

"Listen, it wasn't like—" Noah tried to respond, but a bullet into his side ceased all communication. Basil watched as Noah dropped to his feet. Blood began to pour out of his mouth and

Basil couldn't even look down at his brethren. Basil was losing his mind; the paranoia had set in and had him moving in a way that was unfamiliar. Basil exited the roof, leaving Lil Noah there to die. He picked up his phone and called his Miami connect; it was time for a vacation. He had to get away before Kane's henchmen caught up with him. He had no one left. He couldn't trust anyone fully accept his mother. So many thoughts began to run through his head and a quote of Kane's began to echo in his thoughts. "The streets have no king. The streets are and will always be king. It's only placeholders. One day you can be on top of the world . . . and the next day the streets consume you," Basil said as he made his way down the fire escape. He was on a rampage. He had killed two men within an hour and was on his way to kill a third. He blamed everyone for Moriah's death, so any enemy that he had ever had could get it. Basil was not himself and he could feel it. The sad thing about it was that he didn't care anymore.

CHAPTER TWENTY-TWO

The streets have no king.

—KANE GARRETT

"Momma! Where you at? We have to talk," Basil said as he walked into Frenchie's house. He wanted to drop her off some money because he would be leaving town for a while. He just had a couple more stops before hitting the highway. His plan was to hit Miami and lay low with his connect, Mecca Diamond, for a while. He just wanted to get out of town and figure things out. He had an idea of where the hit came from and he wanted to get things settled so he could face Kane and explain himself. As Basil walked through the house, he yelled for his mother again. He knew she was there because her car was in the driveway.

"Ma! Where are you?" Basil asked as he made his way into the kitchen. He looked over at the table and saw his mother with her head down and instantly felt a knot in the pit of his stomach. He rushed over to her and his hands began to shake as he slowly reached down to put his hand on her shoulder.

"Ma," he mumbled as his eyes began to water. Her hair covered her face so he couldn't see her, but for some reason he felt what was to come. He gently lifted her head and what he saw broke his heart into small pieces. Frenchie's face was swollen with a chicken wire partially wrapped around her neck. Her throat and lower jaw were five times their original size and her soulless eyes bulged as they gazed into oblivion. She barely looked like herself and Basil couldn't believe that he was looking at his mother. Her facial expression was that of pain and it was evident that she died suffering. He totally broke down.

"No . . . No. Ma! No, Mommy," Basil cried as the tears began to flow and his nose ran like a faucet. He hugged his mother's lifeless body and rocked back and forth as he lost the true love of his life, his sole reason for being on earth, his mother. He instantly clenched his jaws and his pain began to turn into fury. He knew who had done this. He slowly laid her head on the table and kissed her forehead. He ran his hand over her face, closing her eyelids for the very last time.

"Landon," he whispered through his clenched teeth as his tears continued to fall like a waterfall. He knew that the death of Landon's son had come back to haunt him and the guilt was like no other pain that he had ever experienced.

"I'm going to kill that motherfucker!" he yelled as he pounded his fists on the kitchen table in complete rage. He heard something jingle as his fists hit the surface. He looked across the table to see a second dagger to his already broken heart. It was a pair of diamond cuff links. He picked one of them up and his shoulders dropped in disbelief as he realized who the cuff links belonged to: none other than Kane. His style was unique and one of a kind. They were the same cuff links that he had witnessed Kane purchase in Miami a while back. Basil knew at that moment that their relationship was at a point of no return. Kane would forever be his enemy and both of them could not exist on the same earth, no matter what. It was the beginning of their end.

Fat Rat downed the glass of scotch and then slammed the glass down on the bar. He shook his head in angst and clenched his teeth tightly. He buried his chin into his chest and slowly shook it from side to side, disappointed. He was at the Irish pub, once again, and was waiting for the bartender to return. He had requested to speak to Landon and was told to wait. Fat Rat's conscience was eating at him as he kept replaying the series of events that had occurred. The last twenty-four hours were like a bad nightmare to him. He repeatedly shook his head in disbelief and glanced at the door, impatiently waiting for Landon to see him. His fingers began to involuntarily tap the counter anxiously. The sins of a man can weigh heavy on his heart and sometimes could be the death of him.

"Landon will see you now," the well-built bartender said as he returned from the back with a dishrag in hand. Fat Rat stood up and buttoned his blazer just before he followed the bartender toward the back to Landon's office. Fat Rat made his way into the office and the pungent smell of cigar smoke hit him as he walked in. The office was laced with mahogany furniture and expensive leather. Fat Rat saw the medium-built Irishman sitting behind the desk, smoking a robust Nicaraguan cigar. The bartender held the door open for Fat Rat as he walked in, looking directly at Landon with eyes of hatred.

"Did you send off that letter?" Landon asked the bartender as he was closing the door behind Fat Rat.

"Yes, sir. I sent it off yesterday," the bartender said as he exited and closed the door, leaving the two men in the office alone to talk. Landon nodded his head in approval.

"Fat Rat, I knew I would be seeing you soon. Well done," Landon said as he put out his cigar and slowly began to clap as Fat Rat approached his desk.

"No need for small talk. I just came to collect what is mine," Fat Rat said with hatred in his tone.

"Absolutely. You owed the house eight hundred thousand from what I can remember. Now we owe you two hundred thousand, after our little deal," Landon said as he reached underneath his desk and pulled out a small book bag. He then tossed it over to Fat Rat and smiled. "That's four hundred thousand. A small bonus for bringing Kane's only child to me. Now she can rest in peace right along with my son. It brings me great pleasure to do to Kane what was done to me."

"You son of a bitch! You said the kid Basil, not the girl!" Fat Rat said as he began to tear up in guilt.

"Well, sometimes things don't go as planned. I am satisfied with what transpired, my friend. I want Kane to feel what I had to feel. He did nothing to try to even the odds when my only child was murdered. I missed the kid, but I got the next best thing," Landon said as anger built up with his every word.

Fat Rat shook his head in disgust as he let his chin drop

down to his chest. The weight of the world was on his shoulders and he had the burden of carrying a secret to his grave. He was the sole reason that Landon knew where to find Basil and ultimately was the reason Mo was murdered. His gambling had made him commit the ultimate betrayal. Fat Rat clenched his jaws tightly and balled up his fist as hard as he could. He wanted to say something but he knew that a deal was a deal. He also knew that he needed that bag of money. He had borrowed from Kane and exhausted all favors in the streets. His bank account was in the negative and all of his bills were backed up. Fat Rat had sold his soul to the devil and the price wasn't cheap. He hesitantly reached down and scooped up the bag. It was a bag filled with blood money; Moriah's blood, to be exact. He peeked in and saw the large bills scattered throughout the bag. He slowly turned on the spurs of his heels and headed toward the exit. Fat Rat began to think about how the money could get him back on track and how it was the perfect time to stop gambling. The money wasn't enough to solve all of his financial problems, but it was a good start. Just as Fat Rat reached the door, he placed his hand on the knob. He paused for a few seconds and took a deep breath.

"Landon," he called.

"Yeah," Landon answered.

"Lions at home tonight, right?"

"Yeah, they have the Packers. It's an even line . . . pays exactly what you bet," Landon said while smiling, knowing that his money had no chance of leaving that office. Not with a compulsive gambler like Fat Rat holding it.

"Who you got?" Fat Rat asked, yet to turn around.

"Sorry, my friend . . . I don't gamble," Landon said as he reached down for his cigar and relit it.

Almost in a hurry, Fat Rat turned around and headed back toward Landon. He tossed the money on the desk and his eyes raced as if he were high on narcotics. "Give me the Lions. For all of this," Fat Rat said as his heart pounded faster that two pistons in a high-powered engine.

"Are you sure?" Landon asked as he blew a cloud of smoke into the direction of the addict across from him.

"What the fuck did I say? Yeah, I'm sure. Book it. I'll be here after the game to pick up eight hundred thousand!" Fat Rat said as he pointed at Landon, his finger trembling from the adrenaline that was pumping through his body.

"It's a bet," Landon said as he chuckled from his gut, letting out a sinister laugh. He watched as Fat Rat stormed out. Landon knew it was a sucker bet. He'd got word that the Lions' starting quarterback had been on a coke binge for the last seventy-two hours. That was the perk of being the biggest bookie in the Midwest. He shook his head in disbelief as he smiled and looked in the bag.

"That motherfucker has some set of balls, I tell ya . . ."

Fat Rat walked back through the bar, looking down at his phone. Kane had just sent him a text asking him to pick up a bottle of scotch for the weekly Sunday tradition. Fat Rat began to check his ESPN app to see the latest news on that evening's football game. His itch had begun, and he was locked in on the game and the potential to double up the bag he had just received from Landon. Fat Rat was so locked in on his phone, he almost knocked down the hooded man entering the bar.

"Watch out, mu'fucka," Fat Rat said under his breath, as the man brushed past him. Fat Rat didn't even give him the courtesy of eye contact. Fat Rat exited out of the door and planned on never repeating the deal that he'd made with Landon that caused the death of his goddaughter.

"The bet is final! Too late to change your mind," Landon said as he was relighting his cigar. He'd seen someone come to his door and assumed that it was Fat Rat returning to call off the dumb bet he had just put in. However, to his surprise, it wasn't Fat Rat. A hooded man holding a .45-caliber gun with a silencer on the tip of it was calmly walking in his direction with the gun pointed directly at him. Landon froze in fear as he looked into the eyes of a man apart. The man pulled the hood off of his head, exposing his face. It was none other than Basil. The same man that Landon had just called a hit on and his henchmen failed to finish the job.

"Do you know who I am? Basil asked in a low, stern voice as he stood directly in front of Landon's huge desk. Landon said nothing, but nodded in confirmation.

"Good. Then you know why I am here," Basil continued as he gripped the gun as tight as he could. "Step from behind that desk and get on your knees," he commanded. He clenched his jaws so tightly that the muscles bulged out of his lower jaw and veins began to form in his forehead. Basil was in a mental zone that he had never been in. He was on a warpath. Landon stood up slowly, but not before touching the button under his desk to notify his henchman in the bar. Basil's eyes were glued on Landon, so he saw the subtle move by his counterpart.

"You think it's a game, don't you?" Basil said as his voce elevated and the rage began to rear its ugly head. Basil struck Landon across the temple with the butt of his gun. Landon instantly fell to the ground as the blood began to leak out of the gash like a fountain.

"Get to your mu'fuckin' knees!" Basil screamed while looking down at him. Landon got on his knees, while holding his head. Basil grinned, getting pure joy out of seeing the blood pour in between Landon's fingers.

"If you're trying to signal your goon, don't bother. I just gave him three hollow-tips to his forehead. His brains are all over the counter, homeboy." Basil gave Landon a swift kick to his midsection, causing Landon to grunt in agony. Basil was positioned directly in front of Landon as he pressed the gun to his forehead.

"So, how did you get the drop on me? How did you know my spot?" Basil asked through clenched teeth. "Boone . . . Lil Noah? Who!" Basil exclaimed.

Landon chuckled. "It was your own guy. Fat Rat told me everything I needed to know. You're own man set you up. I guess your team wasn't as solid as you thought it was, eh?" Landon said with joy. He had lost his only son and the fact that he would make Basil and everyone around him suffer gave him pure satisfaction.

"Stop fucking lying," Basil said as he burrowed the silencer tip deeper into Landon's forehead.

"He told me everything. He knew about it from the jump.

I wanted my revenge and I got it. A gambler will do anything when he's on his last dime and looking for that one bounce-back bet. I sent a letter to Kane claiming the murder proudly and letting him know what went down. His team was responsible for the murder of my son, so he had to pay. He should have given you up when it first happened. But he was too much of a pussy. Therefore, he felt my pain and I'm proud of it. Your whole crew is imploding and I'm satisfied with knowing that. Stop being a pussy and kill me already. I'm ready to see my son," Landon admitted bravely as he put his hands behind his head and closed his eyes and prepared for impact.

Boom!

Kane and Fat Rat were sitting in the den, watching the game as they did every Sunday during football season. Kane sipped on scotch while Fat Rat was on the edge of his seat, focused in on the game. His team was losing and it wasn't looking good for his bet.

"You bet on this one?" Kane asked, already knowing the answer. Kane knew his friend too well and understood that if there wasn't a wager placed on a game, Fat Rat wouldn't deem it even worth watching.

"Just something light," Fat Rat replied, not even taking his eyes off the television screen. Kane looked around and took a deep breath. Sundays Moriah usually cooked for them as they watched the game. Kane looked to the kitchen and could imagine her smiling at him. The wave of sadness overcame him and he couldn't take it.

"I'm taking a walk in the back to clear my head. I can't stay in here," Kane said as he rose up from the leather sofa and then downed the remaining scotch in his glass. Fat Rat looked up at Kane and saw the distress in his eyes and instantly shared his pain.

"It sure is a lot different without Mo, huh?" Fat Rat added as guilt crept into his chest.

"Yeah, it's different. It will never be the same. Somebody took my only child from me," Kane said as he shook his head, still in disbelief.

"I still can't believe it," Fat Rat said as he became teary-eyed as well. Kane placed his hand on Fat Rat's shoulder and comforted his right-hand man.

"I'll find out who do this. Trust me. Just have to prepare to bury my baby girl," he said just before he walked toward the back patio and then out into the backyard. Fat Rat had to fight tears, knowing that he was indirectly responsible for the murder. He thought he was giving up Basil, but Moriah paid the consequences. This was a burden that he would have to carry on his shoulders for the rest of his life. Also a secret that he would have to take to the grave. He wanted to come clean to Kane, but how could he? How could he tell his best friend that he set up the shooting that eventually got his only child riddled with bullets? Fat Rat looked and saw that halftime was approaching and decided to follow Kane outside to help comfort him.

Fat Rat headed toward the back to join Kane. He noticed that Kane was gathering some hay bales with two metal hooks.

Fat Rat saw something that he had rarely seen from his friend. Kane was crying, silently, but tears were streaming down his face.

"You okay?" Fat Rat asked as he slid his hands into his slacks and walked over to Kane.

"Yeah . . . I'm good," Kane said as he dropped a metal hook to the ground and quickly wiped the tears from his eyes. "Help me take some hay to the barn," Kane said as he nodded his head in the direction of the stack of hay.

"Sure thing, Kane," Fat Rat answered as he picked up a hook and struck the bale of hay. Kane and Fat Rat made their way to the barn and then walked onto the steel skywalk that hovered over the oval hog pit. Kane tossed the bale of hay down in the pit and then helped Fat Rat toss his bale over.

Kane stared into the red mud-filled pit and shook his head in disbelief. Fat Rat could feel Kane's pain and placed his hand on his shoulder, trying to comfort him.

"We're going to get through this, family," Fat Rat assured. "I can't imagine the pain of burying your child."

"Especially when your best friend is the reason for it," Kane said, clenching his jaws. He then slid his hand into his pocket and pulled out a handwritten letter from Landon, basically gloating in his glory, breaking down everything that had transpired. The letter exposed Fat Rat for setting up the hit. Landon explained that he originally had called the hit for Basil but it was a bonus when he got Kane's only daughter. Those words were daggers to Kane's heart. To have a man gloating about the death of his daughter was the worst thing that he had experienced in his entire life.

"Wait, Kane," Fat Rat tried to explain as his heart pumped harder than it ever had.

"Wait for what!" Kane yelled at the top of his lungs. "What the fuck am I waiting for?" he repeated as he pressed the letter to Fat Rat's chest. Fat Rat grabbed the letter and looked at it for a while, reading it from the top. He began to comprehend what the letter conveyed and instantly his eyes began to water. He knew that he was the cause of Kane's pain and the truth was exposed.

"I didn't know that she would be there, Kane," Fat Rat tried to explain. Kane swiftly pulled a gun from the small of his back and put it to Fat Rat's head.

"But she *was* there! You . . ." Kane began to break all the way down. "She was there and paid the cost. So now . . . I will not rest until all parties involved in my baby's death is in the dirt."

"But Kane . . . ," Fat Rat pleaded.

"Shut up! Don't say another word," Kane comanded. He stepped back and glanced down. "Jump . . ."

"What?" Fat Rat asked.

"You heard what I said, motherfucker. Jump," Kane repeated. "Five . . . four . . ." He began to count and pulled back the hammer to his gun, notifying Fat Rat that he would have to jump in the hog pit or take a bullet to the head.

"I love you, Kane," Fat Rat said just before he jumped down about twenty feet into the pit. A loud thud echoed throughout the barn as Fat Rat's legs hit the dirt. On impact, his legs instantly broke, causing him to scream in agonizing pain. He immediately fell on his back and continued to scream and rock back and forth. Kane looked down and watched as his best friend suffered.

"I love you too," Kane whispered as he lifted two fingers to his mouth and let out a loud whistle. Almost instantly, the sound of huffs, pattering, and loud oinks invaded the air. Kane looked down and waited for the feeding frenzy to begin. The African warthogs attacked Fat Rat so quick and viciously. Over a dozen oversize hogs bit him all over his body and pulled it in many directions, literally trying to tear him apart. Fat Rat tried to fight the hogs off, but they were too vicious and powerful for him. It was brutal. Kane watched without blinking and was almost in a trance. He tuned out all of the yells by Fat Rat and the horrifying squeals of insane hogs as they mauled Fat Rat to death.

Kane was so zoned out, he didn't see the hooded man creeping up the stairs and eventually sneaking behind him. Kane didn't snap out of it until he felt two hands pushing him in the back with full force, causing him to fall into the pit, joining his partner in crime. Kane yelled at the top of his lungs while frantically reaching, flailing his arms and legs wildly, until he forcefully hit the red mud below. A big thud echoed throughout the barn at the moment Kane crashed flat on his back, instantly breaking it. An excruciating pain shot through his body as he let out a grunt on impact. He wanted to squirm in pain, but he couldn't move his body. He was instantly paralyzed from the waist down. He moaned in agony as he stared up into the eyes of Basil, who had removed his hood and gazed at him intensely. Fat Rat was right next to him, getting dismembered by the warthogs. He was right next to his lifelong partner in crime. They would now be partners in death. The hogs instantly began to work on Kane and it was a bloody massacre.

Basil looked down at the former members of his team being brutally mutilated. He wished that he would have never hooked up with Kane. His entire world was turned upside down. Basil had only told two women in his entire life that he loved them and now both of them were dead. Basil hated the streets. He despised the streets. The streets took everything from him. As he looked down at the horrific murders taking place, he shook his head in anguish. Seeing the man that ran the streets with an iron fist being murdered so viciously confirmed the obvious. He then knew that in the streets, there was no such thing as a king. There were never winners . . . only losers.

For years to come, Flint, Michigan, would remember the name Kane Garrett. His ideologies and principles were the blueprint to the ultimate street dream. Hustlers would use Kane's teachings, as would a particular author. Kane would forever be a legend to the city; a flawed legend but nevertheless, he would be remembered as "almost" king. But you see, that's what he understood that most aspiring hustlers didn't. He knew that his doomsday would come, because the streets had been and always would be undefeated.

"Ba . . . .sil! You are a part of me!" Kane screamed just before a hog violently bit into his neck, severing a main artery, killing him instantly. Kane died while telling Basil something he had longed to tell him. However, it fell on deaf ears as Basil never looked back.

The streets have no king. The streets have no king. The streets have no king...

Dear Parent:

Congratulations! Your child is taking
the first steps on an exciting journey.
The destination? Independent reading!

STEP INTO READING® will help your child get there. The program offers
books at five levels that accompany children from their first attempts at
reading to reading success. Each step includes fun stories, fiction and
nonfiction, and colorful art. There are also Step into Reading Sticker Books,
Step into Reading Math Readers, and Step into Reading Phonics Readers—
a complete literacy program with something to interest every child.

Learning to Read, Step by Step!

Ready to Read Preschool–Kindergarten
• big type and easy words • rhyme and rhythm • picture clues
For children who know the alphabet and are eager to
begin reading.

Reading with Help Preschool–Grade 1
• basic vocabulary • short sentences • simple stories
For children who recognize familiar words and sound out
new words with help.

Reading on Your Own Grades 1–3
• engaging characters • easy-to-follow plots • popular topics
For children who are ready to read on their own.

Reading Paragraphs Grades 2–3
• challenging vocabulary • short paragraphs • exciting stories
For newly independent readers who read simple sentences
with confidence.

Ready for Chapters Grades 2–4
• chapters • longer paragraphs • full-color art
For children who want to take the plunge into chapter books
but still like colorful pictures.

STEP INTO READING® is designed to give every child a successful
reading experience. The grade levels are only guides. Children can progress
through the steps at their own speed, developing confidence in their
reading, no matter what their grade.

Remember, a lifetime love of reading starts with a single step!

To Caffery Garff—J.C.
To Ted—P.W.

Text copyright © 1986 by Joanna Cole. Illustrations copyright © 1986 by Patricia Wynne.
All rights reserved under International and Pan-American Copyright Conventions. Published
in the United States by Random House Children's Books, a division of Random House, Inc.,
New York, and simultaneously in Canada by Random House of Canada Limited, Toronto.

www.stepintoreading.com

Educators and librarians, for a variety of teaching tools, visit us at
www.randomhouse.com/teachers

Library of Congress Cataloging-in-Publication Data
Cole, Joanna.
Hungry, hungry sharks / by Joanna Cole ; illustrated by Patricia Wynne.
    p.   cm. — (Step into reading. A step 3 book)
Originally published: New York : Random House, c1986.
SUMMARY: A simple discussion of the kinds of sharks and their behavior.
ISBN 0-394-87471-4 (pbk.) — ISBN 0-394-97471-9 (lib. bdg.)
1. Sharks—Juvenile literature.   [1. Sharks.]
I. Wynne, Patricia, ill.   II. Title.   III. Series: Step into reading. Step 3 book.
QL638.9 .C59 2003 597.3—dc21   2002014521

Printed in the United States of America   59 58 57 56 55 54 53 52

STEP INTO READING, RANDOM HOUSE, and the Random House colophon are registered
trademarks of Random House, Inc.

Hungry, Hungry
SHARKS

by Joanna Cole
illustrated by Patricia Wynne

Random House 🏠 New York

Millions and millions
of years ago,
the earth did not look
the way it does now.
Strange-looking plants
grew in swamps.
Reptiles with wings
flew in the air.

Everywhere on land were
dinosaurs, dinosaurs, dinosaurs.

Out at sea

there were strange creatures too.

Some looked like dragons.

Some looked like fish.

This big fish

could swim very fast.

It had sharp teeth

and a big fin on its back.

What kind of fish was this?

A shark!

There are no more
dinosaurs left on earth.
But there are still
plenty of sharks.

thresher

tiger shark

angel shark

10

Today there are more than
three hundred kinds of sharks.

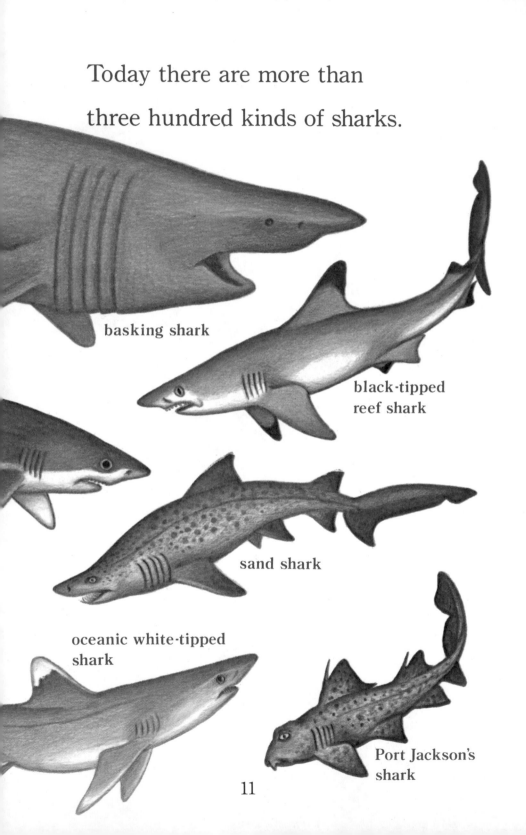

basking shark

black-tipped
reef shark

sand shark

oceanic white-tipped
shark

Port Jackson's
shark

11

Not all sharks are big.
Many, many kinds
are less than three feet long.

The dwarf shark is no bigger
than your hand.

The small carpet shark lies

on the ocean floor

like a rug.

The leopard shark has spots.
It grows to be about four feet long.

The biggest shark

is the whale shark.

It is longer than a bus.

The whale shark

has three thousand teeth.

But it will never bite you.

It eats only tiny

shrimp and fish.

The whale shark is very gentle.
A diver can even hitch a ride
on its back.

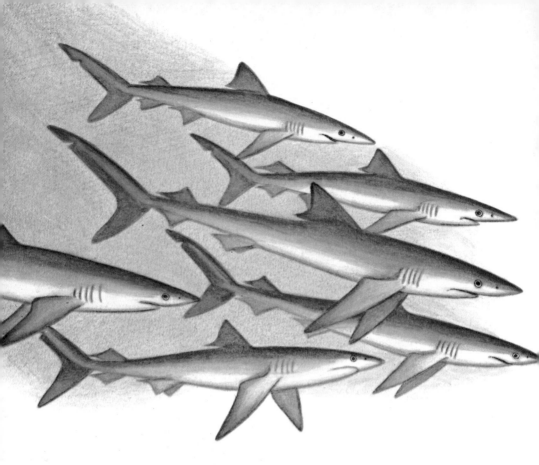

These are blue sharks.

They are far out at sea

hunting for food.

Suddenly

they pick up

the smell of blood.

The sharks speed up.

They shoot through the water

like torpedoes.

In a few minutes

they find a dead whale.

The blue sharks tear off

big chunks of whale meat.

Now the water is

full of biting sharks.

If one shark gets hurt,

the others turn on it.

They will eat that shark too.

In a short time

the whale is all gone.

The sharks swim away.

Nothing is left.

Nothing but bones.

Blue sharks are called
the wolves of the sea.
This is because
they stay together in packs.
Blue sharks often swim
after a ship for days.
A long time ago
sailors thought this meant that
someone was going to die.

Why do blue sharks
<u>really</u> follow ships?
The sharks come
because of noises
from the ship.
Then they stay to eat
garbage that is thrown
into the water.

The most dangerous shark

in the sea

is the great white shark.

It is named after

its white belly.

The teeth of the great white shark

are big and sharp.

Very, very sharp.

It can eat a whole seal

in one bite.

The great white shark is

the size of a speedboat.

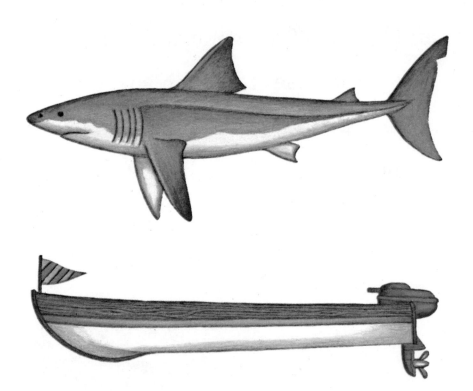

This great white shark

has just had babies.

Most fish lay eggs.

But most sharks do not.

Their babies are born alive.

A baby shark is called a pup.

The pup of the great white shark

is almost the size of a man.

As soon as they are born

the pups go their own way.

It is not safe to stay

near a hungry mother.

The baby sharks swim off
to catch their own food.
One eats a fish.
Another gets a crab.
The pups had better
watch out for puffer fish.

The puffer fish can blow up

like a balloon.

If a shark eats it,

its spines get stuck

in the shark's throat.

The shark will die.

Not many animals

can kill great white sharks.

The stingray

flaps through the sea

like a giant bat.

Its tail has a poison stinger.

The poison can kill most animals.

But a great white shark

can eat a stingray—

stinger and all!

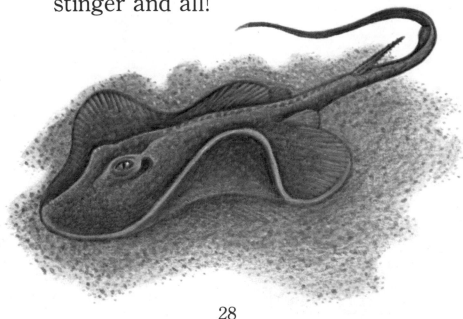

The swordfish is

a very strong fish.

It can cut and stab

with its long nose.

But even a swordfish

almost always loses a fight

with a great white shark.

Another big shark is

the hammerhead shark.

It is easy to see

how it got its name.

Like other big sharks,

the hammerhead never sleeps

and never stops swimming.

Most fish have air balloons

inside them.

But sharks do not.

If they stop swimming,

they sink.

This hammerhead swims
to a group of dolphins.
It tries to catch
one of the young dolphins.
But sharks do not always
get their way.
The dolphins fight back.

One dolphin dives
under the water.
It comes up and
hits the hammerhead.
The shark flies up
in the air.
It falls back on the water.
SMACK!

The dolphins keep
hitting the shark.
After a while
the shark stops moving.
It sinks down into the water.
It is dead.

Dolphins are smart animals.

They can work together

to kill an enemy.

But sharks are not as smart.

They have tiny brains.

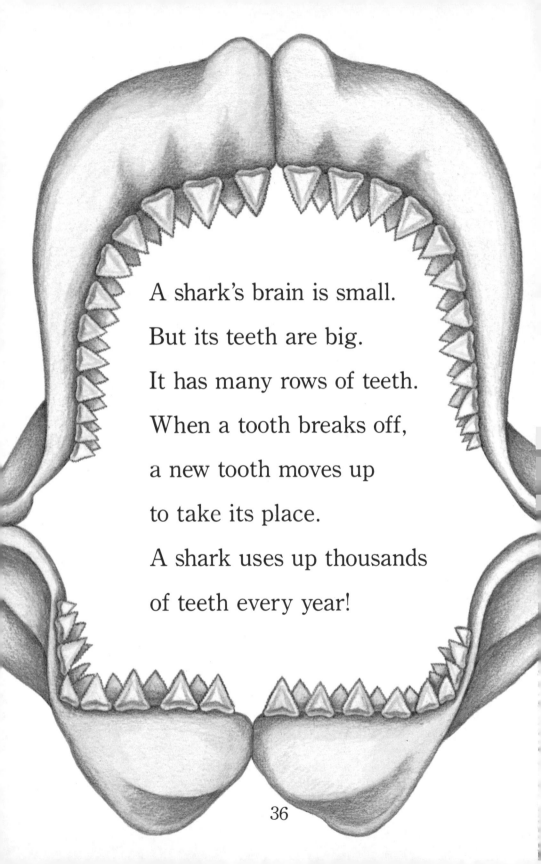

A shark's brain is small.
But its teeth are big.
It has many rows of teeth.
When a tooth breaks off,
a new tooth moves up
to take its place.
A shark uses up thousands
of teeth every year!

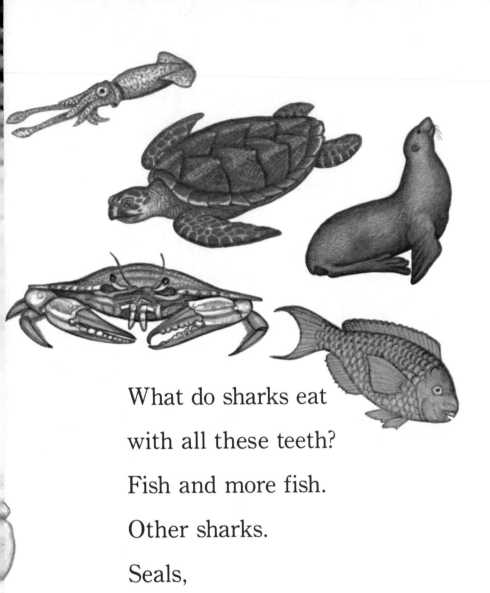

What do sharks eat

with all these teeth?

Fish and more fish.

Other sharks.

Seals,

turtles,

crabs.

Almost anything

that swims in the sea.

Sometimes sharks eat

things that are not food.

No one knows why.

All these things

have been found

inside big sharks:

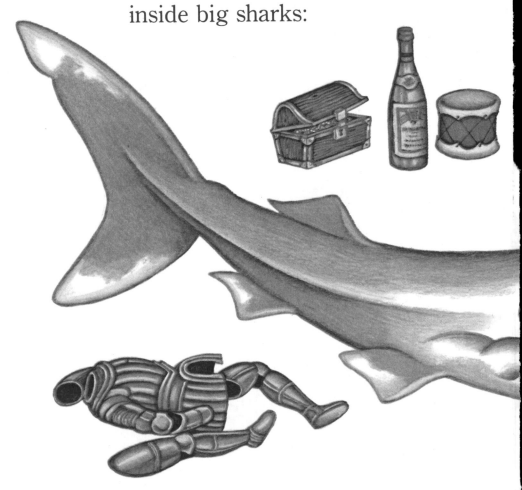

a wallet,

a fur coat,

a drum,

a bottle of wine,

a chest of jewels,

a barrel of nails,

and a suit of armor!

Do sharks eat people?

Yes, they do.

If a person is near a big shark,

the shark may attack.

But the number of people

killed by sharks

is very small.

More people die

from bee stings

than from shark bites!

Sharks do not
go hunting for people.
But people do
go hunting for sharks.
Some people like to go
fishing for sharks.
They have to be careful.
A shark may look dead.
Then all at once
it can "wake up"—
and bite!

Scientists want to study sharks.

But it is hard

to study them at sea.

And it is hard to keep

big sharks alive in a tank.

Once scientists caught

a great white shark.

They put it in a tank

with other fish.

But the shark did not eat.

And it kept bumping into

the sides of the tank.

After a few days

the shark began to die.

So the scientists

took the shark back to sea.

They set it free.

There are many things

we do not know about sharks.

We do not know

how long sharks live.

Or how much food

a shark has to eat

to stay alive.

But we do know that sharks

are here to stay.